T0206859

Holy Hill

COLLEEN ALBERT

The following is a fictional re-creation of certain events in the lives of the author's family when they converge with Father Divine and the Peace Mission Movement. While actual events and historical personages are depicted here, all situations and dialogues are invented, except where direct quotes and photographs are used from items in the author's possession.

ISBN (Print): 978-1-09836-921-7
ISBN (eBook): 978-1-09836-922-4

1

CHAPTER 1

Reverend Major Jealous Divine was holding another open house and banquet tonight at his International Peace Mission West. Admission was, as always, free except for the polite necessity of listening to the Reverend, known as Father to his followers, speak. Not a bad price to pay for the lavish banquets the followers had come to expect.

The Mission is an imposing ivy covered brick Tudor Revival set prominently on the hillside of Berkeley, California's Holy Hill. Named for the prevalence of seminaries and spiritual retreats, Holy Hill is a magnet for seekers of all kinds, and for those who just want to absorb some of the tranquility radiating from the stately old Victorians and Tudors. Only a fortunate few owned these historic estates, many with sweeping views of the Pacific.

The Holy Hill estate was purchased, as with all Father's properties, with cash delivered to the bank in suitcases. The buyer was always a representative of International Peace Mission and the property titles showed the owner as International Peace Mission, or sometimes multiple owners that were followers of the movement. Father himself owned nothing. There were buildings in New York, Philadelphia (his base of operations) and now California. Father had remodeled this one and removed the garish remnants of the former owner who apparently had a fondness for Greek statues in compromising positions. Naked marble men and women were definitely distracting when trying to impress upon followers the importance of modesty. The upper floors of the estate separated the female residents, referred to as Sisters, from the male residents, referred to as Brothers, on the lower floor, making it unlikely they would inadvertently meet unless it was under the watchful eyes of the staff.

This California real estate acquisition was a perfect location for his cause, especially because it was in the city of Berkeley, known for its population of open minded types, liberal thinkers, and activists. He needed to expand his following beyond the poor colored neighborhoods back East if he wanted to establish a more universal appeal. The high educational level in Berkeley with predominantly white college aged residents was a fertile recruiting ground that could pay off many times over and offset the punishingly high cost of the magnificent Holy Hill estate. Most importantly, the Berkeley student population was known for its reactivity to new social movements, and Father Divine's modus operandi of finding an enemy and making sure everyone knew who the enemy was, thereby unifying the group and making them subservient to the leader, was going to be easier here than at more traditional campuses. In Father's teachings, the Capitalistic American way of life was the enemy. True Heaven could only be achieved through a selfless dedication to the group as a whole—in other words, to the International Peace Mission Movement.

The month is April, the year 1947. The atmosphere of the city is electric with University of Berkeley students anticipating graduation and the expected success that surely comes to those who hold a degree from such a prominent institution. Berkeley is remarkably stratified—highbrow educated intellectuals associated with the University, old money types tucked away in the rolling hills, off-beat social misfits with large trust funds, and on the outskirts of the city workers that had to be tolerated because the rich required service—a melting pot in the truest sense of the word.

Tonight it was chilly and the sky's colors mingled from deep blue to orange to pink and the sea released its salty mist. The banqueters made their way up the slow rise to the mission, quietly filing past the rose gardens and jasmine covered brick walls, then along the flagstone path to the entry. Under the porte-cochère a Rolls Royce Silver Wraith patiently waited. A bell sounded from one of the nearby seminaries, marking the passage of time for the theology students.

This was the Heaven on Earth that Father told his followers was already theirs, was right here right now, no need to wait for a distant future, if only they would listen to his message and trust in him—and take some steps to change.

The banqueters were mostly colored people, or Negros depending on who you spoke to, poor but respectable, scrubbed clean and dressed in their Sunday best, ladies in proper dresses and low-heeled pumps and gentlemen in suits. They had come to dine with Father and hear his message of hope. A few white people were sprinkled in, mostly avant-garde types, curious, anxious to let others know how open-minded they were. They were all in their own way seeking something, to fill a void, find a deeper meaning, or perhaps an undiscovered path to fulfillment. Father may help them, so why not hear what he had to say?

The guests filtered into the ornate entry hall and were escorted by mission workers—the Sisters, Brothers, young Rosebuds and young Masters—to their place at the table. A strict seating arrangement was adhered to— absolutely no unnecessary mingling of the sexes was allowed and no segregation of races. Every alternating person was dark complected, seated next to a light complected person. Father did not allow any racial terms other than light complected or dark complected. He believed race was an artificial designation of a human being, an inaccurate label for God's children, and therefore invalid. There were no Negros, no white people, no colored people. A person should be referred to as either light complected or dark complected.

The banquets were always formal and manners strictly enforced. Circulating hostesses discretely corrected anyone that choose the wrong fork or spoon for that course. Napkins in the lap, please, with hands on table only as necessary to partake in the feast. Place settings were on white linen with an abundance of heavy silver, fine bone china accented in real gold, and etched crystal goblets. Intricate floral centerpieces were placed so as not to obscure one's view of the podium or head of the table from where Father would speak. The banqueters sat ramrod straight, alternating dark and light faces expectantly upturned toward where Father and Mother would descend from the landing to bestow their presence upon them.

The last two years had seen an increase in banquet attendance, probably due to soldiers returning home from the war in the Pacific looking for absolution from the horrors they had witnessed. Tonight the banquet hall held close to 100 people, waiting to be filled with the Spirit—HIS Spirit. Tonight he would remind them who HE was.

Lingering in front of his full-length mirror, striking different poses, he was thinking tonight is going to be crucial to not only cementing his existing following, but increasing it. Membership had dwindled, in part due to that nasty business ten years ago when an ex-follower, Verinda Brown, sued him. Sour grapes, that's all it was. Did she think he was her personal money manager? Investments are risks, nothing more, no guarantee intended. Imagine paying every follower who lost money on their investment! The newspapers had picked up the trail, looking for blood, anxious as always to show he was nothing more than a mortal commonplace con man, a crook, a fraud. The press knew how satisfying it was to see the wealthy and successful fall from favor, especially the dark-complected ones.

Then there was that unfortunate incident where one of his disenchanted young Rosebuds had accused him of touching her in the wrong place. A few other silly lovestruck girls, Rosebuds that he had charitably fed, clothed, and housed, had taken up this sordid little theme. Sour grapes again, no doubt caused by petty jealousy over some imagined slight. Incredibly ungrateful for all the opportunities he had given them, that's how he saw it.

On that last thought he gave an angry tug on the vest of his three piece cream cashmere suit. Lately his suits needed tailoring, to be "let out" as his tailor had delicately put it, and he suspected the lavish banquets were to blame. Why did he need to host, or, let's face it, call it what it was—bribe—his followers with food? He had a suspicion that free food was the main reason people came to hear him speak.

He drew himself up to his full height of 5'2" and arranged his face as he imagined people would want to see the source of divine wisdom. The mirror showed a diminutive, rotund Negro man, perhaps in his seventies, with tiny low-set ears. The back of his otherwise smooth hairless facade had annoying folds of adipose tissue descending downward into the back of his shirt collar. His tailor was under strict orders to minimize the neckline by cutting the collars higher. He was surrounded by the trappings of a world leader—brocades, gold leaf, crystal, fine linens, polished rare woods, Oriental rugs and incense. He had come so far on so very little.

He headed purposefully out through the heavy mahogany door of his private suite and glided silently over thick carpet to the landing of the curved staircase. From here he and his virgin wife Mother Divine—formally known as Edna Rose Ritchings from Canada—would make their grand entrance. A hint of lemon furniture oil drifted briefly in the air , assuring him the resident Angels were earning their keep. As expected Mother Divine emerged punctually from her adjoining suite. It always amazed him how a young woman in her twenties could accomplish such a feat and maintain it, convince followers she was the wife of God incarnate. Even with her distracting blond movie-star good looks she managed to be taken seriously by his followers, though some privately grumbled about her very light complexion. Her self-assured bearing, at times imperious, usually discouraged any questions of authority, though. He shocked himself for a moment as he considered *she just might be as good at the God game as I am.*

Her constant companion and chaperone, the prim, conniving, elderly, dark complected Miss Sincere Sincerity, made some last-minute adjustments to the cinched waist on Mother's formal gown—she delicately called it being "let out". He made a mental note that they needed to start taking more after dinner walks. Overweight was not a good signal to send his followers—it showed a certain lazy self-indulgence.

Mother, whom he affectionately referred to as Sweet Angel, put her pale hand firmly on his arm, and together they slowly, deliberately descended the stairs to the dining room to take their place at the head of the table. All heads turned expectantly upwards to receive. What they expected to receive was unclear, even to themselves. Perhaps it was direction, someone to tell them what on Earth to do to find Heaven right now, present tense, not later after they were dead.

He was thinking this evening he would set the tone of the banquet with one of his more mysterious revelations, a speech he had memorized through countless repetitions. It was vague enough that most followers never questioned him, but they pondered it and accepted it because of the thunderous conviction of his voice, his stentorian delivery, his innate acting ability, and most of all his hypnotic ability to hold someone's gaze, to make them believe he was seeing inside them, through them, communicating with their soul.

Tonight was more formal than usual—it was Berkeley after all, not Harlem. There were sumptuous silver serving dishes heaped with roast beef, glazed chicken, braised lamb, candied yams dripping with marshmallow, brown sugar and butter, Waldorf salad, garden salad, steaming bowels of mashed potatoes with boats of gravy, warm home made bread, and small crystal bowls filled with every exotic condiment imaginable.

Father was reverently handed each dish by banquet attendants, served himself and Mother first, then passed the platters and bowls to the banqueter on his right, the gaunt, fawning, light-complected Brother David Devoute, who Father noticed was particularly obsequious this evening. The dishes moved from hand to hand as if on conveyer belts around the tables. The scent of fresh baked bread mingled with candied yams gave one a sense that all was well, safe and secure— a happy childhood memory of festive meals gone by. Food was the universal language spoken here.

Now there was a pause in the activity after the food had been portioned out, and the followers obediently looked to the head of his table. Father stood with Mother, tilted his chin upward and belted out "Peace! God is not only personified and materialized. He is repersonified and rematerialized. He rematerialized and He rematerialates. He rematerialates and He is rematerializatable. He repersonificates and He repersonifitizes. He welcomes you to His table that you might partake in Heaven on Earth!" With that, he and Mother sat down and the feeding began.

No one knows exactly when Father Divine proclaimed himself God. It may have happened gradually over many years on the traveling preacher circuit, when he didn't discourage the notion that he was the Second Coming. Some observers noted he did not exactly claim he was God, he just didn't deny it, and when asked about his past he would say "the history of God would not be useful in mortal terms." He refused to acknowledge relationship to any family—"God doesn't have a family." FBI records show Divine was most likely born in 1870 in Rockville, Maryland as George Baker Jr., the son of sharecroppers and former slaves, and may have lived in a Negro ghetto referred to as "Monkey Run."

Despite an inauspicious beginning, George was a voracious reader. In between odd jobs he became fascinated with theology, particularly The New Thought Movement, a philosophy of positive thinking that asserted negative thoughts led to poverty and unhappiness. George was a regular on Sundays at the local Baptist church, where he was usually asked to say a few words, and he did, incorporating some New Thought ideas along with the usual themes. He was a charismatic speaker with seemingly original ideas, so he was invited to give regular sermons. Attendance at his sermons grew and George began to formulate a plan for a possible future career. He noted people seemed to need him and they had an extra bounce in their step and a smile on their faces after his speeches. "Accentuate the positive" was what people wanted to hear, and they would throw a few extra pennies in the offering plate to hear it.

Encouraged , George worked his way south to Georgia, picking up somewhat of a following on the traveling preacher circuit, a large portion of whom were young women. He was not a handsome man, but he exuded confidence and charisma so people followed him, looked up to him. He preached to Negro congregations across the State on exhaustive tours that were increasingly standing room only. He reinvented and renamed himself—he was now Reverend Major Jealous Divine, remembering a passage in the Bible in Exodus where God declared himself a jealous God to curtail worship of anything or anyone other than Him.

During The Great Depression, 1929-1933, Divine formed The International Peace Mission Movement based in Harlem, New York. During this time period his following increased dramatically and he was feeding up to 300 people a day. The Movement owned and operated hotels, referred to as "Heavens" where congregation members could live cheaply and work in the Movement's various cash-only small businesses. Lavish banquets were held every Sunday. There was free food, free clothing and low-cost housing if one was willing to follow Father's dictates—and hand over their cash at the end of the day. Communal ownership of property and donation of one's labor for the good of the Movement was mandatory to be a true follower rather than just a Father Divine sympathizer. The cash was rolling in, for the most part untraceable, straight into the Peace Mission Movement's coffers.

Divine eventually drew the interest of the FBI during J. Edgar Hoover's time as director. The International Peace Mission Movement claimed to have two million followers. Their corporate base of operations was (and is) Palace Mission Church, Inc., 1622 Spring Mill Road, Gladwyne, Pennsylvania—an estate in the wooded countryside just outside Philadelphia—donated by a wealthy follower. There was a brief, bizarre alignment with the Communist Party when Divine endorsed the Party's commitment to civil rights. Because he was a dedicated Capitalist the association was short-lived but contributed to his colorful reputation. Divine had his hand in real estate, civil rights and politics, small business, communal farms, and the business of being God. He and Mother Divine wore expensive clothes, drove a Rolls Royce, and owned considerable real estate—all paid for in cash. According to IRS records Divine earned zero, owned nothing and paid no taxes. It all belonged to the International Peace Mission Movement—in essence the organization operated as a non-profit corporation, although the term was not widely known at the time. When questioned about their operations, The Peace Mission Movement sold the ideas of accountability, trustworthiness, honesty, and openness to everyone who invested time, money, and faith into the organization.

CHAPTER 2

It was just past noon and Lenora "Nona" Born the tea leaf reader—her latest reinvention of herself—was peering inscrutably into her empty teacup. Tea leaves should be read as soon as the cup emptied to be accurate. She swished them around with the remaining liquid, turned the cup upside down and clockwise three times then flipped it upright. This was the ritual that would absolutely reveal the hidden truth. What she saw now worried her, though—she wasn't the kind of psychic that just saw the good, she could see the dark side too.

The month was October, the year 1937. Her daughter Ann "Dolly" Born had just turned thirteen, officially a teenager. Dolly was a well-mannered girl that seemed unfazed by her striking doll-like beauty. She was actually perfect, tall, blond, blue eyed, polite, passably intelligent. She got along well with her five siblings, got along with everyone in fact. So agreeable. Nona often felt a stab of annoyance when she looked at her daughter. Absolutely no resemblance to her whatsoever. Dolly was unfortunately the spitting image of her father Emil, the no-good womanizer.

Emil, Nona's forth husband - but why count anymore? - was already into the second year of a rather public affair with his dancing instructor. He had decided to take evening dancing lessons ostensibly to take her out dancing to fashionable nightclubs in Hollywood without appearing to have two left feet. He was sinfully good looking and ten years younger than her. She was used to the little flirtations, but who cared? She knew few could compete with her darkly exotic beauty, not to mention her estate at 129 N. Rockingham Drive in Brentwood. This time it was different though, more persistent. Lillian Myers was the woman's name, home-breaker, ten years younger than Emil. Nona was used to a bumpy road with men, and she knew life would go on if this one turned out poorly. Men were like busses—if one drops you off, there will always be another one that comes along to pick you up.

What she saw right now, though, in the tea leaves was troubling. A blank spot where there should have been at least one tea leaf, positioned where a future event should have been. She felt fear as she focused into the cup, like going down an elevator too quickly and the doors open onto a wall. Quickly she attributed it to too much caffeine—tea leaf reading was a hoax anyway, wasn't it? Silly stuff, like Tarot cards and Ouija Board. "Dolly, stop standing there staring" she heard herself say. She wanted to break the spell of the teacup. "You and your sister get cleaned up, you look like ruffians. We're going shopping in The Village today."

Westwood Village was a well kept secret. Even though the rest of America was in the throes of the Great Depression, the West side of Los Angeles felt like a protected bubble, removed from the troubles of the common man. The shops were expensive boutiques, not big department stores, where people in the know went, or the truly famous who actually craved privacy once in awhile. The restaurants were small intimate cafés that served the very best. It was right up Nona's ally, and she wanted to expose her young daughters to the finer things early so they would feel comfortable when they took their places in society. After lunch they would visit Grace Alworth Frock Shop, where the perfect party dress could always be found

Nona's spotless black Buick Special rolled around the circular drive, gravel crunching under the wheels. Tall, thin, pale, gray-haired chauffeur James, whom the family cruelly referred to as Caspar Milquetoast when he was out of earshot, was overly cheerful as usual. "Perfect day for a drive Mrs. Born. Where do I have the pleasure of taking you?" Nona wondered why James annoyed her. Wasn't it good to be so cheerful? She decided James was probably a phony— no one could be that happy, could they? "We're going to the Village James. Drop us off at 961 Broxton Avenue, in front of the theater. We'll meet you back there three hours later." "Will do Mrs. Born. Weather's perfect for walking."

Time to relax now, time to tune out the two fidgety giggling girls. She loved riding in a car, loved her neighborhood and its proximity to the Village. Life was good despite the cheating husband—she had the property and the children, so why worry? Out the window winding Sunset Boulevard rolled by, estates visible only by quick glimpses though thick hedges and stone walls. Now it was right on Bundy, left on Wilshire, left on Westwood Boulevard and into the Village. The tower of the theater rose up grandly ahead against the backdrop of the foothills of Bel-Air. White cumulus clouds drifted across a bright blue dome of sky. The marquis announced *Lost Horizon* was playing. Interesting plot, a Shangri-La where no one ever aged—unless they departed the boundries of the town. She stole a glance in her compact—forty-nine and holding, petite, with jet black hair, large dark eyes—her best feature — hour-glass figure even after six children. She absolutely had a few good years left, and she was going to enjoy every minute.

James eased the car into the loading zone, hurried to her rear door to perform his chauffeur ceremony, overdoing the role in Nona's opinion, and then here they were, in the quaint exclusive Village, a perfect day spread out before them. "Have a wonderful day Mrs. Born. I'll meet you right back here in three hours." Obsequious smile, a hint of Aqua Velva aftershave, and the car swung out and away. Nona briefly wondered where James would go for three hours. Probably to one of the gaudily painted hotdog stands along Santa Monica Boulevard. Then they were off, on a mission, headed straight to Westwood Boulevard where the better shops were.

Nona was proud of her two youngest, Dolly and ten-year-old Genieve, of the dark wavy hair and serious expression. So different, but full sisters nevertheless, unlike some of the other siblings—Eloise Rawizer age twenty-four, Kathleen Cannon twenty, Nona LeCompte nineteen, and her full brother Norman LeCompte eighteen. Legally adults now and out of Nona's hair, starting their own lives and families. Nona had been a mother since age twenty-four, a run of twenty-five years. Each of the four husbands had wanted their own biological children and Nona had accommodated them. She was pretty sure these two of Emil's would be her last, so she wanted to get it just right this time. Besides, they made her feel young again.

"Mother, can we go to the Chitchat for lunch? I love the malts there and the waiters are so nice." Dolly knew that's where they were going anyway, didn't need to ask, but she was always jockeying to be the most companionable, the one everybody wanted to be with, so she went along with virtually everything if she sensed it was the popular choice. The girls were dressed in almost identical pale yellow taffeta dresses with white patent leather shoes, all from Bullocks Wilshire. "Of course we can go there—nothing but the best for you two." Dolly and Genieve skipped ahead, laughing, sharing some silly girlish secrete. Nona noticed that Genieve, as usual, kept to the store side, not so much to look into the windows, but to admire her reflection in the glass. Only ten and already vain.

Westwood Village streets were meticulously manicured by professional landscapers. There were cobblestones, flowering sidewalk trees, smooth iron benches, bubbling fountains, and fringed awnings with bistro tables outside the small cafés. The scent of French pastries and coffee floated on the air as they strolled by. Up ahead the welcoming red door with the black and white striped awning announced the Chitchat Café in gold scrolled letters. Nona stopped outside to check the special board, the girls momentarily distracted by a window display a few doors up, at Grace Alworth Frock Shop. Let them look, she thought. Young ladies should learn how to shop. Anyway she wanted to scan ahead to plan the seating arrangement, one that would give them maximum visibility. Nona didn't like to be stuck in the back—she wanted a table up front and center.

As she scanned the café, a familiar laugh toward the rear caught her attention. It took a moment for her eyes to adjust to the dimness, but yes, it was him, it was unmistakably Emil—and a female friend. There he was, smiling happily, leaning into his lunch partner, arm thrown casually around the back of the woman's chair, moving closer for a whispered comment. From her position Nona was just out of Emil's peripheral vision. She stood there, frozen, the sight so heart-sinking she momentarily could not move, could not breathe. Her feet felt like lead and she was riveted to the spot. Their body language was abundantly clear—they were on a date, and not a platonic one, that was obvious. She recognized the woman as the dance instructor Lillian Meyers—mousy brown hair, slight build, demure posture, simpering smile. "Can I help you? Table for one?" The waiter's voice brought her back to reality. "No thank you, I've changed my mind." She did not want to draw attention to herself, make a tawdry scene, that was beneath her. She would take care of this at the appropriate time, and definitely not in public. She hurried away to gather the girls. They would go somewhere better, that didn't cater to philanderers—and she would save the showdown for later.

Nona had come to Los Angeles, traveling first class, leisurely, by railway from Council Bluffs, Iowa to visit her sister and brother-in-law in Santa Monica. From the moment the train arrived at Union Station in Los Angeles, she was hooked. Union Station was grand, an Art Deco meets Mission Revival style, fringed with one hundred foot palms that leaned into and gently swayed with the warm breezes. After two visits Nona made up her mind that Los Angeles was her true home, the home of her heart. There was such energy here, so many interesting artistic people with new ideas. Los Angeles was the here and now, Iowa the staid past, and Nona was forward thinking, a seeker who lived in the future, always evolving. There was nothing tying her to Iowa. She had two young daughters from two past husbands, one quite older and deceased, the other entirely forgettable, Mr. Rawitzer and Mr. Cannon, but she was already considering a third marriage to Norman LeCompte, a gentleman whom her father had introduced her to. Norman seemed as excited about relocating to California as she was. They were both from wealthy banking families, both in their twenties, both reckless because they had never known failure. They had been born with financial safety nets so they could afford to take risks—money would bail them out of anything, any crazy, wild, daring, reckless undertaking they could think of—they were privileged and free.

They married in 1917 and purchased their dream home, an eight bedroom Spanish style estate set on an acre of land at 129 N. Rockingham Avenue in the Brentwood area of Los Angeles County, only six miles to Will Rogers State Beach down Sunset Boulevard. Nona gave Norman two perfect children, tow-heads Nona and Norman Jr.—miniature versions of themselves except for the blond hair that came from her father's side of the family, the Keelines. They had a full house, with her first two children Eloise and Kathleen, and now Nona and Norman. Life was good but far too routine for her—she was ready for more adventure.

Right now, at this moment, Nona was riding West on Sunset toward the beach with Norman in their new 1917 Chevrolet touring car. It was a perfect summer day, a day like all the others—seventy-two degrees, white puffy clouds, slow floating seagulls against an impossibly blue sky, marine scented air. Fellow motorists waved at the golden couple as the car cruised down Sunset. There were no seasons in California so Nona and Norman had become listless, had reached a state of ennui. It had become an effort to have yet another wonderful day. What to tell their friends? *Gee, the beach was really good today Oliver!* Oliver was their neighbor, a research scientist and professor at UCLA. Talkative Oliver had some stories to tell, that's for sure. Then there was their neighbor across the street, John Barrymore, silent film legend. Mr. Barrymore usually poked his head out from behind the hedge in the late morning to see if there was a reporter lurking nearby to snap a compromising "morning after" photograph for the tabloids. *Good morning Mr. Barrymore—lovely day today for the beach!* How dull their lives were compared to some of their neighbors.

If there was one thing Nona hated, it was boredom—she wasn't cut out for it, putting one foot in front of the other like a drone, so she decided right now was the time to spring her latest idea on her equally bored husband. "Norman, I think we need better grocery stores here, like the ones on the East Coast. You know, where you can get just about any gourmet thing you can dream of, along with regular things like bread, butter, and milk. More expensive, so it never becomes too public, stocked with the very best. Wouldn't that be just a grand idea?" Norman considered this unimportant topic for the required long moment, then politely assented. "Sure thing Nona, an expensive neighborhood grocery store stocked with the best items, where only the best people shop, and where they hire only the best looking people to work there." He winked, Nona playfully slapped him, but later they talked about what to do with themselves for the rest of their lives.

Four years later, in 1921, on the corner of 14th Street and Montana Avenue in Santa Monica, Chef's Market was open for business. It was a huge success with the locals, just what was needed at the time for the burgeoning population of the town. It was convenient to drive there because Montana Avenue wasn't crowded, and parking was easy. Quite a few customers simply walked. It became a flagship for the North of Wilshire neighborhood. Everyone went there, and best of all you usually saw someone you knew.

As they had planned, the market stocked everything upscale one could desire, and practical things too—everything from dragon fruit, hand-picked wild rice, white truffles, special wine vintages, to staples like Campbell's Soup and Wonder Bread. Nona knew just about everyone in town now, especially the gourmet shoppers. Her role in the market was as a floater, smiling, being of assistance, making sure everyone found what they needed, and that all shelf items were neatly displayed—the clientele expected it. Norm monitored the financial details presented to him by the market's manager Robert Wentworth, a recent USC graduate in business management. If anything were wrong, Robert shouldered the blame—but rarely was there a problem. Robert was expensive but he earned his keep.

Today the market had more people than usual. There is spring fever in the air she was thinking, as she watched the shoppers piling baskets of cherries into their carts. She made a mental note that shoppers tended to center in the produce section when it was spring. She was watching fat Mrs. Humphry, the widow, sneaking some cherries into her mouth, sampling too much as usual, before deciding not to purchase. "Hi there Mrs. Humphry—finding everything you need today?" Elderly Mrs. Humphrey's enormous breasts heaved up as she twisted around guiltily, caught in the act. "The cherries are just perfect—I had to try 'em 'cause I'm going to bake a cherry pie for my grandson today. Wouldn't do to have sour cherries in a pie, he wouldn't eat 'em." Nona smiled and moved on graciously—no use embarrassing the woman. Besides, Mrs. Humphry was a fixture in town and had quite a few friends who probably would love to hear gossip about the over-priced market that couldn't spare a few cherries.

Nona headed to the back and up the steps to the office. Today she had two box-boy interviews—they needed one more now that business was really picking up. There were two boys waiting downstairs, so she rang Robert to send the first one up, positioning herself behind the large oak desk, leaning back to give an air of relaxed authority. There was a tentative knock at the office door— "Please come in." She tried to should cheerful because she knew how terrifying interviews could be if you were on the worker's side of the desk. "Hello Mrs. LeCompte, my name is Jack Mitchell." This came out in one long exhalation as if he had been holding his breath all the way up the steps. In front of her slumped a pimply unkempt sixteen-year-old who smelled of cigarettes, looking rather sheepish. After a torturous fifteen minutes she thanked him and said the manager would get back to him. Relieved, he scurried out the door. Jack didn't look the part, and she firmly believed that people who worked around food should look wholesome, clean, healthy.

She glanced at her watch—one more interview to go and then she could get back to making the rounds of the isles. Now another knock on the door, this one assertive, three firm knocks. "Please come in." "Hello Mrs. LeCompete, my name is Emil Born, I'm here to interview for the box-boy position." She blinked, momentarily at a loss for words—was this adult male, an improved version of Douglas Fairbanks Jr. in her opinion, complete with ice blue eyes, sandy blond hair, chiseled features, really applying to be a box-boy? She was sure this was a gag her husband was playing on her, sure it was, remembering how he had laughed at her idea to have only good looking people working at the market. "I know I'm a little old for the job, but I just got discharged from the Navy and live only a few blocks from here. I really need work, I learn fast, and I'm good with people." Emil smiled a thousand watt smile, and Nona smiled back—just to stall, to collect herself, get back in control. He looked like the type who was used to getting what he wanted—there were no nervous twitches, no shuffling, just direct unblinking eye contact, expecting to be accepted, *as if she would be lucky to have him* she thought.

The interview went on for almost thirty minutes, Nona fidgeting over some papers she pretended to consult. She made a quick calculation while Emil was rambling on about how much he was interested in the grocery business—he was twenty-three years old and single, she was thirty-three, with a husband and four children. She could have sworn his glance lingered just a moment too long as she stood up to hand him a sheaf of paperwork. Quickly she re-directed these irrelevant thoughts to the task at hand, making a mental note that the mind does wander when one does not have enough work to do. "Emil, you seem like an earnest young man, and we are all grateful to our boys in uniform—thank you for your service. You are obviously of good character and I believe in giving first consideration to our Veterans. I would like to give you a chance at the job. When can you start?" Emil considered for just a little too long, probably not wanting to appear too needy. "I can start whenever you would like me to Mrs. LeCompte." "How about right now—there's no time like the present." Nona liked the idea of this new trainee—he looked smart, capable of more than just the box-boy position, and his movie-star good looks were a perfect addition to the expensive merchandise. Things were getting interesting here.

Within a month of starting, Emil became indispensable, and Nona kept her new protégé under her wing—she was seriously thinking about promoting him to assistant manager. He dutifully boxed groceries, made pleasant small talk with the customers, especially the female ones, circulated, worked the crowd, volunteered to help little old ladies with their bags—he was almost too good to be true.

Right now, at the lunch hour, he was siting down outside at one of the stone tables with the fringed umbrellas, toward the back door, the last table next to the rear parking lot. From here Nona could look out the second story office window directly over his head, which he was probably aware of. The *Evening Outlook* was spread out in front of him, and from here Nona thought he might be browsing the Help Wanted ads—that just wouldn't do, so she hurried down the stairs and out the back door, slowing just as she rounded the corner. "Oh hi Emil, I didn't know you were out here—it must be your lunch already. Don't let me disturb you, I only came out to get a bit of sun for a moment—just ignore me." "You're impossible to ignore Mrs. LeCompte, and I mean that in a good way." Emil's smiling blue eyes held hers for just a moment too long, the message clear. He had been sending subtle verbal and non-verbal messages for a week now, trolling for a response but so far had got nothing but the stone wall treatment, but the day was so gorgeous, Emil so incredibly looking, and she was in a great mood, so she gave him a break—what harm could it do?—and flirted just as shamelessly back to him. She even sat down and scooted closer, pretending to be interested in the paper—and noticed it was open to the Real Estate section. "Are you looking for another apartment Emil?" Emil sat up straighter. "I'm actually interested in acquiring property in the foreseeable future, so I keep up on prices in the area. I would like to be a landlord one day, have rental income. It's the best way to financial security." Nona didn't know what to say to this, never having had to plan for financial security, and was taken aback hearing this from her employee, her box-boy. Quite the thinker for someone so young, but maybe not so young. He was twenty-three after all, probably thinking of starting a family. There was something in the square set of his jaw and his focused, purposeful movements that told her Emil would not fail to get what he wanted, ever.

"Well, I'd better get back inside—I told Mrs. Humphrey I would help her load the groceries into her car after she finished shopping."

Abruptly he was gone, and Nona was left at the table contemplating what it must be like to make your way up in the world. The *Evening Outlook* was still spread out on the table, corners flapping in the breeze, threatening to lift off on the wind, so she folded it up, noticing a slip of notepaper underneath. She recognized Emil's handwriting from his employment forms. Both sides were filled with numbers, in pencil—long division, decimal points, equal signs. They weren't small numbers, either. Apparently Emil thought in the five digit number range. She didn't know what to think, so simply rested her chin on her hands, enjoying the pleasant hustle bustle of the shoppers, exchanging pleasantries with them as they came and went, noting shopping baskets overflowing with merchandise, and briefly wondered, although it didn't seem important as long as everyone was happy, just how much mathematically the market's profits would pencil out to.

After the humiliating Westwood Village discovery of Emil's covert lunch date she had a whim to see the place the ill-fated Emil affair had started. "James, would you please turn left on 14th and pull into Fireside Market? I need something there." "Of course Mrs. Born." Vague shade of irony in his voice—he must know the tawdry story, the simpering phony—let him smirk—she couldn't resist driving by the market occasionally, still owned by the nice couple that purchased it in the LeCompte divorce sale. They had renamed it Fireside Market but stuck with her original idea of gourmet foods. She wished them well, she really did—they were lovely people. Why did she come back time and again to this corner, drawn against her will to look at a building that just made her sad? Because the market was her tie to a life she should have never given up, a concrete representation of a moment in time, a choice, where she could have easily gotten back on the high road, instead of being pulled down—*when you lay down with dogs, you get up with fleas.* It was one of her mother's favorite sayings, which she should have taken to heart.

Now, in her Buick as James guided the car into the parking lot, Nona reminisced about the early days when she had Emil, Norm, the business and her children compartmentalized into neat packages. What a horrible mistake it had all been—she had been greedy, had expected too much out of life. She already had it all before Emil came along—doting husband from her same background, four beautiful children, estate in Brentwood, and a thriving business. Why had she been so thoughtless? A two-year affair with a penniless young employee, the pregnancy, the hurt in poor Norm's eyes—she had begun to think of him as Poor Norm back then—as she confessed the trouble she was in, how sorry she was. She didn't blame Norm one bit for leaving, packing his bags and retreating into the familiar safety of the family estate back home in Iowa. Months later came the divorce decree from the LeCompte family's expensive attorney demanding Norm be paid one half the current value of Chef's Market or that the business be sold and one half the sale proceeds be returned to him along with his initial investment. At least he let her keep the house to ensure his children would be raised well, in an appropriate neighborhood.

Fall air, bittersweet and chilly, needled into her open window and she quickly rolled it up, pulled on her coat, turned up the collar, put her sunglasses on. Maybe no one would recognize her—she didn't want to be seen as a has-been haunting the places where once she was someone of significance, accomplishing something, at the hub of the community, a force that mattered. With sudden recognition she realized how unhappy she was, had been for a long time, and she had taken to daydreaming about the times when she was happy, looking back in the way elderly people did, dusty memories that seemed to get better with age and invention. Really all that she was doing now, let's face it, was waiting, but for what she had no idea. Maybe the tea leaves would tell her.

Later in the evening, at home in front of the fire, Emil upstairs quietly avoiding her—they didn't talk much anymore—she reached for the pile of mail. Maybe there was a nice card or letter from a family member, some good news she could hear from someone.

Nothing could have prepared her for the letter from the bank, dated October 1st, 1937:

> Dear Mr. Emil Born,
> This letter is a formal notification that you are in default of your obligation to make payments on your home loan, account #4339620. This current account holds the sum of $10,000, due and payable by November 1st, 1937.
> This amount has been overdue since July 1st, 1937 and you have ignored multiple requests to make a payment or reconsolidate your debt.
> Unless the full amount ($10,000) is received within 15 days, we have no choice but to begin the foreclosure process on your home at 129 N. Rockingham Avenue, Brentwood, California.

Emil had finally done the unthinkable—he had stolen from her. She had married a liar, cheater, and thief—she had given up Norm, a good man, to marry—and here she had to admit what had happened—a playboy, a gigolo, someone after her money all along. And he was definitely on the winning end.

CHAPTER 3

The rest of that evening would forever remain a blur to Nona, a thing the mind blocks out because it is too painful to recall. Only now, two years later, is she able to mull over her mistake, far worse than she originally thought and more obviously foolish in hindsight. Naively she had put Emil on her property title as a wedding gift, in effect making him a full half owner of the estate—which allowed him to take out loans against the property, the bank loan officer never thinking to ask the wife if she agreed. There was something she saw in Emil that simply wasn't there, in fact had never been there, an honesty, a forthrightness, a frankness in the blue eyes. How one can delude oneself when one wants to believe in something. Yes, he was a good father to Dolly and Genieve, his two biological children, but how difficult is that? She should have known, a handsome man ten years younger, falling in love with a married woman ten years older with four children, getting her pregnant, and he so anxious to marry her as soon as the LeCompte divorce was final. What a fool she had been in hindsight. She had even given him the means to become financially independent by paying for his landscape architect degree, his expensive equipment, his employees. Living near his customer base of Bel-Air didn't hurt either—his charm and looks allowed him access to the gated estates of the fabulously wealthy, whose landscapes were immune to the problems of the Great Depression. He was now the designer of choice and doing very well financially. Lillian Meyers, dance instructor, was now Mrs. Lillian Born, wife and part-time Avon cosmetics saleslady. They married right after his divorce was final, and through mutual acquaintances Nona learned they were head-over-heels in love, traveling up and down the coast of California to all the romantic places young couples went.

It was already 1940, the beginning of a new decade, America just coming out of the Great Depression, and here she sat, a fifty-two year old divorcée, with sixteen-year-old Dolly, who looked like a female Emil, a daily reminder of her tragic misstep, and sassy, bratty thirteen-year-old Genieve, in her rented bungalow North of Wilshire—at least it was the better area of Santa Monica, she had that much left. The divorce from Emil had cleaned her out and there was only a small savings left—her own father blamed her for the fiasco so he cut her trust fund in half as a lesson, her Brentwood estate was sold, her housekeeper had been dismissed, and she actually was ordered by the judge to pay the bum Emil out of the estate sale.

"Mother, Daddy has not sent my allowance yet, has he? I checked the mail today and there was nothing from him at all." This from Dolly, who faithfully checked the mail every day, looking for something, anything from her father, that would make this all disappear. Dolly had grown into a striking statuesque blond teenager, and people were starting to stare at this vision of Nordic perfection, turn around and look as they passed on the street. It was really quite annoying—no one gave her or Genieve second looks, other than to try and figure out what the relationship was—could the tall blond goddess be related to these two shorter dark-haired people, or were they of service to her in some capacity? "Mommy, Daddy has started sending my allowance at the end of the month, instead of at the beginning, like he used to. I hope someone else isn's getting my allowance, like Genieve, because she is too young, she doesn't need money yet, and I need to start saving for college, right?" Geneive scowled and challenged,

"I do more than you around here, so I should get an allowance too, right? I never had to sweep before, Tilly did it, she said it was maid's work. Tilly got paid, how come I don't?" Tilly was their housekeeper in Brentwood, the tidiest person Nona had ever met, and a nice lady too, size large, gracious, middle-aged, happy of be of service. It was heartbreaking to dismiss her when the house sold. "Okay, enough, the two of you, or I'll wash your mouths out with soap. Both of you go right this minute and finish the homework assignments, you have plenty to do for school. I need a little peace now, a break, so I'm going for a walk. I expect to see the homework done when I get back."

Nona hurried out the door before she could change her mind. She needed to stay in shape. Fifty-two wasn't that old as long as you were in top physical condition. You never knew who you were going to meet, so it was imperative to always look your best. To that end, she had assembled her outfit for today, black and white plaid Bermuda shorts, white sleeveless blouse, white tennis shoes, black cardigan thrown over her shoulders in case it got chilly. She is headed to Lincoln Park on the corner of Lincoln Boulevard and California Avenue, going at a pretty quick pace, down 12th Street, right on California toward the ocean. Pine trees lined one side of the street, tall palms the other. A few cars were slowly motoring along California, not in a hurry because it was Saturday—probably going to Chef's Market—*no, Fireside Market now.* A horn tooted and she turned to see who was in the car. Was that a former customer from the store, Bessie or Betty, or—she caught herself going back to the past and stopped it. The future was her habit, not the past. She had even pasted a reminder note on her dresser mirror: *Don't look back, you're not going that way.*

Winded, breathing in the salt air till it filled her lungs completely, as her physical education teachers had taught her, she slowly inhaled and exhaled rhythmically until her heart slowed, then stretched down, legs straight, trying to lay her palms flat on the warm sidewalk. What she wouldn't give for a See's butter cream—there should be some kind of reward for all this perspiration. Nearby a park bench beckoned, so she strolled over to enjoy the moment, listening to the seagulls as they floated low and circled the park hopefully, looking for picnic leftovers.

"Hello there sister, may I share your bench with you?" She is startled, uncomfortable, even a little alarmed to see a colored woman north of Wilshire, unashamed, almost as if she belonged there. It was an unspoken rule that colored people were supposed to stay south of Santa Monica Boulevard—and calling her sister, the nerve! The woman didn't wait for an answer, just sat right down and started reading a newspaper—*The New Day.* The woman wedged her face in the paper, holding both edges up like a shield, the paper making a rustling sound every time the page was turned. Must be a fast reader. Nona had an opportunity to surreptitiously glance at the print on the back page. Something about the layout and size of the print looked childish, simplistic—probably a publication geared toward colored people. There was no way Nona was going to be pushed off her bench, so she waited for the woman to try to initiate some conversation to break the uncomfortable silence. Oddly though, the woman seemed at ease as she read the newspaper, humming, nodding occasionally. She got the feeling the woman was waiting for the right moment to start a conversation with her—probably selling something, maybe a subscription. The sound of the rustling pages took Nona back to when her father used to bury his face in the morning paper, the business section, and would give her the funnies to read.

Fifteen minutes passed. "I've finished reading sister and have to move along. I'll leave you the paper so you have something to enjoy on this beautiful day. My name is Meekness Simplicity, and if you want another newspaper, they're only five cents at the newspaper stand on 4th and Wilshire, in front of Thrifty Drug Store." Nona wanted to be polite, and was relieved Meekness was leaving, so she took the paper, and was taken aback again as green cat-like eyes stared back, a bit glassy but pretty nevertheless. A mulatto, mixed race, milk chocolate skin, green eyes, wiry black hair with ribbons braided in, wearing a baggy blue cotton shirtdress and dumpy flats. Unusual person, but she enjoyed the occasional odd-balls that peppered Santa Monica, so she took the paper—there was nothing else going on and maybe it would have some entertainment value, a peek inside a little known Negro press, if there was such a thing. "Thank-you Meekness. My name is Nona, nice to meet you. I do enjoy reading. Have a nice walk. I have to be getting home now." She tucked the paper under her arm and backed away before the conversation could go any further.

Later, back home, while the girls finished their book reports for school, she browsed the paper, idly curious. The cover page had a photograph of a small Negro man, very dark, feeding chickens—probably fattening them up for the kill—and the paper was filled with little homilies, a sort of Reader's Digest for colored people, all smiling blissfully, frozen in time shaking hands, hanging laundry, cooking a meal—meant to be comforting, attainable, average Joes, happy and simple. The caption beneath the cover photograph proclaimed that every race, creed, and color would have peace, abundance, and assurance while living in the promised land on a farming commune. The man feeding the chickens, one Father Divine according to the caption, wore a white three piece suit, his Fedora tilted at a comical angle—weren't farmers supposed to wear overalls? Maybe he was the overlord. This was nutty stuff, just the thing for a little diversion. The date header of the paper was odd too—it was stamped with the volume, number, date, then A.D.F.D. Maybe she would ask Meekness about it, if she ever saw her again.

Genieve came in from the kitchen, hands on hip, authoritative. "Mother, the meatloaf is ready. I put potatoes and carrots next to it so it's like a full meal in one pan. Dolly didn't do anything, and she wouldn't even peel the potatoes when I asked for help." Genieve was a surprise, the bratty one was actually turning into someone useful.

She loved to cook and was pretty good at it too, but you darn well better heap on the praise for whatever she put in front of you. She had a huge ego even at her young age that needed to be stroked or she would become pouty, wouldn't cook for a week. Nona was sure Genieve would make something of herself. The divorce affected her only minimally—she seemed secure in the fact that her doting Daddy would not be far away, and she had taken a liking to Lillian the new wife. Lillian heaped Avon samples on both girls, trying to stay on their good side, and it seemed to work with Genieve, who especially loved the miniature lipstick samples. Emil and Lilian had rented a small pink wood framed house on 17th Street and California, only six blocks away—Nona often wished they had moved out of Santa Monica, but no such luck. Emil doted on his girls, was a good father—not the sort who would pull a disappearing act with a new young wife. Nona had heard a rumor from her friends that Lillian could not have children of her own, so Dolly and Genieve may be all the children Emil and Lillian would ever have.

Dolly had become more petulant and demanding with her Daddy, probably competing with Lillian, whom she blamed for the divorce. Nona didn't know what to make of Dolly, who had become remote, introverted. One of Dolly's friends from school had told Nona she was weak-minded, always willing to do what was suggested to her, but had no ideas of her own. She had a vague idea that she should go to college, but lacked interest in her classes at Santa Monica High School—she was just going through the motions. Nona was thinking Dolly would make a good wife for someone, would produce beautiful children, and she absolutely had the looks to catch someone that did well financially, like a lawyer or doctor. Toward this end, Nona encouraged Dolly to focus on Home Economics classes.

Almost a year went by, Nona falling into a daily routine of managing the girls, running the house, and jogging, now making it easily to Palisades Park and back, almost exactly two miles, in under thirty minutes. Today, though, she decided to go only as far as Lincoln Park, maybe sit on the same bench again and relax. She deserved it, taking some time to smell the roses as they say. She saw that her favorite bench was open and headed right for it. At the same moment she saw a female figure emerge from behind the old knotty pines, wearing a baggy dress and heading at an angle toward the same bench "Nona, hello there, how are you? Remember me, Meekness?—we met before in this same park. I come here often but never saw you again." Nona was stuck now, couldn't get out of a conversation without appearing rude. She noticed Meekness was carrying the same paper, different edition, and was probably going to read it again on the very same bench as she did before. Strange but she even appeared to be wearing the same clothes—was this woman a hobo living in a park?

Meekness clutched her newspaper, *The New Day,* close to her chest. Evidently this was a treasured source of information for her. Nona remembered the odd header showing the unusual date of publication. "Meekness, I noticed the paper you gave me before had a date at the top that ended with A.D.F.D. I wondered what it meant." "Sister, it means in the year of the Lord Father Divine. See, here he is giving a feast for his flock at the communion table in Philadelphia." She proudly held up the front page, where the same small Negro man from last year's paper was presiding magnanimously at the head of a long formal table filled with smiling people, colored and white mixed together. Nona thought she would play along, humor Meekness to pass the time—she liked esoteric topics like tea leaf reading, Ouija boards, witchcraft, automatic writing. She thought of it as the science of ideas, systems of belief, visionary theology. Only in California could you have a conversation like this with a stranger—in Iowa they would throw you in the loony bin—it was part of what attracted her to California. "I didn't realize the man feeding the chickens on the cover of the paper you gave me was the Lord. I thought Father Divine was a preacher who ran a commune." This opened up a long dissertation from Meekness about all the good works, charity, healings, magical happenings, and unexplained events that could only mean one thing—God had appeared again on Earth in the form of a small colored man, a preacher, benefactor to the poor, someone with a plan, a formula on how to live in Heaven now, not later. As Meekness spoke, Nona noticed the glassy-eyed far away look, as if she were seeing Heaven open up right above them. She seemed to disassociate from the park, blocking out the occasional car horn and children's laughter from the playground, and go into an alternate reality from where she extolled the virtues of being a true follower of Father Divine. Nona played along with polite questions for awhile, but she was waiting for her chance to break away, so she asked for another newspaper to read to learn more about Father. Meekness was overjoyed to give her the paper, thinking she may have reached someone, shown them who God really was, saved them. "Meekness, thank you once again for your gift. I'll read it and let you know what I think the next time I see you. I come to this park often on my walks. Have a wonderful day." Seagulls cawed overhead, mockingbirds chimed in, and the scent of the sea was hopeful, empowering. Nona wondered why Meekness Simplicity needed to look further for Heaven when it was right in front of her, right now.

CHAPTER 4

Father Divine was hovering, in avuncular mode, over the shoulder of his current favorite Rosebud, Miss True Light. True, a light complected young woman with wavy red hair and porcelain skin was primly sitting at one of the study desks, wearing her Rosebud uniform—knee-length black skirt, white blouse, and form-fitting cropped red jacket with *V* for Virtue and Victory over Carnality embroidered on the lapel—in the deserted library at International Peace Mission West, writing a prayer for Father. He noted approvingly that she had remembered to date the composition correctly—April 15th, 1947 A.D.F.D.— Anno Domini (in the year of the Lord Father Divine.) He mused that as long as A.D.F.D. was properly credited to him, the rest of the message may very well be of secondary importance.

True Light shyly handed Father her letter, leaning in close—and now he was trying, he really was, to block out what George Baker Jr., former self, wanted to do at this moment. "Thank you for your prayer Rosebud. I would like to read it right now, while I am near you, so I can feel its energy." The small looped cursive handwriting with a pronounced right-handed slant was difficult to read in the dimness, but here it was:

> Father you are so precious to me and millions of others. Father you are the Rose of Sharon and Lily of the Valley praise your holy name. You are God and the only God...and Mother is our Mother and we never had another. Praise your holy name Father and Mother dear. Thank you for the blessing of the past day and safety of the night as well as of the other days of this week. Thank you Father and Mother to see how lovely you both look and thank you for revealing yourselves to your children. Thank you for coming in the flesh which is such a help to us and Father and Mother dear forgive me of all my sins today. I love you so much I cannot tell in words how much. Thank you Father and Mother dear. Love, True Light

Father Divine, a.k.a. Reverend Major Jealous Divine, a.k.a. George Baker Jr. was touched, yes he was. Miss True Light—he thought of her frivolously as Miss Delight—was a true believer in his godship, his embodiment of divine fatherly love. She and the other young Rosebuds in his movement never questioned anything. They just followed the rules, happy to be taken care of in style—the banquets, the mansions, the clothes, the jobs, the communal family they were part of—all their needs were met by his movement and the income it generated. Their income went straight into Father's Heavenly Treasury and he doled it out as he saw fit. They were truly like children, dutifully avoiding the evils of the Capitalistic, prejudiced, self-serving American way of life. The mature Angels and Brothers, and some of the young boys, referred to as Masters, sometimes stepped out of line, but not often—the threat of losing their livelihoods and roofs over their heads usually kept them quiet.

"I love you too, Miss True Light, and don't you ever forget that. You are my child and I will take care of you the rest of your life, you have nothing to fear, you are safe." His small dark hand cupped the back of her smooth neck and disappeared under her hair, lifting it up, releasing True's sweet scent—did he feel goose bumps? He heard a shuffling just then and his name spoken from the doorway right behind. "Father dear, they're waiting for you in the conference room." Miss Sincere Sincerity, Mother Divine's personal chaperone, had come up on him just a little too quietly as usual, stooped over and silent, far too humble—he could almost feel her disapproval of him, her pursed lips, her dark expression. She wouldn't dare say anything though, because she held one of the highest positions in the International Peace Mission Movement, as close to the top as you could get, the constant companion, chaperone, and personal assistant to the seemingly delicate but formidable Edna Rose Ritchings, better known as Mother Divine.

Sincere Sincerity was what he thought of as a lifer—too traumatized to even pretend to live a normal life, she easily came to terms with Father's rules, becoming a convert while still a young woman in the Deep South. While walking home from school one day she had been dragged into the bushes at the side of the road and raped by a group of white men to the point of internal injury. Later her school books were found strewn across the road, the information in them rendered irrelevant now to the young girl. The doctors performed a hysterectomy, causing her to be considered damaged goods in her culture. She would never give birth so was doomed to live life as an outcast, no children, no family. The white men went unpunished and Father Divine suspected the doctors performed the hysterectomy to prevent her kind from reproducing. Stories like these were common and plagued his people continuously, the crimes for the most part going unpunished and usually unannounced in the news. His own parents, former slaves, were treated brutally by whites at every turn, especially his own mother. Divine deeply resented the injustices white people perpetrated against those of a darker complexion, but if he had to use them to further his cause, give it legitimacy, so be it. Thus far it was working beautifully and the increasing number of whites attracted to his movement gave him the credibility he needed if he was to proceed with building his following— and financials—of his Peace Mission Movement.

The conference room at Peace Mission West was designed to impress. This was where Father Divine met with advisors—and smart attorneys—to work out his business plans. A huge rectangular carved mahogany table dominated the center of the room, polished to perfection with scented lemon oil and placed on a palace-sized Persian rug, giving the room a muted, quiet quality. At the head of the table Father Divine's hand carved lion's head chair with red velvet cushions presided. The chair's legs were a little longer to make Father Divine appear taller and more imposing—at only 5'2" he needed a lift in stature to match his booming voice. Floor to ceiling leaded cut glass casement windows scattered prisms of light at certain times of the day. The pool and cabana were off in the distance, over the rolling verdant lawn, in line with the vast blue of the San Francisco Bay.

Today the topic was the downtown area of Berkeley, specifically the areas where people congregated, where they spent money. The backstory was always racial integration, how to accomplish it without raising the deep hostility of whites against Negro-owned businesses. Divine knew that people found it difficult to resist incredibly cheap prices regardless of the complexion of workers, so his method was to either buy or lease store space in a commercial area, then undercut nearby businesses. It worked every time—whites grumbled about the colored folks working in the neighborhood but soon gave in and spent money because the prices were unbeatable, the quality was good, and the workers, all followers of Divine, were preternaturally nice and spotlessly dressed, always prefacing and ending a transaction by cheerfully saying "Peace." At Peace Mission restaurants you could get a well-rounded meal for 15 cents, at their barber shops a shave, haircut, or shoe shine was 10-15 cents, and the laundries and seamstresses were top-notch and practically free compared to existing businesses. The domestic workers were hired out to fine homes through his temporary agency The Courtesy Employment Service—they flawlessly performed their duties without resentment and with a smile. The small businesses had become an integral part of his International Peace Mission Movement.

Divine convinced the followers who worked for him that they were profit-sharing and payment was a communal model—meaning they handed over everything they made to Father Divine. He told them they were part owners of the businesses in which they worked, part owners of the buildings Divine purchased with the proceeds from their endless, often back-breaking labor. They were told they were a part of something larger, part of their new family The Peace Mission Movement. The businesses accepted only cash, and where the cash ended up no one knew and few cared. They had their needs met, ate well, wore nice clothes, lived in beautiful surroundings with other followers—they were, in their minds at least—a happy family with Father and Mother Divine at the helm, taking care of everything, buffers against an unkind world.

Now here he was, at the head of the table again, in his conference room, with two real estate attorneys and an accountant—all white men well established in the city of Berkeley, all liberal minded. They weren't followers, but just as well, he thought—he needed to be advised by business people—certainly these types of men would never buy into his divinity nonsense. They were here advising him because he paid them well—they all had that in common, the quest for the all-mighty dollar—how to get it, how to spend it, how to control it, how to keep it.

"Gentlemen, I thank you for coming today. The International Peace Mission Movement would like to move forward with the new gourmet grocery store for downtown Berkeley. I believe you gentlemen have some papers for me to sign regarding this matter?" One of the attorneys, a Mr. Sperling, shifted his large bulk forward in his chair and slid a packet of papers across the table to Divine, carrying with him a thin trail of citrus aftershave. "Please sign where the red stickers are sir, then we're done. You are set to take possession of the building in thirty days."

They were all looking at him when the other attorney, Mr. Fletcher, a thin efficient looking young man, stuck his chin forward, pausing significantly for effect—his moment to shine with knowledge no one else had. "The other grocery store in town, Giuseppi's, is making noises with his property owner because his lease says no other grocery store will be able to open up in competition with him within a certain distance."

In an entirely different voice than he used for sermons he hit back, "Gentlemen, I do not intend to compete with Giuseppi's, I intend to put him out of business. An Italian grocery store cannot and will not compete with a gourmet grocer—the people of Berkeley are tired of common food—they want truffles, not pizza. All I need to know is that my supply chain is in order and ready to deliver products at below cost to our charitable endeavor. My food procurement management staff has opened many stores for me and they know what to do."

"Your suppliers are ready when you are sir. Just give us the word when the space is ready." This from the accountant Mr. Alan Moskowitz, C.P.A., a tall elegantly thin dark-haired Jewish man who had been with him for years. Every time he did any kind of transaction with Alan, he felt safe, like he was protected not from the Devil, but something worse—the Internal Revenue Service, whose agents were always lurking in the background, waiting for a slip-up, a mistake, a clue as to how much cash passed hands and where it ended up, a shred of a paper trail so they could nail him to the cross. It never happened, but they watched him with an almost religious fervor, in his opinion—and he knew religious fervor when he saw it. It was because of Alan's intricate knowledge of the tax system, specifically charities, non-profits, and religion-based tax laws, that he managed to remain a free man.

"Anyone have anything to add? Seems like we're done here, and things are in order. I think you all are going to see that the people of Berkeley are sick of graft and greed, and are ready for a fine gourmet grocery store with fair prices—something they've never seen before--with good, honest, humble working folks serving them."

"I need a breath of fresh air Brother. I'm going for a walk in town." Brother David Devoute, who was never very far from him, nodded in acknowledgement. Devoute was almost like a sponge, Divine thought, but he had come in handy more than once. If there was anything going on at the mission Devoute almost certainly knew, and would wait for an opportune moment when he was out of earshot of everyone to humbly mention with downcast eyes the latest gossip. He thought of Devoute as his second set of eyes, although he would never admit this to Devoute—Divine, as God incarnate, would of course already know the goings on—so he usually just thanked Devoute for being a faithful Brother with no comment on the controversy. He was less than one hundred percent sure Brother Devoute believed he was God incarnate—he was around him too much. Devoute had become a follower when still a young man who wanted to start a family but was unsure or unable to take control of his life due to excessive indecisiveness and low self-esteem. It was so much easier for him, after learning of the options Father Divine's followers had, to just give up control and join the International Peace Mission Movement and serve. He was now middle-aged and gray, a soft pear-shaped man that had worked his way up in the movement to become something of a fixer, or a man Friday for Father. He neither had nor wanted any other life.

Divine headed down the stone path to the sidewalk and turned right in the direction of downtown Berkeley. He was thinking he would do his best to blend in—a Negro in a three-piece suit was a rare sight in this part of town so it was difficult—but today he was representing his business, after all, and needed to be an ambassador of good will. Prejudice or not, he would just keep walking, smiling, as if everything were perfectly normal. And observing. His small stature made his Fedora look ludicrously large, and his very small dark hands protruding from shortened coat sleeves made him appear somewhat misshapen, almost dwarf-like. His walk was a bit stilted as he tried to minimize the bounce in his step—he believed a self-contained gait would make him appear more dignified. It was warm today, and he started to perspire but he didn't dare take his coat off—it would look too informal. He wanted to walk the area of his new building, where his grocery store would be. As usual, many white people did not make eye contact with him, pretended not to see him, or looked right through him, which must have been difficult because he cut such an odd figure. He never let any emotion show on his impassive face other than peace, because in the near future these same people would be customers of his mission's grocery store. Even though they may not become converted followers, they would most likely become what he thought of as Father Divine sympathizers—and sympathizers spent money at his businesses and donated to his causes.

He was walking the quaint tree-lined downtown area, smiling at this happy thought, when his reverie was interrupted by a blustering little Italian man with a thick accent, obviously Giuseppi himself, appearing out of nowhere, ambushing from behind. "Hey, you the guy who gonna open a store near me? Waddaya think you doin'?" It was definitely Giuseppi—Divine knew this because Giuseppi had imprinted his shopping bags, pizza boxes, even his store sign with his likeness—round cheerful face, perfectly waxed Italian mustache with jaunty pointed ends, black hair parted in the middle and slicked down just so. At this moment, Giuseppi looked anything but cheerful, in fact he wondered if he was going to have to call for help—he had no idea how to fight, only talk—so he quickly searched for a verbal side step, something to calm and placate the man while he thought of a way out of an embarrassing confrontation. *Money, of course—that's what he's worried about.* "Mr. Giuseppi, what a pleasure to meet you. We were just discussing today how lucky we are to have an Italian speciality grocer nearby because we're not going to carry any Italian products—they're in such short supply—may we refer customers to you, the ones that inquire about Italian products?" Giuseppi paused for a moment, hands on hip pugnaciously, and pondered. "I don' need any more business, we doin' great, but I guess it's okay if you send 'em my way. We got plenty for anybody wants Italian, for sure." They chatted for a bit, Divine allowing the faintest shade of the ghetto to color his usually well-modulated voice. They moved their impromptu meeting to the side to allow people to stroll by, people who glanced at them curiously—two oddball characters amidst young educated white college students and well-to-do locals. Giuseppi was hardboiled and rough, something Divine felt more comfortable around than the usual hoity-toity types he encountered in this town—at least he was direct and you knew where you stood, unlike the snide overly educated locals here. They would get along just fine for now. Maybe when Giuseppi went out of business he could buy his products at closing sale prices.

A week later Divine was again in front of a group of people, holding his standard pep rally that always preceded his request for free labor. He had memorized the confusing meaningless words, but more importantly, had perfected the style of delivery—loud intonations, swaying body movements, waving hands, emphatic grunts—because it was effective with his particular audiences. "The harvest is ripe but the laborers are few. Let's bring our mythological concepts of brotherhood into reality—have not you seen the meaning of true Christianity as it comes forth into expression in the person of Father Divine? We are overcoming, um, the impracticality of misrepresented Christianity by putting them in their respective places. Fo' as long as they are over-privileged and, um, subjected to the spirit of dictatorship and lordship they cannot be prosperous, healthy, and happy and they cannot have a victory over difficulties, um, that come in opposition to mortality." Here he paused significantly and reared back dramatically to look around the room, on fire, seemingly making eye contact with each individual after delivering his dénouement. One timid soul mustered the courage to raise her hand to announce, "Father dear, I would like to volunteer to work every single day and night if need be to help in the store so we can let the people buy food at fair prices. Just tell me what to do and when to start." This from a new young Rosebud, Stella something he believed, who had just moved into the mission from an impoverished Negro enclave near San Francisco. He guessed she had no other options judging from her appearance—still young but very overweight and unattractive. He would take care of her because she was willing to work for him, was filled with enthusiasm to start life with her new family, and had few other choices in life. "Thank you Rosebud, you make Father and Mother very proud." Stella almost swooned and sank back down into her hard wooden mission chair by force of gravity, overcome with the spirit of goodness. She was going to change with world, starting with Berkeley. Divine made a mental note that she could probably be trusted at the cash register.

Over the years he had studied many preachers and picked up a little from each, learning from their successes and failures. George Baker Jr., a mimic even as a toddler as his mother had told him, had learned that people who gravitated toward gurus, new thought movements, preachers, gods incarnate, saviors in the flesh, or the like, actually admired the fact that the words spoken by their leader were mysterious and the meanings muddled—it meant the concepts were so deep that it forced you to stop and think—they may even be parables if you only opened your mind. If you didn't understand then you were not worthy to receive the message yet—or close minded, or worse, dense—all the more evidence the words were divinely inspired since only the enlightened understood. What absolutely did matter was the emphatic delivery of the sermon, your conviction, and very importantly, your appearance—did you look prosperous? If so, then obviously you were someone that knew more than the average Joe and you were to be taken seriously. Followers gravitated and wanted to be associated with success because they did not have their own, or at least did not feel successful. One of the psychoanalysis books he had picked up called it "identification with the aggressor"—he understood that concept. You, the leader, their god even, were their role model, their father figure, especially if they could imagine—and you didn't discourage the idea—that you were in fact God incarnate.

Tonight, after the pep rally for Mission Grocery Store workers, Father Divine was feeling his age—he was no spring chicken after all. Mother Divine wasn't much help in business, supposedly had no interest or talent for it, or so she claimed. Much of her time was spent counseling Rosebuds, gaining their confidence, getting them settled and outfitted, indoctrinated into mission life—she seemed to take even more of an interest in the Rosebuds than he did. Edna Rose Ritchings—Mother Divine—understood people, especially women. So to take some of the pressure off, he had instructed his office staff to advertise in his publication *The New Day* for experienced management help in his grocery store, which was scheduled to be open very shortly. Already today large crates of boxed and canned foods had been delivered to the loading dock and the shelves were probably being stocked with the non-perishables tonight even as he sat in his bedroom suite and perused applications. His brass banker's light cast a reassuring soft glow over the papers spread before him at his writing desk. He reminded himself that he had to be very careful whom he chose because this was a trusted management position—they needed to be a Father Divine sympathizer at the very least and preferably a full-blown follower—a conundrum because his followers were usually unskilled domestics or lost souls with few job skills.

The papers rustled quietly as he turned them over, mulling over each, giving the applicants an equal measure of his time. Now here was an interesting application from a woman who had relocated to Berkeley with her husband, a Mr. Herschel Twining, along with her two adult daughters, from Santa Monica about two years ago—it even had an introductory letter written on fine stationary with an educated hand. He held the paper up to the light—sure enough, it had a watermark and the warmth of the lightbulb caused the paper to emit perfumed scent. Expensive perfumed fine stationary for a job application—was this a gimmick? If so it worked, and now he investigated the specifics in greater detail. Amazingly, the woman had experience not only working in, but owning a grocery store! Her letter stated that she wanted to remain a productive member of society, wanted a meaningful job where she could use her brain, rather than sit around home all day while her husband worked—Divine took this to mean the woman probably wanted to be financially independent from her husband. She also stated she had been reading *The New Day* for years and admired his work with the poor. The letter was signed by a Mrs. Nona Twining. After further reading he decided to make sure Mrs. Twining received an answer in the form of an "invitation to interview" letter placed in the mission's outgoing mailbox by tomorrow morning—he hoped she had not found other employment yet because she sounded like his perfect candidate.

CHAPTER 5

Nona tried not to think how old she was—if anyone asked, her standard answer was "I'm as old as Anne." If you took the bait and asked who Anne was, the response was always a significant roll of the large dark eyes, then silence—you got the message. Anyway, she was in perfect shape and exercised regularly at Vic Tanny's Gym near Muscle Beach in Venice. She loved hanging around Muscle Beach—what you saw there just couldn't be duplicated anywhere else, she was sure of it. One of the local oddballs, an elderly woman they called Gravel Gurty, walked up and down the beach all day long wearing only a gunny sack. Occasionally the gunny sack, worn in lieu of a mumu, would slid down to her ankles—you got an eyeful of tanned leather skin, sagging breasts, and deflated buttocks as she stooped over to tug the sack back into place, a scary reminder to the young beach crowd to spend less time in the sun. She had a few casual gym acquaintances, but in general she didn't dilly-dally long at Venice Beach—just long enough to get her fill of oddballs for the week, enough to have something to giggle about with her daughters.

In the blink of an eye Dolly had turned twenty-one, Genieve eighteen. Where had the time gone? It was so easy to let days slide into years in the California sun—will it be Sorrento Beach, Venice Beach, or State Beach today? The girls—women now actually—gravitated toward State Beach, lifeguard station 17, at the end of Chautauqua

Boulevard in Santa Monica Canyon. Genieve, always aware of appearances, maintained this is where the better people—code for wealthy eligible young men—went to the beach. Dolly went along wherever Genieve decided to go. Nona guessed that way Dolly didn't have to think.

Nona's savings were getting very low, and she was worried sick. They had stayed in the rented bungalow on 12th Street in Santa Monica so the rent had not been raised much—they were exemplary tenants and the little bungalow had become home, but paying rent was beginning to be a concern. Accordingly, she had become very, very friendly with a mature gentleman, a Mr. Herschel Twining, who managed First Federal Bank on 4th Street and Wilshire in Santa Monica. Mr. Twining was tall and thin, thick black hair, in his sixties, wore dark business suits, looked important and resembled an undertaker—an unkind thought but true. Nona was not adverse to the idea of a fifth husband if it could help their situation. She suspected Herschel had analyzed her account and noticed how it had dwindled from a very substantial savings to one that could only be referred to as—and she hated this word—average. Maybe Herschel saw this an an opportunity to be of assistance to a still attractive divorcée. As she stood in front of the full-length mirror, choosing an outfit for today's lunch date with Herschel, she noted approvingly she looked quite a bit younger than him and he was lucky to have her. Herschel looked rather shop-worn, poor man. He was a widower whose wife had passed away a few years ago from a lingering illness and he was terribly lonely, and like most men was not doing well on his own without a woman to tell him what to do.

"Mother, you look like like a movie star. I like the teal and black striped blouse, black high waisted skirt, and the black strappy wedges—plus, they're easy to walk in. Is he taking you to the Pier? If so, you want something nautical looking, not something frilly. Take the mohair cardigan in case it gets cold, and wear the hat with the brim so you don't have to squint." This from Genieve, fashion expert, avid reader and collector of Vogue and Glamour Magazines. Genieve was all for Nona's alliance with Herschel, even though she idolized her daddy Emil. Herschel had money and a career Genieve could relate to—bank accounting manager. Genieve had enrolled herself in a correspondence course with Merritt College of Business. The physical campus was up North in San Leandro, just outside of Berkeley. The course was what Genieve chose to spend her baby-sitting and odd-job money on. She knew instinctively that it was going to be up to her to become a success because she didn't want to have to put up with a man supporting her, as she adamantly stated to anyone who listened—she was going to make it on her own so she didn't have to answer to anyone for anything. Nona noted how like Emil she was in her love of numbers and accounting—"the blood will tell" her own mother would have said.

Just then came a forthright knock on the door, exactly three firm knocks, and Nona visualized Herschel on the other side adjusting his tie and straightening his posture. Genieve swung the door open dramatically while Nona hurriedly dabbed a dot of Arpège perfume behind each ear, then glided casually across the living room. "Herschel, you look so handsome today! I haven't seen that suit before—it's perfectly tailored for you." After a few minutes of pleasantries with Genieve—Dolly was hard at work this afternoon scooping ice cream a few blocks away at 31 Flavors on Wilshire—Nona gathered up her purse, hat and cardigan and sailed out the door, with Herschel dutifully following her to his car. You couldn't miss the car, she thought—a new shiny red 1946 Buick Super with white wall tires—a little gaudy for her taste but then few shared her tasteful background. Much of California was new money after all, so one should loosen up and just enjoy. The car and the man seemed mismatched, but perhaps there was more than meets the eye to staid Herschel Twining.

"Where are we going for lunch? Or is it a surprise?" She knew it was important to Herschel to be the decision maker, so she would go along with anything he suggested.

"To The Lobster, my treat of course, a reward for being so beautiful." His chin jutted forward a little, the captain of his own ship.

She raised her eyebrows approvingly—very generous for a lunch date. The Lobster was a fixture in Santa Monica, right at the head of the Pier on Ocean Avenue, a tried and true date destination if you wanted to impress someone.

Herschel pointed the car down 12th Street to Wilshire and turned right, Nona leaning back and just close enough to Herschel to make him aware of the Arpège applied in his honor—a non-verbal communication in any language. Now it was time to just relax and take it all in. Wilshire was one of her favorite streets. She loved the fact Santa Monica was a city, with most of the action of an important city where things were happening, but with only a few high rise buildings, and those were historical buildings with beautiful detail, not cement monoliths. Tall fan palms swayed all up and down Wilshire, all the way up to Westwood Village and beyond, and down to Ocean Avenue with the vast blue of the Pacific in the distance beyond Palisades Park. The city had escaped the post World War 2 tract housing boom because it was already built out—it had maintained a beautiful mix of predominantly Spanish architecture, with a sprinkling of Art Deco, Victorian, and Modern. Not a tract house in sight, no sign of anything average, no sameness, just original buildings and homes, each one different, each with its own special character, populated with interesting people.

Now they were in the restaurant parking lot, Herschel stiffly twisting his upper body, turning his head to back in—right next to the "head in only" parking sign—"I want to be able to leave easily without backing up in case I have a glass of wine." She nodded silently—never tell a man how to drive she thought—and tried to decide beforehand if she should indulge in wine in the middle of the day. The Lobster had an extensive wine list along with its five-star menu. It opened in 1923 and had become an icon as deeply embedded in the landscape surrounding the pier as the nearby authentic 1861 Rodman seacoast cannon gun that pointed mysteriously out over the ocean. The Lobster had survived the Great Depression and World War 2 by never compromising quality—entering the restaurant enveloped you in a warm heady mist of lobster and drawn butter, freshly baked sour dough bread, and pecan praline pie right out of the oven.

They were ushered to a table with a view—the best view she noted with satisfaction. Herschel had a way of getting people to attend to him—he looked like someone of note, and people that banked at First Federal, which was most of Santa Monica, recognized him. "I'll order for both of us, if you don't mind my dear." "Of course Herschel, you must know what's best. The hostess seemed to know you." They made small talk while waiting for the meal to arrive, but Nona had a distinct feeling there was something important Herschel wanted to tell her. He seemed to be waiting for the right time, getting closer to the bottom of the wine glass, before opening up. Abruptly, "I'm transferring to the Berkeley branch of First Federal in one month. I really don't have much choice in the matter because of the significant monetary advantage that has been offered to me. It's an honor, frankly, and I am originally from San Francisco so I am familiar with the area. I wondered if you might be at all interested in accompanying me. I truly enjoy your company and have become quite attached to you. As I understand it, there is nothing tying you or your daughters here. Perhaps a change of scenery would do you all good. It's a very forward-looking town, so I am sure you would enjoy it."

Nona was floored. Was this some sort of proposal, or did he think she was just going to shack up with him and hope everything went well? How could she have given him that impression? Herschel was half Jewish on his mother's side—maybe this was a Jewish cultural quirk, living together outside of marriage—why should he buy the cow if he could get the milk for free?—her mind was spinning and her frown was deepening. "Of course, you would have your own flat, obviously, for appearances. I can help you find something if you are at all open to this arrangement." Arrangement! She was furious but her wheels kept spinning all the same. She forced the frown into a more attractive facial expression so she would appear neutral on the subject while she thought. And thought. How could this benefit them all? She did in fact feel safe with Herschel, and he certainly didn't seem flighty—just the opposite in fact. She knew that if a Jewish person liked you, they would give you the shirt off their back. She wondered if converting to Judaism was required for this so-called arrangement. She had tried Catholicism, Lutheranism, a vague Protestantism, Eastern Thought, Occultism, and lately even New Thought—thanks to Meekness Simplicity's pushing Father Divine's dogma every time they met in the park. "Herschel, I have to admit, I'm honored you think enough of me to ask. Tonight I will discuss it with the girls—you know how fond of you they are, so I'm sure they will be thrilled." Herschel was a good catch, really— especially at her age—and she didn't want the fish to get away, but she needed to stall a bit to think.

The young waitress, blond hair pinned, rolled, styled and secured by a hairnet, bent forward from her tiny waist with a smile to deliver two huge plates of lobster tail with drawn butter. For now it was time to enjoy, and put worry aside. Nona knew how to do that—compartmentalize—if you couldn't do that, you were sunk, as her father had said many times. Nona's eyes drifted out to the beach beyond the pier, and an image materialized in front of her, a scene she had witnessed in the 1930's—she thought she had long forgotten it, but there they were now, as if in a dream, right there on the sand beside the Pier—the Okie family camping on the beach, all their worldly possessions piled around them, spilling out of the battered black makeshift tarp they had fashioned into a tent. The Dust Bowl Migration route out of the Midwest was Route 66, which ended right at the head of the Santa Monica Pier, right where they were sitting now. The people, hillbillies or Okies the Californians called them, had never seen the sea before and stopped to admire the incredible sight and breath in the salty air of the Pacific Ocean after a lifetime of seeing only the endless dusty plains, mostly barren now from the drought. She could see that Okie family now clear as day—the mother, stern, solidly built, capable, thick ankles and wrists, not an ounce of fat on her sturdy frame, and the man, rawboned, tall, hawkish face, lean as a coyote, and their four children ranging from toddler to teenager, all in rags but somehow persevering. They were going to be okay, you just knew it—they were survivors, not quitters. She and Herschel were probably enjoying the very potatoes grown and sold by the Okies right now, smothered in butter next to the lobster. Nona admired The Okies for their strength, their connection to the Earth—her life was ridiculously easy compared to theirs. She leaned over the table and squeezed Herschel's arm. Opportunity was always available if you knew where to look—and here it was, right in front of her.

The rest of the day went by unnoticed because Nona was thinking, planning on when and how, or even if, she would tell the girls about Herschel's proposition. Dolly would go along with anything, as long as it made her seem agreeable, but Genieve had lifelong friends in Santa Monica, ties that would be hard for her to break. Nona was used to change, but her children were not. They had all been born and raised in Santa Monica, and her older daughters and son had moved only as far as Malibu and Pacific Palisades, or stayed right in Santa Monica. But Berkeley had such a nice ring to it—she had never been there but envisioned it as a haven for the educated, old money set, even the intelligentsia. Someone once told her the downtown area resembled

Westwood Village—you had the advantages of close proximity to a University so there was culture along with more than enough retail for those who loved to shop. She became conscious that she craved a change of scenery, something new, to feel as if her life was moving forward instead of stagnating.

Later that evening, after dinner, in the small living room, among the lingering smells of one of Genieve's home-cooked meals—spaghetti this time—they discussed the prospects, Nona opening with all the positives.

"If you stay in your hometown all your life, you'll become close-minded and ignorant, dull. What would your conversation be about if you never experience new things. You want to be well-traveled and conversant don't you? Let's try it for a year—if you don't like it you can come back. You have nothing to lose, and you can stay in touch with your friends—maybe they would even like to come up and visit. Everyone wants to see Berkeley—there's so much going on there."

"Well, I guess it would be better if I was closer to Merritt College—then I could pick up my course material in person, or even take a few classes on campus. She hesitated, not voicing her concerns about moving away from her lifelong friends and the rest of her family.

Dolly held back, measuring her sister's and mother's reactions, before committing to a statement. "I guess it would be okay, but where would we live, where would I work? The only work experience I have is with 31 Flavors Ice Cream and some babysitting jobs. What about Daddy? When would I see him?" No mention of Lillian of course—Dolly had chosen to block out Lillian, home-wrecker, the person responsible for the entire divorce and money mess—but of course she would never admit it. It might make her seem like she actually had an independent opinion rather than just being agreeable.

Nona pointed out, "You can write your Daddy—you know how he loves to write letters, and you can send pictures back and forth. He has a telephone now too. It doesn't have to be forever, and it will be good for you to have a change of scenery—maybe you'll even meet someone nice." They both looked at Dolly significantly—she was twenty-one now and not even seeing anyone, no prospects. "Well girls, let's think it over tonight and we can talk about it more tomorrow evening.

In the morning Nona picked out a nice exercise outfit and headed out on her usual route. She was feeling better about the adventure, more confident. Why not try something different? Nothing worse than doing nothing but the same thing day after day, getting older, going nowhere—look how fast six years had gone by. Sometimes she would see the same people around town that used to come into her grocery store. She always noted how much they had aged, and she hadn't aged at all—but that was impossible of course. She had a theory that new ideas and travel kept one's mind and body young. She needed to move forward, see new things and have new experiences before her time was up.

Winded but feeling good, she went over to the drinking fountain in Lincoln Park, her usual rest stop before Ocean Avenue. Sure enough, there was Meekness Simplicity on her bench, reading the paper. Maybe she would run the new idea past Meekness—odd people often had alternative insights on things that proved to be something one would never think of—a divine madness of sorts.

"Hi there Meekness. Do you have time for a chat? I don't want to interrupt you if you are reading though." Meekness was thrilled to be asked anything, considering she was normally ignored at the park, even though it was her regular routine, for years now, to read the same publication on the same bench at the same place. She had become a fixture at the park, just like Gravel Gerty at Venice Beach—a character.

"Peace Nona, please tell me what is on your mind today." Nona filled Meekness in on her new opportunity, trying to keep it as simple as possible—they really weren't personal friends, but she had grown used to seeing her, and they sometimes discussed the ideas put forth in The New Day, Meekness often sharing her feelings for Father Divine and his Peace Mission Movement. Nona always tried to keep it light because she didn't want to push an oddball off the deep end, but the conversations did have entertainment value for her, so why not listen? In this new religion, there were no depressing threats of punishment in the afterlife—the teachings always accentuated the positive in the here and now, which Nona liked. She had been trying the New Thought for some time now—for the most part it cheered her up, and at least it wasn't doom and gloom, sin, Hell, the Devil, and so forth. Nothing wrong with being happy now, while you were alive—why wait for Heaven?

"Father Divine teaches you need to cut loose from your worldly ways to get to Heaven on Earth. You supposed to make a change in yo' life, get away from your ol' self to get to see the world as it is, as he wants it for you. To my mind that means change fo' the better. You doin' the same thing every day, year after year, means you thinkin' the same things too. You gonna be too old befo' you knows it and wishin' you had tried somthin' different."

There it was, the droplet of prophetic wisdom Nona knew she would hear from Meekness Simplicity—too old before you know it. It confirmed exactly what was gnawing persistently in the back of her mind—time was running out for new opportunities. A decent financially secure man with good intentions wanted to give her and her daughters a fantastic opportunity, a second—or in her case fifth—chance at happiness. She thanked Meekness for her insight and quickly jogged back home to tell the girls to start packing. She was going to start a new life.

CHAPTER 6

Mrs. Sweet Angel Divine—born Edna Rose Ritchings in Canada—or Mother Divine, or just Mother, depending on who you were talking to, wandered along the shiny new shelves delicately touching the perfectly arrayed rows of boxes, cans and crinkle ribbon wrapped goodies. Each section had its own particular scent—right now she was in the chocolate scented isle so she slowed down to admire the merchandise. Gourmet chocolates galore, boxed cookies, tins of imported powdered bittersweet baking chocolate. The store was a veritable Horn of Plenty, a Cornucopia of any good thing you could have a craving for. And practical items too—bread, cheese, milk, vegetables, fruits in season. And all at prices meant to discourage competition—why would anyone shop anywhere else if they could get the best for very little money? She continued to float around the isles, the store not yet open for business but getting close, probably by the end of this month, April 1947. Mother and her assistant Sincere Sincerity had carefully chosen the workers to mind the store, taking special care to select those who would handle the cash—several signs had been placed strategically around the cash registers: PEACE. WE ACCEPT CASH ONLY, NO CHECKS, NO CREDIT. There was one position left to fill—the store manager. No one associated with International Peace Mission West had experience in managing a grocery store, so they had placed a help wanted advertisement in The New Day, which had a fairly large circulation. The lady who was interviewing for the manager position today had been reading their publication for a few years all the way down in Santa Monica, and had continued to read it up here in Berkeley—she wrote in her application cover letter that she saw the advertisement in the Help Wanted section of The New Day. Mother Divine had gone over Mrs. Nona Twining's cover letter in detail, and was looking forward to meeting with her. She had decided in advance that she was probably a light complected do-gooder, an ideologue—and that was just fine with Sweet Angel Divine.

Today, at Sincere's suggestion, Mother was wearing a tailored business suit that she saved for the occasional times she was required to attend meetings related to Peace Mission financial matters—lightweight tan wool suit with an A-line single-pleated skirt that draped beautifully to just below the knees, matching two-button blazer with a paisley silk pocket handkerchief, white silk blouse, and sensible but expensive brown pumps with a little bow tie fastening. The only jewelry she wore today was her gold wedding band that showed she was married—in spirit only of course—to Father Divine.

She drifted over to the produce isle, deep in thought, when a female voice from behind said "What a beautiful produce layout. I would put the salad items closer together though, and have the refrigerated salad dressings nearby so they can be selected easier—and the bakery breads should be within view of the produce because the shopper will probably be planning on dinner with salad and fresh bread. Quite irritating to bring home dinner ingredients without remembering the fresh rolls." Mother Divine quickly arranged her face into her signature serene toothy smile and turned to greet whom she knew was probably Mrs. Nona Twining, store manager applicant.

Nona walked confidently toward Mother Divine. Her first impression was of a tall very light complected young blond woman, probably around her daughter Dolly's age. There was something vaguely calculating about her—she smiled, but not with her eyes, which were watchful, icy blue and piercing—she was a little heavy, with thick wrists and ankles—working class disguised with expensive clothes, inelegant—a bit masculine even, and remarkably self-assured. She held eye contact far too long to be polite. Nona quickly redirected her thoughts, switched gears to remind herself that this was Mother Divine, Father Divine's wife—the couple that had done so much for the poor, the disadvantaged, the colored people who were downtrodden, born into poverty. Nona was a crusader, a forward-thinker, an idealist who wanted the world to be righted, and at least these two—Mother and Father Divine—were working toward that end. By managing the Mission Grocery Store, Nona could simultaneously help people, do something of value for society, and make a little money—all while alleviating the boredom that had once again slipped into her life. Since Nona wasn't a true follower but only what was known in the press as a Father Divine sympathizer—at least she hoped she could pass as a sympathizer—she would be paid in money, a very modest amount, and not in food, clothing, and shelter as were the core mission workers and residents—the Sisters, Rosebuds, Brothers, and the young Masters, the true followers of Father Divine that were completely taken care of by the Peace Mission Movement.

Mother Divine moved toward her, holding out both hands, and said "Peace. We do not use the word hello here because it begins with Hell." She took Nona's hand in a two handed handshake—Nona made a mental note to inquire of Herschel what that was supposed to convey—and the two moved toward the back of the store to sit down in the new office—her future office she hoped—and have a get-to-know-you session. Hello did in fact sound like Hell, come to think of it—she made a vow to herself to try and remember that next time a hello was in order.

The past year Nona, Herschel, Dolly, and Genieve had been living in a perfectly beautiful leased home in Berkeley on Benvenue Avenue, in the better part of town—a dark wood shingled ivy covered Victorian with a generous front porch furnished with white wicker chairs and loveseat, overstuffed cushions, and potted scented geraniums in all colors. The stone stairs leading up to their house were polished in the middle from many generations of footsteps. It was just so picturesque, everything Nona hoped it would be. There was a feeling of timelessness here—you could sense the history and the people that had come before—it was like you were a part of them, contributing to the story. The quiet streets were lined with mature maple, oak, and elm trees, some coming together to form a canopy overhead that filtered and dappled the sunlight. Students rode by on bicycles, baskets filled with books, everyone well-dressed in the Northern California way, not like the Southern Californians—they had an East Coast chic style here. She and Herschel had quietly married at the local courthouse in a civil ceremony rather than having a formal wedding. Herschel was husband number five after all so they felt a bit past a white wedding ceremony. He was an excellent provider with an impressive nest egg—true to his banking background. Together they had purchased a magical cabin on a sizable piece of land in the Country—Whispering Pines near the famous Whispering Pines Resort, hideaway to the occasional Hollywood celebrity who wanted a vacation away from the limelight, a chance to reconnect with nature, greenery, bubbling streams. Things were pretty good, pretty stable—a little too staid for Nona's taste, but she made up her mind to stick with it because she told herself it was well past the time to start behaving like an adult and settle down. Herschel was nothing if not normal, the definition of it really, and Nona's mind would occasionally wander to more interesting times. That's when she came up with the idea of taking a job at the grocery store—it would be her very first job working for someone else. She was not required to work of course, but because the store was at the center of a controversial new business model in town—and Nona thrived on controversy—and just happened to be a grocery store, how could she resist? Plus, she was familiar with The International Peace Misson Movement and believed they did nothing but good. She came up here to try new things, after all, not to just sit around waiting to shrivel up and die.

Genieve had adjusted quickly in the way young people do to new surroundings. She was absolutely thrilled to be near Merritt College where she could pick up her studies in person. She was going through the lessons like wildfire, receiving high marks on her tests. She even got a part-time job working at Capwell's Department store in Oakland, so she was in retail and shopping heaven—she made good use of her employee discounts, that was for sure. Even if she was just going for a walk around the block to take in the Bay Area's sharp invigorating sea air, she made a concerted effort to look like Ava Gardner, her idol and fashion role model—actually she did resemble Ava Gardner as she matured. Nona was so proud of her.

Dolly on the other hand was developing into someone very different from Genieve, and very different from her old Santa Monica self. Soon after she landed the job at University of Berkeley in the Admissions Department, she began voicing new ideas about religion, politics, and social justice theory—it wasn't like her. Usually she wasn't a deep thinker—but who really knows the inner thoughts and workings of the quiet types? She had a group of friends from the University that she went swimming with on her lunch hour. The rest of her free time was usually spent at the University library where she had employee privileges. Dolly was a follower at heart—Nona noticed this even when Dolly was a toddler. In the past Dolly clung to her Daddy Emil, who doted on her, and as Emil got a little distracted with his new wife, Dolly had started clinging to Nona. Now that Nona had a new husband that took most of her attention, Dolly had no one—but she was twenty-two now, and Nona wondered why Dolly had not married yet. There was a young doctor, Bob Wallen, that Dolly dated occasionally, but he was a straight and narrow traditional type, and some of Dolly's ideas were a little off-beat—this was second-hand information from Genieve, who relayed that Dolly found Bob a little boring and Bob really didn't agree with most of Dolly's theoretical ideas—in Genieve's opinion the guy was just looking for a beautiful wife with mainstream traditional ideas, a trophy wife. Dolly had adopted a social consciousness which many men found unappealing and incongruous, especially in a beautiful blond woman—women who looked like that weren't supposed to have strong opinions. Dolly had always mildly irritated her, she was ashamed to admit, because she looked like Emil incarnate-- a daily reminder of how duped she had been by that no-good bum. Emil absolutely worshipped Dolly and they sent cards and letters back and forth without ever mentioning it to her—again information from the observant Genieve, who made sure to meet the mailman at the door if possible.

Overall, though, it could be said that everything was going well. At least Nona felt like she was in motion rather than stagnating. She and Herschel were compatible and she loved their Country home—something to look forward to as a regular get-away. Genieve was thriving, and Nona might even get the grocery store manager job, perhaps be at the center of something again. Up here in Berkeley there was an underlying feeling that one was at the core of new ideas, a vortex where things were happening, being created, put into motion by the people that made things happen. In Westwood Village students and even professors had certain priorities—like going to the beach, being seen at the right restaurants, spotting a Hollywood celebrity. Nona didn't want to agree with the general impression up here that Los Angeles was shallow, but she had to admit things were a bit more academic in Berkeley, more urbane. And she was happy to be away from daily reminders of her divorce from Emil—the taste of sour grapes for some reason still lingered.

The office was so sparsely furnished that it reminded Nona of Van Gogh's Bedroom painting—unadorned dark wooden furniture and one bare window that looked out onto the street. "May I ask who the third chair is for, Mother Divine? Will this be a group interview?" A chair with a gold framed 8 x 10 inch photograph of Father Divine propped up on the seat back had been pushed up to the table—Father's staring eyes appeared to be looking straight at her, assessing her. "This is Father's chair—he is always present, so we are never alone—he's here with us right now, listening." Mother smiled and nodded at the photograph as if it were animated, in communication with her. Nona nodded her head in agreement and easily held the extended eye contact with her unfathomable large dark eyes. From regularly browsing The New Day in Santa Monica and talking to Meekness Simplicity, Nona knew many people truly believed Father Divine was God come to Earth again to save humanity. She had her answer carefully prepared so as not to offend. She wanted the job, and got a kick out of off-beat characters, so she thought it might be fun to play along—what could it hurt? At least it wouldn't be boring. Really, the Father Divine Peace Mission Movement had actually helped people, and what was wrong with that? The movement, or cult as she secretly thought of it, gave people a chance to believe in something, have well-regulated lives in the midst of the chaos created by injustice and poverty.

Mother Divine took out a list of questions to be directed to manager applicants, topics relating to the Earthly business of taking care of the money—Nona noted with approval they seemed to care vary much about the financial side of the equation. She answered these questions easily, noting with interest they did not seem very sophisticated for an organized cult—no, *movement* she firmly reminded herself. The behavior expected of the workers was very regimented—they were to be called by their chosen names only—in Nona's mind they seemed like nicknames—absolutely not their birth names, because they had disassociated themselves from former lives and family members. Salutations to be used were Sister, Brother, Miss, or Master—they prefaced the chosen names but could also be used alone. The word hello was forbidden—upon entering and exiting a room one was required to say peace, never hello. "Is there a name you would like us to call you that describes how you feel about your new family Mrs. Twining?" Nona, prepared for this question thanks to reading various articles in The New Day said with as serious an expression as she could muster "Faith Noble."

"What a lovely name—we shall use that name for you always." Mother Divine smiled briefly and slipped the pen and papers back into the desk drawer, apparently finished with writing. She folded her hands together and leaned forward confidentially.

"Now, about money and hours—Father took six days to create Heaven and Earth because he did not believe in a short work-week. He could have done it in one day," confided Mother, her eyes shining inward, in another place altogether "but he made it in six days so that his children would also work six days. He planned it that way. Hours at the store are 7:00 A.M. to 7:00 P.M. six days a week. Sundays we are closed because Father gives services and communal dinners then—which we hope you will attend. You will be paid in cash, but part of your income, which you will never see, will go directly into Father's heavenly treasury so we may continue our good works. You are part of something now, Faith Noble—welcome to the International Peace Mission Movement." Mother nodded at the photograph of Father Divine as if answering a question, then arose, extending both hands again to conclude the meeting with the double handshake.

Nona wasn't about to start speaking of money, questioning the amount, negotiating—it sounded common in her opinion. If she didn't care for the compensation, she could just give notice and find something better. Herschel mentioned he could find her a position at First Federal, but banking was so unbearably dry. The grocery store position was supposed to be enjoyable, and she didn't really need to work, so let them keep a little for their treasury—she would probably have donated it on her own anyway.

The room had suddenly become close, the humidity level rising unaccountably to the point where little beads of sweat were forming on the back on Nona's hands. There was a sickly sweet smell coming from somewhere—rotting fruit?—with an underlying odor of fresh garlic that seemed to suck oxygen right out of the air. She guessed they may have left a delivery sitting somewhere in the store without unloading it. She wanted to get moving. Relief that the interview was over revived her—really, this was supposed to be a diversion, and not anything to be taken seriously—she had something new, eccentric to look forward to, and perhaps she could even help people that needed it too, make the work meaningful. It couldn't be anything weirder than Venice Beach, after all, that endless parade of oddballs that she loved for their entertainment value if nothing else. As Mother walked her to the door, bidding her "Peace", she glanced back at the photograph of Father. Who had turned the photo to face the exit? Father Divine's calm black eyes followed her impassively out the door.

Later that evening she and Herschel, Genieve and Dolly had a dinner prepared by Genieve—her speciality of meatloaf, potatoes, carrots and onions baked and glazed in the same Pyrex baking dish. They all wanted to hear about the eccentric religious nuts that were opening a grocery store. "That's so unkind, to speak ill of people who help others," Nona admonished Herschel, who threw a few uncharitable words toward Father Divine—charlatan, crook, con artist, swindler, hustler, confidence man. "If he took the money and ran, that would be different, but he feeds, houses, and clothes thousands of people who otherwise would have very few prospects in life. He's even gotten people off the welfare roles. They say he has millions of followers just in the United States alone, with more in other countries."

"He has to be making huge amounts of money for himself, otherwise how could he afford to dress the way he does, own all those estates, and drive a Rolls Royce? Have you seen the way Mother Divine dresses? It's obvious what's going on, anyone can see that. I read in one of the papers that the IRS is investigating him because he doesn't pay taxes." This from Genieve, ever conscious of material possessions.

"I think the movement provides positive direction for lost souls. So what if Father Divine makes money—he should, really, if he is rescuing people that otherwise have no hope—I think what really bothers people most is that he is a Negro who is successful. We all know that isn's supposed to happen, don't we?" Dolly looked smug with her moral high ground stance of social justice verses prejudice. "I've seen plenty of preachers talk, but at least this one is doing something. Actually, I went with some work friends to a dinner he gave a few months ago—he is a very powerful speaker who makes a lot of sense, and his followers love him." They were all surprised to hear Dolly voice a strong opinion, or any opinion at all—it had been her lifelong habit to see which way the wind was blowing in a conversation, then go with that, agree, always agree, anything to get along, to be seen as nice and not controversial. "In fact, Mother, now that you'll be working there, I have a perfect excuse to go in and shop for food. We can probably save money too. I'm tired of the inflated prices people charge in this town for everything just because they know people here can pay it. They take advantage of people—it's about time they learned a lesson. We have choices now."

Nona, Genieve, and Herschel just stared at Dolly. They didn't even know Dolly had gone to such a dinner, much less sympathized with what most people thought of as an eccentric cult for colored people. "Why Dolly, I had no idea you went to one of Father Divine's speeches—why didn't you tell us before? We're your family, after all. We care about you and what you're interested in."

"They say at the Peace Mission your family and friends will always try to discourage you from getting involved in anything outside the norm, that if you deviate outside your normal conventional behavior pattern it will be met with suspicion and accusations of unethical behavior. I can see by the way you all are looking at me that's exactly what you think. Well, sorry, I just felt like doing something different without consulting my family—and I'm glad I did because it opened my mind." She picked up her fork and continued eating, clearly not open at all to any further discussions on the topic. The rest of the dinner was consumed in contemplative silence.

Back at the International Peace Mission West Father Divine was mentally preparing for one of his informal after dinner meetings—office talks he called them, and they weren't mandatory like most of his meetings. He could pretty much predict who would or wouldn't be there, and he was rarely wrong. Brother David Devoute never missed an opportunity to be near him so his presence was a sure bet, and the old busybody Sincere Sincerity would absolutely be there just so she didn't miss anything at all interesting or controversial to report back to Sweet Angel Divine. There would be the usual core group of followers with the probable addition of Stella, the newly minted Rosebud, who worshipped, literally, the ground he walked on.

He mulled over which memorized speech he would repeat tonight, wondering how he was going to put energy into it once again, going over his notes in his private suite, his king sized bed beckoning him, tempting him to just relax, sleep for a week, no thinking required. He was feeling his age, already 1947 and he in his seventies—he would be dead before he knew it and welcomed it, actually. He was so tired of the charade—he wanted to simply retire, but how does one retire from being God? There were thousands, no millions, of people depending on him, living off him. There was no going back—the play must continue until the finale. His own Sweet Angel Divine had once called him a performance artist in one of her rare candid moments—but Sweet Angel loved the charade more than anyone, loved the power, the homes, the clothes. He—George Baker Jr.—had let the attorneys, real estate people, and tax experts take over—they had created a new world, a movement, a thing with a life of its own, and he was at the head of it all. He owned so much real estate and small businesses he'd lost track. There was no turning back without risking being exposed as a charlatan, a con artist, a thief who would undoubtedly be locked up with the key thrown away. He imagined the thousands of followers who would demand their money back that they had been led to believe was invested in his Heavenly Treasury so they too could own a piece Heaven on Earth, part of an estate, hotel, grocery store, whatever. He rationalized investments were always a risk, but at least they found happiness, didn't they? Of course they did. They didn't have a Rolls Royce or estate homes or businesses, but at least they were content, which was an improvement over their former selves, wasn't it?

A discrete knock at his door interrupted his reflections. "Father, are you in there? I have a message for you." It was the young Rosebud True Light, the red-haired Devil incarnate, temptress of the flesh, come to visit him in his hour of weakness—just like it says in the Bible, they come when you're at a low point, unable to resist.

"Come in Rosebud, what have you got there child?" True shyly shuffled in carrying a letter, dressed in her spotless uniform with *V* for Virtue and Victory over Carnality emblazoned on the lapel , the cropped jacket a little too tight around the chest area—he tried to keep his eyes focused on her face, yes indeed, he was trying his best.

"I wrote another prayer for you Father dear. Would you like me to read it to you? I want to make sure you like it before I give it to you."

"Yes Rosebud, I will hear your prayer." He was mesmerized by the way the light of his reading lamp caught the red highlights in her hair, bounced the light back at him. He thought he smelled a hint of patchouli oil, but that was not possible was it?—no perfume of any kind was allowed for the followers, no cosmetics, nothing to encourage the opposite sex from becoming overly interested.

She held the letter close to her face and softly recited the letter. "Peace Father and Mother Dear. This has been a very wonderful and peaceful day. I am so grateful to you and Mother for coming in your bodies to save us from the sins of the world. You are so wonderful and we worship you our King and Queen of the Earth. I dearly love you both and try every day to obey your word. Praise your holy name. Father, help True Light each and every day and tell me what I should do and how to do it." She looked up at him then, tears starting to form around the thickly lashed blue eyes.

"Why child, that's a beautiful letter, why are you crying? Come here to me." He could't believe this was happening again, wondering if this one was going to complain to the authorities like some of the others had. But of course no one really believed them—they were oddballs after all, cult followers of Father Divine, obviously mentally unstable. His attorneys had thought of everything—the living arrangement policies, posted in public view around his properties for all to see, made it clear that men and women were to be kept apart as much as possible, with no unnecessary mingling of the sexes. Sometimes contact was necessary though, for example in the course of cleaning his suite, delivering a verbal message, or in this case, delivering a letter.

"Father, I love you so much, you are so beautiful, so perfect." Overcome, crying, she came in close, threw her arms around his neck, and hugged him as he twisted her around and slipped her onto his lap. Not even Superman could resist such temptation he's thinking. Sweet Angel down the hall surprising him would not be a problem, because she spent most of her time with the Rosebuds, gaining their confidence, avoiding men just like the policies recommended—she had never yet knocked on the door of his private retreat in any of the mansions, and he had no carnal knowledge of her—this suited both of them, each having their own private lives with the public appearance of a Heavenly virgin marriage—they were business partners, nothing more.

True Light was so moved by the spirit and so carried away with the works of the flesh, just like it says in the Bible—sexual immorality, impurity, sensuality—so grateful for his personal attention, that she only minimally resisted his embraces. Father had his rules for these occasions—hands and mouth only, no genital to genital contact because that could only end in disaster, and absolutely no telling afterward. With one eye on the clock—he didn't want to miss his office talk—he allowed the works of the flesh to take their course.

CHAPTER 7

The city of Berkeley is home to the oldest campus in the entire University of California system— the University of California at Berkeley, founded in 1868. Ten years after the founding, in 1878, the city was incorporated and the name changed from Ocean View to Berkeley, named after the 18th century Irish bishop and philosopher George Berkeley. Before World War 2 it was a typical college town filled with smart kids from well-to-do families, with the quirky addition of theologians from all across the religious spectrum—seminarians,, Zen masters, Fundamentalists, Nature Worshipers, monks, Druids, religious philosophers. They gravitated to the woodsy hillsides of the city, establishing themselves in eccentric but architecturally important estates dotting the hillside. The area eventually became know as Holy Hill, a sort of alternative University of Berkeley where the institutions operated under their own, often off-beat, rules.

During World War 2 thousands of new people moved into the area, drawn by high-paying jobs mostly in the shipbuilding industry. The city of Richmond, just to the North of Berkeley, home to the Kaiser shipyards that were pumping out Liberty cargo ships, saw its population quadruple in just a few years. Mr. Kaiser recruited workers from all over the United States for his shipyards, even hiring women and minorities. Many of the newcomers were Negros from the South. In 1940, there were under 1,000 Negros living in Richmond; in 1945, there were over five times that number. Oakland's Negro population has almost tripled, and San Francisco's from fewer than 5,000 to 32,000. Also recently arrived are large numbers of whites—who the locals call hillbillies, hicks, or Okies— from Oklahoma and the South, come to escape the poverty still evident from the Dust Bowl blight in the 1930s.

Plenty is going on now in 1947, enough to keep one rushing to the newspaper stand to see the latest headlines, or keep the radio or television tuned to the news channel. Some highlights (and low points):

A downed extraterrestrial spacecraft is reportedly found near Roswell, New Mexico, dubbed by the media as the Roswell UFO incident.

US announces the discovery of plutonium fission, suitable for nuclear power generation—J. Robert Oppenheimer, a physicist at U.C. Berkeley, and later the chief scientist for the Manhattan Project, worked along with Edward Teller and others to produce the hydrogen bomb.

In California, the designer and airplane pilot Howard Hughes performs the maiden flight of the Spruce Goose, the largest fixed-wing aircraft ever built. The flight lasts only eight minutes, after which the "Spruce Goose" is not flown again.

The Tennessee Williams play *A Streetcar Named Desire* opens in a Broadway theater.

Jackie Robinson, the first Negro professional baseball player since the 1880s, signs a contract with the Brooklyn Dodgers.

The House of Un-American Activities Committee begins its investigations into Communism in Hollywood.

American financier and presidential adviser Bernard Baruch describes the Post World War II tensions between the Soviet Union and the United States as a "Cold War".

An explosion at the O'Connor Electro-Plating Company in Los Angeles, California leaves 17 dead, 100 buildings damaged, and a 22-foot-deep crater in the ground. The blast was felt 15 miles away.

Elizabeth Short, an aspiring actress nicknamed the "Black Dahlia", is found brutally murdered in a vacant lot in Los Angeles.

The movie *Miracle on 34th Street* hits the theaters, winning three Academy Awards and posing the idea that Santa Claus just might be real.

Nona was in her element, in the middle of a flurry of activity and controversy. Things were happening and she was right there, in the vortex, living it. She was alive during interesting times.

A simple wooden sign over the door read MISSION GROCERY STORE, and in the window beneath the striped awning the salutation PEACE was stenciled in plain block letters, but one would think they were selling something controversial. The gossip around town was that the store was owned by a cult. Odd people came into the store under the guise of grocery shopping but were really there just to gawk at the supposed cult members, hoping to see something creepy. They were confused and disappointed when they were greeted by cheerful shiny faces, both dark complected and light complected, in spotless starched white smocks and bibbed aprons. The store was laid out in an appealing open bistro French market arrangement. The items for sale were obviously high quality and there was nothing junky or tacky at all—and they didn't sell incense and gongs like cults were supposed to. The gawkers were disappointed. They did get a shock, however, when they checked the prices on items that tempted them. How could they sell so low? Was there a catch? Did you have to donate money or something at the checkout stand?

As she stood there on this perfect brisk spring morning, surveying the cast of characters in the store, she felt a momentary stab of sadness for times gone by, and a little déjà vu. The salt air wafting in when the front door opened and the tinkling of the little brass doorbells reminded her of her former store and her former life. She quickly switched gears, thinking, don't live in the past, and don't look back, you're not going that way. She flashed her most cheerful smile as she circulated the store, mingling with customers, being seen—this was the fun part of the job. Suddenly, from too close behind her a falsetto male voice asked "Do you carry Italian squash? I only see zucchini." Startled out of her reflections, she spun around to see a tall thin man with a protruding Adam's apple towering over her, hairless, pale eyes, pale skin, looking at her quizzically, head held cocked to the side on his long neck, his whole face a question mark. Was this one of the eunuchs living at the monastery she had heard about?

"I believe they are the same thing sir—some people call them Italian squash, but we label them zucchini—which is the proper Italian term for them."

"Great, then I don't have to go to two separate markets. My soup recipe calls for Italian squash and cannellini beans and I thought I was going to have to go to Giuseppi's for the real Italian ingredients."

"We have both of those items here, and the produce is fresh off the truck this morning—like it is every day. I understand Giuseppi's only gets produce deliveries twice a week—I'm not sure which days—because they have less turnover." She could see his face register this fact, and she surmised this customer was definitely finicky about his ingredients. She was certain she had just reeled in another faithful customer. And why not? They were the new market in town and this was the crucial time to change people's shopping patterns, divert them here, create a habit pattern so they automatically started shopping here first. The man smiled happily, slipped some items into his cart and floated away down the aisle.

Nona had been at the store about two months, and it was keeping her occupied. Now in the evenings she had something to converse with Herschel about instead of just his daily report from the bank, which was a pretty dry topic. Herschel was just so staid—that was the word that always came to mind when she thought of him. The other day she got a half hour lecture on the vagaries of interest rates and how they affected home prices. But she was grateful to have been rescued from the fate of the discarded divorcée who never managed to have much of a life after the husband traded her in for a younger woman. She was also happy for Genieve, who was juggling school, work, and a promising boyfriend. Genieve was resilient, determined, good natured and gregarious—Nona had no doubt good things would come to her because she made them happen, not content to let them just fall into her lap—she created her own world rather than taking cues from those around her.

Dolly was the one who troubled her. Within a year of moving to Berkeley, she was gradually transforming into someone new and different. She had always been weak-minded, petulant, relying on her stunning looks and her ability to pout to get her way, especially with Emil—Genieve coddled her too, let her get away with anything, called her both a best friend and a sister. But everyone had something to do now, they were preoccupied with the business of living, so Dolly had no one to lean on. Bob Wallen, Dolly's doctor boyfriend, whom everyone hoped she would marry, had gone down to Los Angeles to interview for a position at one of the hospitals—they didn't hear much from him after that. Office workers and academics from U.C. Berkeley that she met in the course of her employment in Admissions had become her new group of friends—but they never seemed to be available to meet Dolly's family—they always managed to be too busy. Just the other night she renounced her past and said it wasn't part of who she wanted to be, that she just wanted to forget everything, although she didn't specify what she wanted to forget. She gave money and clothes to a mysterious charity, and to those who, in her words, needed it more than herself—but who they were she never mentioned. She had talked briefly about doing fundraising for the International Peace Mission West, saying it gave her life meaning to help others. She was suddenly adamant about being called Ann—her given name—instead of her nickname Dolly. Per Genieve, spy that she was, Dolly still signed her letters to her Daddy as Dolly. Her clothing and hairstyle had changed to become almost stodgy, the opposite of the stylish young woman she was. She often referred to names of people she called friends that her family had never met. She spent much of her spare time in the library at U.C. Berkeley unwilling to share what she was studying there. She was drifting off in another direction, but Nona didn't know where, and she realized once again that she viewed Dolly, and her father Emil, as thorns in her side, one of those people who made you feel sad or uncomfortable to think about, instead of making you smile.

The brass doorbells tinkled just then, opened a crack and a blond head peaked in, then pushed open the door wide to enter. Dolly, in a frumpy dress Nona thought she had long ago donated to the thrift shop, looked around, searching for someone, and Nona ducked behind one of the isles to watch through a vantage point in the shelves.

"Hi Stella, can you go to lunch yet? We're going to meet at the bookstore on Shattuck Avenue."

Stella, deftly maneuvering her considerable bulk around the counter to come out from behind the cash register, hurried over to Dolly, smiling broadly, hands out, saying "Peace Sister Ann. You're looking well today. I'll be off in about five minutes, and I get an hour and a half for lunch today because they know I'm going to the meeting."

"Me too Sister. They gave me an hour and a half for lunch today because they know attendance at the meeting is important to the Movement. Everybody will be there, even Mother."

Nona was aghast—Mother? She had no knowledge of any meeting at a bookstore, so Dolly couldn't possibly be talking about her. The only other person she could be referring to would be Mother Divine.

"Have you seen my Mother today Stella? I think she must be here somewhere."

"Yes, she's around here somewhere. Last time I saw her she was circulating the isles."

Dolly wandered away, clearly contemplating something. Nona knew all her daughter's postures—she had given birth to her, after all—and Dolly was stalling, probably to prepare a different face to meet her. Nona popped out from the isle as if by accidental timing. "Dolly! What a nice surprise. Doing some shopping for dinner tonight on your lunch hour?"

Backing away, hooded eyes, hiding something, Dolly said in a strained voice "Oh hi Mother. No, I just wanted to say hello. Some of us from the office are going swimming in about 30 minutes when the swim team is finished with the lap lanes. We got a long lunch break today as a bonus so I just thought I would see how you're doing."

"Lucky you caught us in a lull. This store is really getting busy, thanks in large part to me. I don't know how they would have managed without my professional insight. Good thing they hired me. Now all I have to do is get them to pay me—I haven't received a dime in almost two months. I'm not in the habit of groveling for money as you know, so I'll give them some time to realize their mistake—it's a new store and most of the people have no experience. It's fun here though, something to do instead of just rot, like I was doing before."

"Maybe they don't have the money to pay you yet because they're using it to help people who need it more than you."

"Then at least they could tell me instead of just not.....oh hi there Mrs. Porter, so nice to see you again!" Nona backed away from Dolly to attend to a new customer whom she had met before. She needed to make sure Mrs. Porter had a stellar shopping experience so she would pass the word along to her friends.

Dolly's new social consciousness was more than a little irritating—it was like she had turned her back on what she came from and had redefined herself, become one of the downtrodden, the disadvantaged, the victims, never missing a chance to try to make others feel guilty for doing well. Sure, there was the divorce from Emil but that was an unfortunate fact of life, one that most people were able to overcome. Dolly had gone from Brentwood to Santa Monica, and now to Berkeley—with a Country home thrown in for good measure. How sad was that really? Nona resented Dolly for drawing attention to herself, managing to be petulant even in the face of so much to be grateful for. Maybe Nona had spoiled her, or maybe when someone is that beautiful anything less than perfect is just not enough for them. In any case, she was determined to be happy, she, Herschel, and Genieve. Let Dolly be disgruntled about the lack of social justice—it's not a perfect world, after all.

When Nona turned around to find Dolly, she saw Mother Divine standing close to her daughter toward the back of the store, hand on her shoulder in a protective way, both young women in their twenties but frumpily dressed as if in costume, both eyeing her with odd expressions. Her daughter became unrecognizable to her for just that instant.

Nona finished the closing ritual of the grocery store, saying a longer than usual goodnight to Stella, who she now looked at with different eyes—Stella and her daughter shared some common interest, as yet unknown. She decided to take a walk the short distance to the bookstore, find out more about the lunchtime meeting if possible. She couldn't shake that image of Mother Divine and her daughter standing close together, sharing a confidence of some sort—it made her uncomfortable, and she was going to get to the bottom of it. She was an excellent actress when the situation called for it, and she had a plan. Tightly wrapping her soft camel hair coat around her against the breeze coming across the sea, her best low wedge walking shoes with steel taps clicking rhythmically on the sidewalk, she leaned into the misty spring evening air of the Bay Area and marched forward. In a few blocks she passed a tall apartment building that housed mostly undergraduate students—reluctant to stay in their small rooms, they spilled out onto the street, many affecting the insolent poses of Left Bank artist types—black turtlenecks, bérets, tight pants, hips slung forward and cocked to the side. The posture of the determinedly disenchanted—Liberal Arts majors without a doubt, not Physics students, that was for sure. Taking up space in an expensive college just to pass the time on their parent's dime.

Up ahead, a black valanced awning with a stenciled sign in gold block letters on the window announced BODHI TREE. Stacks of books in the windows were the only indication as to what was within. It was obvious this off the beaten path store considered itself a bookstore for the intelligentsia—a sign indicating that it was a bookstore would have been just too brash, too obvious. You were supposed to know about it by word of mouth—it you didn't know, don't enter, you probably aren't hip enough. Nona ascended the steps and walked confidently in. Doorbells tinkled and the wooden floor creaked, prompting movement from behind the tall counter—the clerk probably had been reading something terribly deep, knowable only to the enlightened—or maybe he had been sleeping. A thin white slow moving stream of smoke rose from a small brass cylinder on the countertop—incense, the thick pungent mysterious kind that lingers in your hair and clothes long after you have gone home—the good stuff, from India. Nona had been an incense burner in her tea leaf reading days.

"That's the best incense there is. You have good taste."

The clerk rose higher from behind his protective counter, eyes opening a little wider in bored recognition that this might be someone enlightened. He was a little past student age, but still managed the know-it-all literature grad student affectation. He brushed his long triangle of sandy bangs back with a finely boned white porcelain hand. He looked for all the world like an ineffectual idler, but she suspected he may be the manager or even the owner—relaxed, assured, superior.

"We got a shipment last year, but not very much so we use it sparingly. Can I help you find something?" He reared his head back a little and looked down his nose, hoping to be asked what he thought of the latest James Michener novel so he could excoriate the public's poor taste in reading material.

"I came to see if there's any literature left from the lunchtime meeting I missed today. We were so busy I couldn't get away, but I thought I'd come by to pick up the material if you still have any. Then I think I'll just browse, see if I can find something to read." She wanted to make sure she lingered, not in a hurry to rush away, to build trust and dig for more information.

"Yah, I think there's some on the bottom shelf here." He ducked down behind the counter again and then surfaced with a few thin booklets which he slapped on the counter. "This what you're looking for?" Nona took one and read a line from the cover:

—and shall lose themselves in the Unity of the Spirit, of Mind,
of Aim and Purpose—

She briefly wondered how one can lose themselves and find aim and purpose at the same time. "Yes, thanks so much—that's exactly what I'm looking for. I usually don't miss meetings if I can help it."

The clerk nodded appreciatively and his eyes slid away from her, clearly remembering what he was doing before she walked in. Nona turned and casually browsed the shelves, the incense hanging heavily in the air, carrying her back to the past. Really, though, she was quite anxious to see what sort of information was in the booklet, wondering why Dolly would lie about going swimming to come here during her lunch hour—and Stella too, along with Mother Divine who probably organized the meeting. After browsing a few isles of books on esoteric topics, opening the dusty and brittle volumes, she paused at *Une Saison en Enfer—A Season in Hell* by Arthur Rimbaud. She was familiar with the poem and it gave her an unaccountable feeling of foreboding . As casually as she could she slipped out the front door, brass bells announcing her departure, then hurried out into the damp night, into a town that had come alive with the nocturnal habits of the college crowd.

Later that evening Nona disappeared deep into the overstuffed damask sofa, sliding right under the beaded silk fringed lampshade of the floor lamp to analyze the booklet with laser focus, not wanting to miss a single innuendo or message that could be extracted from the odd information. The punctuation was atrocious and there were capital letters throughout that didn't belong. The cover had a photograph of the International Peace Mission West. Under the photograph of the Mission the caption read:

> The Mountain of the House of the Lord - "International Peace Mission West" —
> We shall have a RIGHTEOUS GOVERNMENT! But it shall not be bound to this democracy as it stands today, alone, but

> other democracies or countries shall merge into this one, and shall lose themselves in the Unity of the Spirit, of Mind, of Aim and Purpose, until there will not be any division among us nationally, neither will there be any division among us internationally! - Father Divine

Inside the cover it got right down to business, detailing a talk given by Father Divine:

> OFFICE TALK Given by FATHER DIVINE TO SOME OF HIS CABINET IN HIS PRIVATE OFFICE STUDY of the INTERNATIONAL PEACE MISSION WEST, HOME And TRAINING SCHOOL, APRIL 24, 1947 A.D.F.D. TIME - 6:45 P.M.
>
> This significant Office Talk given on this occasion depicts the fulfillment of the Scripture to the letter by the great FULFILLER, GOD ALMIGHTY, FATHER DIVINE, for automatically, without premeditation, as the time and season warrants it, the fulfillment takes place and the Scripture is revealed.
>
> FATHER opened the Bible at random and pointed to a certain verse, which MOTHER read, and as it was very stressful in FATHER'S consideration, HE asked MOTHER to read it again at this particular time, which SHE did, and FATHER brought forth this marvelous revelation which had been hid through the ages, hid from man's understanding, awaiting the day of the fulfillment, which is here and now. (FATHER speaks as follows:)
>
> Then Solomon began to build the House of the LORD at Jerusalem in mount Moriah. Then the LORD began to build the house of the LORD in Berkeley in International Peace

> Mission West; where the LORD appeared at the signing of the Declaration of Independence and at the drafting of the Constitution and its Amendments; where the people proclaimed Liberty throughout all the land and the Pilgrim Fathers came in the name of the Quakers and made Berkeley, through the signing of the Declaration of Independence and the drafting of the Constitution and its Amendments—the City of "BROTHERLY LOVE" and the Cradle of Democracy, making it the COUNTRY SEAT of the WORLD! And thence HE starts to build the Temple of GOD. Not at Jerusalem in mount Moriah, but at the NEW JERUSALEM, better known as Berkeley, at International Peace Mission West!
>
> How I happened to stress this so vividly, is because I opened the Bible at random, and without any premeditation or reconsideration it came pointed out; II Chronicles, third chapter and first verse; and reading it volitionally in MY Cabinet, I brought out by interpretation of the Mystery of the repetition of history, showing quite definitely by inspiration and by interpretation, that as it was with the building of the Temple of the LORD in Jerusalem, in mount Moriah, so it is in the rebuilding of the Temple of the LORD in Berkeley, or at Berkeley in International Peace Mission West.
>
> So the Scripture is now being fulfilled in your hearing. It is quite vividly depicted and it can be seen and observed, as this is the Crowning Day! The Country Seat of the World and the Cradle of Democracy and the City of BROTHERLY LOVE has been crowned as Berkeley at International Peace Mission West!

Nona stopped to reflect. It was interesting that if someone took the trouble to print information in a booklet or flyer, no matter how ridiculous, there were always people willing to read it and try to make sense of the nonsense—in other words, if it's in print there must be some truth to it. She wondered at the psychology behind this. She herself had been open minded when she first read The New Day back home in Santa Monica, but mostly out of her lifelong curiosity for new ideas—that's all it was to her, a new idea to be analyzed and considered, or a new fashion to be worn and discarded when it went out of style. All the religions had some truth to them, some commonality—but this Father Divine seemed to be taking it to a new level, actually claiming to be God, and his followers thought of him as God incarnate here on Earth, and he did his best to not discourage that idea. Maybe he had even started believing his own lie about who he was—had he fallen over the metaphorical cliff of reality? But she thought not, he was smarter than that—he had managed to build a large empire of followers, businesses, and properties. It was obvious what was going on, just as Genieve had said—he was living off his followers, living off their labor and their naiveté.

Just then she looked up and caught the flash of shiny blond hair through the front window—Dolly coming home from the library, at a late hour for her, 9 p.m. Her clothes looked shabby—even though U.C. Berkeley paid a very good monthly salary, Dolly had started to look like she was on her last dime. She was thinking that Herschel can check on Dolly's savings account at First Federal—that was the surest way to find what someone was up to—start with a money trail.

"Oh hello Mother, I'm surprised you're still awake. I just finished at the library—they have the most fantastic books there, ones that you can't find anywhere else. I'm worn out from reading—can't wait to get to bed." She backed away a little hoping to not have to answer any questions. Her mind was filled with new ideas and she didn't want to be brought back to reality by her Mother.

"I have some interesting reading material myself. I went to Bodhi Tree to find something to read and ended up becoming more interested in some flyers left on the counter." Nona slid the Father Divine booklet across the coffee table to her and used the full power of her large dark piercing eyes, the look she used that signified a liar would be immediately found out and punished.

"You're spying on me! I can't believe it—I'm an adult and you're treating me like a child!" Dolly changed quickly to fight mode, a rare sight indeed in someone so wishy-washy.

"Dolly, we're all worried about you. You look different, you're evasive, you've lost your doctor boyfriend—a great catch by the way—we don't know your friends, and now you seem to be taking that Father Divine character too seriously—he's just a crook, you're smart enough to know that. You're only twenty-two, this is supposed to be the best time in your life and you're wasting it on oddballs, riff-raff, and rough trade. You don't need a mission—remember who you are! You're very different from these people you're associating with. I've told you many times—when you lay down with dogs, you get up with fleas."

Dolly, face contorted, uncharacteristically furious, "I remember one of your other favorite sayings too Mother—don't wrestle with pigs, they enjoy it and you just get dirty. I feel like I'm getting dirty right now! I'm sick of your elitist attitude while people are starving around you and don't even have shoes to wear. At least we are doing something at the mission to help people instead of just thinking of ourselves. And another thing—I've talked to Daddy about you, and he says you are the most self-centered person he's ever met. I wouldn't be surprised if you try to get a raise from the Mission Grocery Store—it's supposed to be a charity, but you don't understand that word, do you? The mission is just another one of your nutty fads, isn't it? You don't even believe in what we are doing. I'm going to recommend they find someone more committed! Dolly spun around, the beads on the silk fringe lampshade clicking to the rhythm of her angry footsteps, stomped upstairs, and slammed the door behind her. She had gone beyond petulant and was approaching militant.

At dawn Nona awoke with a jolt and a touch of dread, but she knew what she needed to do. She arrived early to the Mission Grocery Store, on foot with no ride from Herschel because she needed to walk and think, the exercise clearing her head, oxygen coursing through her brain, crystallizing her course of action. She knew that either Brother David Devoute or the elderly sneak Miss Sincere Sincerity—or both—would be there—the two highest in the mission hierarchy, right under Father and Mother Divine. They were always the first to open the store and the last to leave, dutifully taking care of the cash register, counting the money, protectively hovering over their ledgers like ferrets with a catch, hunching over the books so no one could look over their shoulders, always carrying two money pouches. One evening after staying particularly late, she heard ripping paper at a register—did they distain money to the point of destroying it? Nona boldly strode past the register to see Sincere tearing up receipts—too quickly she mumbled a vague excuse even though Nona never asked about it.

Now she carefully opened the front door so as not to set the brass bells tinkling and lightly walked toward the registers. Sure enough Brother Devoute was at one of the registers transferring money from one of two pouches into the cash drawer, his gray head bobbing as he counted.

"Miss Faith, what a surprise! I didn't hear you come in—and you're early. You are truly driven by the spirit of our Lord Father Divine, I can tell."

"I am, Brother David—I'm driven, but when I give my expertise I expect to be compensated. When can I expect the payment due to me that we agreed on when I was hired? I've been here almost two months and haven't seen a dime. My employment forms, which I went over last night, specifically state either you or Sincere Sincerity must give the okay before payment is made. My family is planning a nice long vacation at our country home in Whispering Pines as a surprise for my daughter Dolly and it would be nice to have extra money for our trip." She wasn't going to grovel—she wanted to make it clear that it was money owed to her as per her agreement to run the store for the mission business machine—she didn't need the money, she expected it—huge difference.

Devoute lowered his bushy gray eyebrows and darkened his expression in deep contemplation before answering. "Miss Faith Noble, there are so many people in need now, people still suffering from the Depression, still out of work due to the social issues of our time of which I am sure you are aware. You and your family are the lucky ones. Most of our people that we help are grateful to even have three meals a day and a roof over their heads—they don't get to go on vacation. By the way, I am sure your daughter, the one you call Dolly—our Sister Ann—would be the first to agree that it's more important to help people in need than it is to go to a country home in a resort town. If I know Sister Ann, she would have a hard time enjoying the vacation if she knew she was taking food out of someone's mouth. So, that's a long way of saying that, no, we don't have the money to pay you this month or even the month after because we are scaling up our food and clothing drive in this city—every day, more and more poor people arrive here and they need help more than ever. By the way, if you read the fine print at the bottom of your hiring forms, it says this business is a non-profit charity and we are not obligated to pay if it's not in the best interest of current funding projects."

Nona thought it was better not to say anything because she was fuming, livid, beyond any civil reply. The room had turned black in front of her and she had an acidic taste in her mouth, the sign of an impending explosion. She was known as someone tolerant and forward-thinking, but that was going to change—they had suckered her, played a shell game with the money, and now this David character was instructing her about her own daughter Dolly. The undercurrent was foreboding, a struggle with a cult that had begun to tighten its noose around one of her children. With all the dignity and restraint she could muster, she turned on her heel and left, bells tinkling angrily after her.

CHAPTER 8

True Light had secluded herself in the mission library again, tucked into the blue velvet window seat overlooking the gardens. At this moment she was reading one of the archived versions of Father Divine's magazine publications, The Spoken Word. On the cover was a photograph of Father Divine, nattily dressed as always, reclining against a giant Horn of Plenty, hand caressing the mouth of the horn, out of which tumbled what looked like thousands of gold coins imprinted with various words such as Truth, Joy, Love, Peace, etc. She loved this picture of him—the history of Africa seemed locked inside his eyes—she let out a long sigh. She scanned the article, trying to refocus her attention away from matters of the flesh, as Father had advised:

> "The question is often asked, Where does FATHER DIVINE get HIS money from? The Corn-Copia or Horn of Plenty extends back into what may be known as the Infinite or unknown of the SOURCE of all things; it's flow is ceaseless from its unexhaustible SOURCE. At first glance the Substance flowing from this horn appears to be in the form of money, but a closer glance reveals these tokens are: Truth, Love, Kindness, Faithfulness, Righteousness, Justice, Brotherhood,

and thousands of other tokens. When one is led to ask again where does HE get all HIS money from, they might say instead, where does He get all his Truth, Love, Kindness, Wisdom, and so forth from. For this Precious metal is the current coin of the New Jerusalem, with the KINGS Own Mint mark upon it. There must out of necessity be an Abundance of that which is needful, and it might appear in the form of that which we call money."

True paused to contemplate the meaning of all this, but all she succeeded in doing was daydreaming of Father and how much she loved—and wanted— him. No one had ever known a love more pure, she was sure of it. He was God, but God had bodily needs, just like she did. With that thought her hand drifted down to discretely caress herself in the deserted library. She had not seen him in a week except from afar, at the Sunday Communion banquet, sitting at the head of the table with Mother Divine. She could barely look up from her plate at the occasion—guilt and desire were at war within her.

Just then movement in the garden caught her eye—it was Father and two of his followers. Father was walking them across the lawn, making sweeping gestures around the garden, while the two followers absorbed every move and gesture like sponges, mesmerized. True thought she remembered their names—young Master Robert and his sister, Rosebud Lilly. Lilly was a silly girl who enjoyed acting childish when she thought she had the spotlight. She didn't look like a child though—she looked to be in her late teens, like True, and was definitely a head-turner, with long straight black hair and green eyes all atop an ample bust line. Currently she was her tossing her long black mane with exaggerated movements to follow Father's hand pointing across the rolling lawn, throwing her head back to look at the sky. Showoff movements, and Father Divine seemed to be paying attention. Then they moved off, down the rolling lawn and out of sight.

True Light continued her studies, but somehow she felt vaguely troubled—she was not a deep thinker and couldn't put her finger exactly on the cause of the ill feeling, but it was there all the same. She came to the logical conclusion that she needed to compose another letter to Father and deliver it herself again. Since Father was also God that meant he could see inside her heart at all times, so he would know she was coming to him tonight.

Back in his study, safely hidden away from the wants and needs of the masses, free from the pressure of being expected to have an answer for every trial and tribulation that plagued humanity, Father Divine struck a match and thew it into his fireplace. There was a soft pop as the match caught the kindling and then the fireplace came alive with orange flames and the smell of charred oak, enveloping him in warmth and goodwill as he settled into his favorite recliner. There was a nip in the salty air coming in from a window that had been left open—a perfect evening for sitting by the hearth. He briefly wondered how many people had a fireplace in their bedroom, but who cared? He had worked hard all his life for luxury—unlike most people who didn't really want to work at all— and deserved every ounce he could squeeze out of this lifetime. Living up to his own legend had taken away most of his true self, and he relished every moment where he could take back some measure of privacy to reconnect with the man formally known as George Baker Jr.

A timid knock on the door came at the appointed hour, 8 p.m. Rosebud Lilly was right on time for her counseling session. She pushed the heavy mahogany door open and slipped in. She had told Father earlier in the day that she had been having problems of an embarrassing nature and wanted to speak to him, Father Divine, since he, her Savior, would know what to do. He had assured her he knew what was in her heart but it would help if they had a prayer session together before she retired for the evening. He reassured her that in the morning she would feel much better after confessing, getting it out in the open.

"Where shall I sit Father?" Lilly look terrified in the presence of God but was determined to carry out her confession so she could be cured.

"The proper thing to do when you are confessing to God is to get down on your knees to pray and receive my message. Please child, kneel close before me and tell me in your own words what is troubling you." He put his hand on her bowed head to comfort her as she started her confession.

But something felt wrong, discomforting, a prickly feeling at the back of his neck—he became aware of a presence behind him near the door—a small noise perhaps, or a cold draft of air suddenly come into the room, causing the floor length brocade curtains to undulate across the windows. In that moment his eye caught the woman standing just inside his peripheral vision—True Light!—standing there frozen, not knowing how to proceed.

In a constricted voice that struggled to keep from quivering she whispered "I, I, just wanted to deliver another prayer to you Father." With a contorted betrayed face that looked ready to let loose a dam of tears, she placed the letter on his desk with stilted movements, quickly spun around and hurried out the door, leaving behind a faint scent of patchouli oil.

At the same moment, down the hallway in Mother Divine's suite, Sincere Sincerity was attending to the wardrobe selection for tomorrow, her arthritic hands giving each item full consideration, carefully fitting the outfit to the intended message the occasion warranted. She wondered what the all the foot traffic in the hall was—usually this time of night it was quiet as a, well, church. She pulled on the heavy brass doorknob and as unobtrusively as she could poked her grizzled head out the door, but quickly pulled it back in—quick enough, she hoped, to remain undetected. In a flash of recognition and understanding she had seen Father in the hallway looking nonplussed, frantically glancing toward the winding staircase descending to the community rooms, clutching a throw pillow to himself. She didn't like that man a bit, didn't buy for one moment that he was God anymore, but her position in the mission hierarchy was such that it gave her certain privileges she knew she could never achieve anywhere else. She recognized there were times when things should remain unsaid, and this was definitely one of those times—she would immediately file this into her category of useful information that may come in handy in the future. She had been with this organization for a long time, most of her life actually, and knew she would get her chance later to leverage information—but right now it was time for her to mind her peace, if you could call it that.

The next morning Miss Happy Word, a faithful elderly follower of Father Divine and a full-time cleaning woman at the International Peace Mission West, was slowly going about her usual business of cleaning the ladies' community lavatory, pushing the mop over the black and white honeycomb tiles, marking each swipe by the pattern, pushing to a slow rhythm, softly humming songs to Father. Out of the corner of her eye as the mop rounded the row of pedestal sinks she was startled by the lady in the bathtub. She instantly recognized the thick red hair spread out across the water—Miss True Light must have fallen asleep there. But wait, something was wrong, this was stiller, deeper than sleep. True's face was pointing up toward the ceiling with eyes open beseechingly, unseeing, her body partially submerged in rust colored bathwater except for her forearms, each hanging over the smooth sides of the antique clawfoot bathtub as if to hold herself above the waterline. There was no steam in the room so Miss Happy knew the bathwater had gone cold. She walked around the tub, noting the pool of blood that had formed under the right hand, congealed over the gash in the wrist, and the unmistakable metallic smell enveloping the scene. Miss Happy Word was terribly sorry for the young woman, but knew she was looking at a person who had failed to fulfill the requirements of the Peace Mission Movement—the inevitable outcome was death sooner or later, not the everlasting life promised by Father to those who adhered to the International Modest Code of celibacy, good works, and pure thought. She noted disapprovingly that those of a lighter complexion seemed to have a harder time adhering HIS principles—they either went astray completely or only progressed to what they called sympathizers—those who gave money to the movement and then went back to their highfalutin lifestyles. Fly-by-nights all of them, and here was another one floating in the bathtub. She would have extra cleaning to do. Miss Happy darkened her expression, shook her head and ambled off to notify her superiors of the situation.

By the morning after that, there was no trace of True Light or the fact that she had ever been there. Followers that entered the mission as residents were required to renounce all family ties or anything that bound them to their former lives before they entered mission life. They were required to turn over their property, savings, and wages to the International Peace Mission—they would be penniless if they tried to leave. Most came with nothing though, so it seemed to them they were gaining, if nothing else, security—a place to live, a job, clothes on their back, and three square meals a day. If they couldn't work anymore due to disability they were evicted and told to seek help at the local Salvation Army. They were encouraged to change their names, making the chances of a family member or friend tracing them extremely low. If a family member managed to find the follower's location and contacted the mission, they were advised the family member didn't want to speak with them, or that they had never heard of them, or that they had died many years ago. Officially there was no one to notify in the event of any life circumstance, even death. Upon their inevitable demise they were quickly buried in a potter's field or cremated.

Father Divine was notified about the True Light situation by David Devoute. "Thank you once again Brother Devoute. My heart goes out to these young people that are so confused by the temptations and evils in this world. Let us not speak of this again though. Looking back into the past will only bring sadness, bring useless memories into your consciousness. We live in Heaven on Earth here, and we cannot let the fallen pull us down into a Hell created by their own wrongdoing. "

"Agreed Father. I keep my mind on purity only. There are always those that would bring you down but I'm not having any of it."

Father put his hand protectively on Brother Devoute's bony shoulder and together they walked down the hallway, Devoute continuing on toward his quarters in the men's area, head lowered in submission, and Father going up the winding staircase to his suite. Both men surreptitiously stole a backward glance at the other to gauge acceptance of the validity of the exchange. Divine didn't like what he saw.

He, Father Divine, alone again with George Baker Jr., sighed as he closed the heavy mahogany door behind him, retreating into the safety of his private suite. Never show weakness or indecision, he knows that—after all he is God to his followers. But he didn't need this, another controversy surrounding one of the young Rosebuds. Enough of them and people would start wondering if there was something funny going on here at the Peace Mission. He decided to take the usual route and not acknowledge a problem at all, let it blow over—after awhile people forgot anyway. Who would remember an inconvenient and inconsequential death of an unknown person after a few of his lavish communion dinners? Who would even care? And the surroundings his followers lived in, his estate and the grounds, had the effect of making people stuporous, indifferent to the outside world and its problems, enveloped in a cocoon of quiet luxury and drunk with the wealthy trappings of his life. At this point he felt immune to all the controversy that had been thrown at him over the years. They resented his success, and yes, were jealous of his lifestyle, but they couldn't pin anything on him—nothing stuck. And no one would miss True Light—after all, she had arrived out of the blue, no past addresses, no friends, and had indicated no next of kin other than the Peace Mission family. They were her family and her death would be dealt with from within—it was none of anybody else's business.

He would have to be careful for awhile, not ruin an entire lifetime of hard work by throwing it all out the window for a few moments of pleasure. He would stay away from the Rosebuds, but not too far because he understood the attraction young girls had for a father figure—he needed that to maintain control. Psychology had always interested him, and years ago something had caught his attention because it seemed such a simple concept but yet such a powerful tool. In one of the psychology books it said that a narcissist doles out attention in small doses so he can better control those around him. The book defined a narcissist as a person with an exaggerated sense of self-importance, a need for admiration, and a lack of empathy for other people. To him this sounded more like the qualities of a leader, which he was—it was his destiny to lead and guide others, and too much empathy for one person would put the entire flock at risk. He knew that casualties and fallout were inevitable to carry out his mission—there were bound to be winners and losers—and he refused to be on the losing end, ever. He would just keep marching forward, stepping over the bodies of the fallen.

CHAPTER 9

Herschel positioned the pince-nez precisely on the bridge of his aquiline nose as Nona tilted the lampshade to cast better light onto the pile of papers—Dolly's bank statements —a year's worth, enough to see if her personalty change and evasive behavior coincided in any way with a financial factor. They were in their bedroom huddled over Herschel's family heirloom cherrywood writing desk. It was a full moon evening and they had just come back from dining out at one of the picturesque little sidewalk cafés. For a suspended moment in time, over a glass of wine, music drifting in from a nearby nightclub, Nona was absorbed, present, alive, as if she and Herschel were alone on the San Francisco Bay, sailing languidly over the water without a care. She had such a nice life, really, so lucky that Herschel had come along. Nona couldn't help but resent Dolly for managing to ruin things—if only she had not asked her to come with them. She was so like her father Emil who had been the ruination of her perfectly fine marriage to Norman LeCompte.

"I do feel guilty snooping Herschel—I place a high value on privacy and it seems very wrong to do this, even though it was my idea. Dolly really should be able to make decisions on her own. If she makes some mistakes she'll learn from them. She's an adult now, after all." Nona was thinking that Dolly had actually progressed to almost ruining her new life here in Berkeley, her lovely country home in

Whispering Pines, and had taken Herschel's attention away from her in a negative way. They shouldn't have to be thinking about this, the problems of her adult daughter from another marriage, but Herschel seemed determined to get to the bottom of Dolly's strange evasive behavior. Nona noticed that Herschel had an uncharacteristically strong dislike of Father Divine—maybe it was because he was in the banking business and thought of Divine as a financial swindler and wanted to get to the bottom of the con man's cash-flow, maybe even report him to the Internal Revenue Service. For a long time Herschel kept his head lowered over the figures—he was in his element, noting every detail of every date, time, amount, deposit, and withdrawal. What they were doing had to be kept secrete from the bank too—it violated privacy laws because Dolly was legally an adult.

Nona was tired from the wine. It had gone straight to her head as usual which was why she rarely drank. Looking at all the numbers made her eyes droop. The bed looked awfully inviting so she gave in, dove under the covers, and as soon as her head hit the pillow she was asleep, but the last thing she remembered was seeing Herschel's back still hunched over the bank statements, in deep concentration, doggedly determined to get to the bottom of it all.

In the morning she woke up to the sound of the coffee grinder, the aroma of the crushed beans ascending the stairs and drifting into the bedroom, giving her an imagined jolt of caffeine even before it hit her bloodstream. Herschel was making coffee, and if she was lucky, buttermilk biscuits and jam, or maybe if she was very lucky, his famous pancakes with real maple syrup. Straight and narrow as he was, not fascinating, he was dependable, solid, and resourceful—someone you could count on. She glanced at the clock—7:30 a.m., Sunday, still early enough to acceptably wear the white Turkish bathrobe from Capwell's Department Store Genieve had given her for Mother's Day last year.

"Mornin' Chef, what's on the menu?" They had a blackboard menu in the kitchen, Herschel's idea, and this morning it announced

Buttermilk Pancakes with Blueberry Maple Syrup in Herschel's ornate cursive script. A box of Bisquick pancake mix, a stick of real butter, a quart of buttermilk, and eggs balanced precariously near the edge of the countertop were arrayed neatly in line with the stovetop griddle. A pile of hot pancakes with melting butter, a pitcher of heated syrup, and a coffee mug were waiting at her place setting in the kitchen's bay window breakfast nook. She slid right in, no invitation needed. The first bite melted in her mouth and went straight to her head, same as the wine had last night, elevating her mood considerably away from the looming issue of Dolly. What an embarrassment to have your grown-up daughter causing problems like this, so unnecessary.

His back to her, focused on flipping the pancakes at the precise moment they bubbled and turned brown around the edge, he said "As you know, Genieve and Dolly left for an early morning tennis match and swim, so it's a perfect time to discuss what's been going on without having to whisper. I'll do the talking so you can eat—I confess I've already had a few pancakes to make sure I got the batter right."

Leaning back in his chair at the breakfast table, he crossed his arms over his chest in preparation to deliver the unwelcome news. "So, here it is, the low-down on what I see as a slow money drain that started a little less than a year ago. I went back one year's worth of statements and calculated forward. Dolly is making about the same hourly wage as Genieve—I pulled Genieve's statements just for comparison, but Genieve works part-time because of her studies, and Dolly is full-time. Both of them have the same low living expenses because they live with us—Genieve's savings is growing even with part-time work, but Dolly's statements show paycheck deposits and then fairly large cash withdrawals. She's not writing checks, so I can't trace it. She's spending cash somewhere. I don't see evidence that she spends any money on herself, do you? At the rate she is earning, she should have five thousand dollars in savings, but instead she has less than half that—looks like over half her earnings are disappearing into thin air after she withdraws the money."

Nona tried hard to savor her breakfast, but the bites were turning sour, drying up, forming a lump in her throat that wouldn't go down. She had a horrible suspicion what Dolly was doing with her money—especially after reading the Father Divine pamphlet she got at the Bodhi Tree bookstore. Upon reflection she had come to the conclusion that the Peace Mission Movement was really an imitation of the Communist Movement—didn't the Communists ever give up? Hollywood was loaded with them according to the latest news reports—now here they were in Berkeley, disguised as a new religion. She remembered reading the definition of Communism, and it sounded pretty close to how the Peace Mission Movement operated: a theory or system of social organization in which all property is owned by the community and each person contributes and receives according to their ability and needs. It troubled her that under such a system, one central person or a few people at the top were able to dole out resources—or not—to all those under them as they saw fit. That was putting way too much faith in those at the top—or not giving enough credit to those below—unless, of course, the person at the top managed to convince people he was God come to Earth.

"Herschel, you have gone above and beyond trying to help. Without you I would have no concrete idea what was going on with Dolly. Based on recent events I'm going to guess she was convinced to give a lot of her earnings to the Peace Mission. You shouldn't have to worry about this though, you've done so much for us all. Unfortunately this is something I need to discuss with her father Emil, as much as I dislike having to communicate with him. Maybe he can talk some sense into her—I'll call him this evening and let him know, and ask if he can reason with her." She loathed the idea of calling Emil, but why shouldn't he share the burden since he was her father? Emil and Dolly adored each other, so she may listen to him.

She hoped that two-faced phony of a second wife, Lillian the former dance instructor, didn't answer the phone.

Later, in the early evening, as soon as Dolly departed home again for one of her frequent visits to the library—even though the library was closed on Sundays— Nona rehearsed in her mind what to say to Emil. Genieve was up in her room studying for an upcoming test but she would still have to speak quietly—the telephone was seldom used and she didn't want Genieve asking who she was talking to. Calling Emil would definitely arouse interest, which is exactly what she wanted to avoid. She peeked around the corner into the living room to see Herschel at his station on the corner of the couch browsing the latest edition of Reader's Digest, simultaneously listening to news commentary on the radio, something about Howard Hughes' connection to the Hollywood film industry. She dialed the number, waited for what seemed like forever for someone to answer. Then he picked up the receiver, his hello sounding very satisfied and relaxed. She hated him.

"Hi Emil, it's Nona. Sorry to interrupt your evening, but we have a problem." Silence for a time while he no doubt made hand gestures to Lillian.

"So great to hear from you Nona—we hope everyone is okay up there. Judging by the letters I get from the girls it sounds pretty ideal. Say hello to Herschel for me." He now sounded stilted, uncomfortable—no doubt Lillian was a few inches away, leaning close into the handset of the pink Bakelite desktop telephone she knew Emil had pilfered from her during the divorce. Nona could almost smell the cheap Avon perfume Lillian peddled door to door in her pathetic career as an Avon saleslady.

Nona quickly delivered the bombshell to get his full attention. "I'm calling about our daughter Dolly, and I think it's pretty serious." There was silence on the other end as Emil held his breath in, preparing for the worst. She gave him a summary of recent events, behavior changes, and the evidence of the bank statements with the disappearing cash. There was a long pause while he considered—Nona knew it took him a while to form thoughts into words, but when he did, everyone listened—Emil was a smart man and people knew it, respected it.

"Let me think about it overnight—I also want to check the Santa Monica Library. They may have some books on cults so I can figure out what we're dealing with. I'll call tomorrow. Say hi to the girls for me, tell them I miss them."

Nona knew Emil would take action, have a plan. He was never one to just stand aside and wring his hands. And he loved his daughters, especially Dolly. She felt better after getting off the phone—something would be done.

When the phone rang the next evening and Long Distance said it was Santa Monica calling, she felt relief, something she previously didn't associate with Emil. "Hi Nona, it's me. I spent the whole day in the library researching religious cults and Father Divine. This Divine character is masquerading as God come to Earth, and the doctrine he preaches is not even his own—it's related to the New Thought Movement, and the Communist Party, plus a few of his own nutty twists thrown in. I won't bore you with the details, but believe me, the authorities are watching him. He's been put in the looney bin for saying he's God, and he's been arrested and jailed for fraud. One of the judges who threw the book at him died of a heart attack right after the trial, and Divine had the nerve to take credit for it, telling the press, "I hated to do it." Can you believe this creep? His crazy followers bought right into it, hook, line, and sinker. He gets rich off of his poor dumb follower's labor, houses them in communes, feeds them, sends them off to slave labor jobs and then takes all their money. That's just the half of it. How in the heck did our daughter get involved with this crook? Were you off on one of your nutty philosophies and Dolly jumped on the bandwagon with you? You know how weak minded she is—maybe she was trying to please you? We all know how impossible that is."

The conversation had taken a bad turn. She would definitely not tell him about her Santa Monica friend from Lincoln Park, Meekness Simplicity with her New Day newspapers, or that she had briefly worked at the Mission Grocery Store up here until she was positive they intended to stiff her. "That's right, lay the blame on someone else—of course it's my fault. Your daughter is an adult and I can't control what she believes—but you know what? I wish I had never given birth to her. She's just like you, a chip off the old block—all she brings into our lives is problems. I wish you could talk her into going back home to Santa Monica—but then she wouldn't have an easy life living off Herschel and myself, and our nice Country Home to go to when she gets bored. She can afford to indulge herself in the latest counterculture philosophy about how horrible the wealthy are, how abused the poor are—she has a safety net in case her new ideas about how the world should be don't pan out to her advantage."

"I've had enough for tonight Nona. I think I know what I'm dealing with. I'll have a talk with Dolly within the next few days." Lillian murmured something from nearby and Nona could picture her gently taking the receiver away from Emil, playing the dutiful concerned wife to a hilt. The receiver clicked then, leaving a lot of what she wanted to say unsaid.

Herschel walked up behind her just then and put his hand on her shoulder. "I couldn't help but hear a lot of the conversation Nona—it sounded like Emil was right here in the room because you were holding the receiver so far from your ear. I'm so sorry this is happening to Dolly, but she is an adult and should be making a life for herself, thinking of a family. At this point, she doesn't give back much, does she? I am not even sure why she needs to live with us. Genieve I can understand—she's in school and working part-time, she's only nineteen—and she's happy and well-adjusted. But Dolly is twenty-two and acting like a rebellious teenager. Maybe she should be out on her own to see what the real world is like. She'll probably drop her crazy ideas pretty quickly once she gets a taste of reality. And Nona? I don't want Dolly and Emil to come between us, okay? What do you say we take off for a couple weeks, go to our Country Home? Nothing like Whispering Pines to clear the air—what do you say?"

What could she say? There it was, the choice was put in a nice way but still firmly clear—Herschel and a settled life, or Dolly and her problems.

Now, two weeks later, Nona knew what she had to do. The time alone with Herschel in Whispering Pines had cleared her head. He was so centered—she envied that, someone who could pick out a path and stick to it, guided by logic rather than emotions and whims of the moment. In their marriage bed he was slow, tender, considerate. She would not put their relationship in jeopardy like she had her other marriages, not this time. He gently pointed out that she had six adult children and only one was a problem—that was an excellent record. He reasoned that she shouldn't get stuck on the negative aspects of just one person when she had such a large family to be proud of. He assured her Dolly would find her own way, would in time tire of her Father Divine fad. In the meantime, maybe she was inadvertently fueling the fire by arguing with Dolly, who maybe was starring in her own drama, intentionally focusing everyone's attention on herself. And, she was enabling Dolly's adolescent fantasy of the world by allowing her to live almost free.

Halfway through their vacation Genieve had called to report the low-down on the latest happenings with Dolly. Apparently she went out often in the evenings after work to go to meetings. Both Sundays she told Genieve she was going to the International Peace Mission West to attend the weekly communal banquets and hear Father Divine speak. She tried to talk Genieve into going but didn't get very far—Genieve saw the whole thing as a con and said she would rather eat cold cereal than give that crook the satisfaction of listening to him—Dolly didn't say another word about Father Divine to her again. Genieve continued to worry over Dolly—they used to be best friends as well as sisters, but now they were becoming estranged. Dolly was moving closer and closer to her mission family, lured by the idea that she was making a difference, helping people that had not been given a fair shake in the world.

By the time they arrived back home, Nona's plan was more clarified. She decided to push Dolly out of the nest—it was getting too crowded in the little Victorian house. The rooms were small and getting smaller—there was no room for unhappiness. Tonight was the night she and Dolly were going to have their talk—keep it short, logical—Nona told herself. She knocked on Dolly's bedroom door, three soft taps to indicate good tidings. "Come in." In that moment Nona felt another flash of resentment for Dolly—who did she think she was to take up an entire bedroom in a nice house, almost never come down except to eat and go out the front door to work, to tennis, to swim, or mostly now to her mission friends—her fellow cult members. "We need to have a talk Dolly. You know we can't go on this way and you know exactly what I mean. We are happy for you that you have found a purpose in life, but we think you'd be better off, happier, if you found your own place to live. You earn more than enough money at work. Maybe you can get one of those darling little studios near the college closer to work. You'd also be closer to the pool and tennis courts—maybe you'll meet a nice young man who likes tennis, like your last man friend Dr. Bob Wallen—whatever became of Bob? He was such a great catch."

Dolly rolled her icy blue eyes up, sucked her cheeks in and pursed her lips —a move so familiar to Nona she could almost see her daughter at five years old trying to mimic the bored look of adults. "We just didn't see eye-to-eye on things. He was too interested in material things, which is great, but he couldn't really understand wanting to give back, help others less fortunate, unless he got paid well for it. He called me an ideologue. I didn't call him a name back but secretly I feel fortunate I didn't get stuck raising a family for him while he went off every day to do more important things. I don't want to be a dependent housewife for anyone. Genieve doesn't either—that's why she's working so hard at Merritt College. We're each going about it in different ways though—I want to be of service to others, stand for something, have a cause. Genieve is going to do it through financial independence, but I can't see her ever helping anyone but herself, she's so selfish. I don't see why you're always picking on me and not Genieve.

Good point, thought Nona, but Genieve was not in a cult, giving her money away and isolating herself from her family—Genieve could be considered normal, mainstream, motivated to make something of herself. Dolly had gone off the deep end with the Father Divine cult. There was a way to help people and still get paid without giving your money away—take Father Divine for example. He doled out a lot of social justice tokens but obviously managed to do very well for himself financially.

They talked until the wee hours. Nona managed to gain Dolly's trust enough to learn, shockingly, that she was strongly considering moving into the International Peace Mission West to become a Rosebud. She envisioned herself as a social justice warrior in the fight against poverty and discrimination. Foolish as it sounded, she said she liked the Rosebud uniforms, wanted to wear one so everyone knew she stood for something. Nona had a sudden déjà vu of eight-year-old Dolly and how proud her daughter was to wear her uniform when she was in Camp Fire Girls in Santa Monica. She wore that uniform all the time, even when there was no meeting. In a flash of understanding Nona recognized Dolly was born to be a follower, had always been waiting for someone to tell her what to do, to hear marching orders. She would never find her own way because she didn't have one—she moved with a herd mentality, a member of the hunted, never the hunter.

"Well, Herschel and I think it's better at this point for you to have your own place, and since you're thinking of moving into the mission you must agree too—it's time for you to have your own space. At least we're all in agreement with that, right?"

Dolly's face suddenly whitened and became small and pinched. "Well, that's true, but I don't want to feel pushed out, in a hurry to leave just because your fifth husband doesn't find my presence convenient for him. My Daddy would never consider such a thing—who does Herschel think he is? I guess I'm odd man out for your new little family—but guess what? I'll leave when I'm good and ready—you and Herschel can't do a thing about it, because, as you may have forgotten, I'm on the lease here as a legal adult. I could legally ask you and Herschel to leave too if it came right down to it. And maybe I will. Genieve and I can stay here and easily afford the lease without you two nagging us all the time. I wish you would have stayed in your expensive Whispering Pines cabin on a permanent vacation. I just can't believe what you choose to spend your money on when there's so many people in need—it's disgusting!" Dolly had changed again, generating an anger Nona didn't know she was capable of, eyes narrowed, bouncing light back but not letting anyone in, brow furrowed, spitting words out cruelly. In one shocking moment, Nona was transported to that final blow-up with Emil her mind had blocked out for so many years—his threats of ruining her financially if she didn't pay him his legal share for agreeing to marry a woman ten years older than him with four children, against his better judgement—he wanted to be paid for putting up with her! Right now, in this moment, Emil was back with a vengeance, an unwelcome vestige from the past come to life in female expression, an off-shoot of the same person—and wicked as ever, if not more so. Just as she had put Emil on her Brentwood estate's property title so many years ago, now she had put his daughter on her Berkeley home lease and was about to be stung again—but not this time, no way—this time she would fight to win. She wished she could give that bum Emil his rotten daughter back.

Dolly escorted her mother to the bedroom door with a cold rough hand firmly gripping her arm, no trace of feeling whatsoever. Nona was pushed into the hallway, the door slamming so close behind her she felt the rush of air from the the swing of the door. It was a finality that would set the tone for a new chapter in their mother-daughter relationship.

"She's on the lease because it's required that all adults living in the house be on a lease, but I sure didn't put her on the property title for the cabin, especially after what you told me about Emil. I was hesitant to say this before, because she's your daughter, but it's well-known that some behavior traits are inherited. Looks like Dolly may have received a bit of the bad seed." Herschel was being very careful, peeking out over his pince-nez to gauge her reaction, treading water into dangerous territory because he knew mothers are biologically linked to their children after all—husbands and boyfriends, friends in general were always second to that biological imperative. He didn't want to get involved, but he had no choice.

"You don't deserve to be in the middle of something so sordid Herschel—you're a good man. I can assure you, this is unthinkable behavior for anyone in my family—we are all decent people. This is absolutely the work of the Father Divine cult—and let's call it what it is, a cult. I've heard these cults take over people's mind, hypnotize them until they don't even know who they are anymore. But I'm a firm believer in free will, and somewhere along the line Dolly made a choice to go down the wrong path. The followers I met working at the Mission Grocery Store were so very different from Dolly—they came from poor backgrounds, were the truly downtrodden until they found food and shelter at the mission. Dolly has absolutely no excuse, so I have no sympathy for her—in fact, I've had enough of all this. The best thing for her is just to let her go, forget about her until she comes to her senses. Living at the mission with all the oddballs may just be the thing that she needs to face reality."

Hershel raised his eyebrows high, let his mouth drop open a little, sucked his breath in as if to convey a sudden thought had occurred to him, but Nona knew better. There was very little about Herschel that was spontaneous, and she knew he had mulled this one over for a long time—"Do we really need to continue this lease my dear? I only need to make an appearance at the bank about once a week. I can do most of the paperwork from home—I'm the manager after all. If I want to be there more often all I really need is a small apartment, just enough for one person. We really should spend more time in Whispering Pines—after all, we're not getting any younger. We can help Genieve find a studio near her Merritt College—she'll probably love it, and she can find a room-mate if she gets lonely."

"I thought you just signed another year's lease term. The owner seems to be very anxious about money, so I doubt he'll let us out of the lease."

Dramatic pause, as if Herschel was in deep thought. "I'll take care of that, don't worry. If he won't let us out of the lease, he'll be happy to be rid of us if I start paying late, or better yet, forget to send checks at all. A month or two of that and he'll want us out of here in a hurry.

And who cares? It's not as if I need the reference—I already own a home and I manage the main bank in town—I have more than enough character references. And he can find other tenants pretty quickly in a college town even if he raises the rent, so he'll not even miss us."

She hugged him, secretly grateful he had not suggested moving out on his own to escape her family problems—he was taking her with him. The crowded nest syndrome was about to be end. If one's problems would not leave you, then you had to leave them, leave them in the dust, roll over them and don't look back. Just keep moving forward.

CHAPTER 10

He woke up in a sweat, just little George Baker alone and terrified in the night. He sat up as if jerked forward by an unseen force, satin sheets sliding to the ground in a damp heap, pulling himself forcefully out of a dream state into consciousness. He tried not to look at the bedside clock because this would set him worrying—could he get back to sleep or would he suffer all day from insomnia, confusion—he couldn't afford that. He had a congregation to lead, sermons to give, words of wisdom to share that people with pens and paper hurriedly scratched out as he spoke. He was frustrated he couldn't control his own mind when he controlled the thoughts and actions of so many followers.

The bad dream—nightmare really— was back again, same topic, same script. How was it possible to have the exact same nightmare over and over again? And what did it mean? In his suite, right now, on his hand carved highboy dresser, was a child's porcelain bank in the likeness of the cartoon character Sylvester the Cat, the coin slot right on top of the cat's head. The bank held a few gold coins which he occasionally verified were still there by rattling it to hear the reassuring clinks inside. The bank and coins were a wedding gift from Sweet Angel Divine—he was vaguely aware she may have meant the bank to be a spoof of some sort, a statement of vague smug intention, but he chose to ignore that and allowed it to become a fixture on his dresser.

His nightmare always began with a white door slamming shut in front of him. Then he somehow was materialized inside his grandmother Baker's musty apartment with the same highboy dresser, the same Sylvester the Cat bank. There was one small dirty window that looked out onto the brick wall from the neighboring building, filtering in yellow light that reflected slow moving dust particles drifting in the air. His grandmother was in the next room and he thought he heard her call out to him, but he was alone with the bank, which began to move, rattling and shaking, a thin dark line of smoke rising from the top of the cat's porcelain head. The eyes turned evil, looked down upon him hungrily from its perch atop the dresser. It was alive and going to kill him—he felt a stab of fear too real to be a dream, a stab deep into the pit of his stomach, so real it took his breath away, and the sinking feeling of not being able to move. The cat figure ballooned out into a black cloud and mutated into the Devil clutching a pitchfork aimed right at him. He had to find his grandmother—where was she? He moved to the kitchen to find help, too slowly as if dragging his legs though quicksand, his arms leaden and useless, hands numb. He looked up to see butcher knives floating and bouncing across the ceiling through a cloud of mist, glinting, nice and sharp—if they fell they would kill him, slice right through him one by one. Where was his grandmother, who would save him? Then there was a turn for the worse—the bank had morphed into his mother, whom he feared worse than the Devil—the evil bank and his mother had melded into one horrible entity and he knew he was going to die, be stabbed and eaten, and he knew his grandmother was dead and couldn't save him. He tried to make his way to the door but he was unable to get control of his limbs, was glued to the spot by something heavy, suffocating over and around him. Cold fear gripped him, he was desperate for this to be a dream but it wasn't, gasping for air as the evil overtook him just before he reached the door. That's when he fought his way back to consciousness. But it was too real to be a dream—some part of this was real or else how could it be so vivid, cause his body systems to seize up like this?

He laid back down, heart racing, sweating out fear, and switched positions on the bed, turning on his other side so the dream would't come back. It never did after he switched sides. But it would return another night, that he knew.

This morning he was headed on foot to the center of town at a brisk pace to clear his head from his poor night's sleep. The recurring nightmare puzzled him but the threat faded with the chilly morning light, the smell of the sea, salt air whipping him alive, seagulls squawking overhead. Everything always seemed more hopeful in the morning. He fiddled with the buttons on his suit, rolled his shoulders up and back, sucked his stomach in and proceeded forward, his signature Fedora cocked at just the right angle. He tried to remember not to bounce too much when he walked—move slow, dignified, self-assured, radiate Peace, he told himself. By now people in the town were used to seeing the diminutive Negro gentleman, and lately some people were giving him grudging admiration for his charity work and successful grocery store with the low prices and quality goods. The new customers who previously had come in with frowns trying to find something wrong now smiled as they passed through the tinkling brass doorbells. It was okay if they didn't buy into his Divinity, as long as they came to shop, maybe even donate extra to his cause and feed the mission's coffers.

Up ahead he thought he saw someone familiar—was that the pugnacious little Italian grocer Giuseppi? Divine slowed his pace down—the man would be even more pugnacious now that many of his customers had switched to the Mission Grocery Store—which had decided to carry Italian products after all. Giuseppi ducked under a short red awning and disappeared inside The Piedmont Tobacconist. The store window was large, too large, so he ducked his head as he passed, holding his breath so he didn't have to inhale the cigar smoke billowing out the door, hoping Giuseppi wouldn't be looking out. Father Divine had a difficult time blending into a crowd and sure enough, the door opened back up quickly, doorbells tinkling angrily. "Hey, you, Mr. God—I guess you don' believe in keeping your word, you crook! Waddaya think you doin' buyin' up my supplier's goods so I get only the seconds and a lotta times now, nothin'! I got a family to feed—what am I supposed to do? You gonna rot in Hell for playin' God, cheating honest businesspeople like me, you son of a bitch, come back here..."

He didn't miss a beat, just kept walking, didn't want a showdown with this little has-been. Whose problem was it if the man didn't know how to stay in business when a little competition came along? A few people turned around to see what the shouting was about and he looked around too, arranging his face into a puzzled look, as if he too was seeking the source of the upset. He walked on, shaking his head, just minding his own business, going with the easy flow of the crowd,—he was an accomplished stage performer after all. He walked on, determined to enjoy the day—maybe a surprise visit to his grocery store would be the thing to do. It was only a few more blocks.

A horn honked, startling him out of his musings. A few minutes later a falsetto male voice rose up from behind, a little out of breath. "Father Divine, excuse my intrusion, I just wanted to introduce myself and comment what a wonderful difference your store makes in this town." Father quickly arranged his face into his signature benevolent smile before turning around to see a tall, thin, very pale complected man with dark sunglasses, completely hairless, looming over him, fawning and smiling sheepishly. "Sorry to startle you, but I felt I must say something because I'm sure no one else does, even if they think it. People are habitually ungrateful in this town, but some recognize all the good you're doing. It's about time that nice things become available to the less fortunate." The man raised his sunglasses to make deeper contact. He was startled at the man's eyes—pale blue, almost colorless, no depth at all—only a diamond hard reflection, quizzical, analytical—Divine felt guilty all of a sudden, and a chill ran through him. "Allow me to introduce myself. I am Grand Archdruid Ichabod Leach of the Ancient Order of Druids in America. We reside up the hill from you, in the temple of the Seventh Ray near Druid Grove. Occasionally we can smell your feasts—tell me, do they work well for you, this method of feeding people to draw them in?"

He was taken aback, flustered by a very rare lack of words. What did the pale man want, what did he mean? How could he get away fast while at the same time appearing gracious?

"I just noticed the time Mr. Leach—sorry but I'm late for an appointment. I hope we meet again soon—I'm looking forward to it." Divine glanced concernedly at the town clock across the street.

Backing away, fully aware of the man's eye's boring into him like cold knives, he heard the falsetto intonation, "We will meet again when we are both like clouds upon the wind."

Druids! Weren't they the ones who wore long white robes and gathered under the moonlight in a circle, chanting and carving Celtic crosses into tree trunks? Reverend Major Jealous Divine, also known as God to his followers, was anxious to be safely inside his grocery store—he was starting to think he was one of only a few mainstream religious leaders around Holy Hill.

Sincere Sincerity was looking for Brother David Devoute, her male counterpart whether she liked it or not. Her job was to take care of Mother Divine, watch out for her, wait on her, even advise her if asked. Likewise Brother Devoute with Father Divine. David Devoute, in her opinion, was obsequious and closed mouthed with information to a fault. If he knew anything he held back and waited to top your information with his own in a sort of one-upmanship. But he did it in an annoying overly humble way. What a phony. Why were light complected people so phony? This unkind prejudicial thought immediately made her felt guilty, and she quickly redirected her mind away from race in accordance with the International Peace Mission code of ethics. But it was hard not to think that way because she knew it was true.

Right now she was making her slow careful way down the winding staircase that led from Father and Mother's suites, the lush carpet muting her steps, her gnarled hand firming gripping the polished mahogany banister for balance—she was entering her dotage, getting frail. But she was still tough, a survivor. She had done well for herself considering. She rounded the corner to the right toward the men's wing. Normally she would never go there because interacting with the opposite sex was discouraged unless absolutely necessary, again in accordance with Peace Mission code of ethics. But Brother Devoute had not been seen since yesterday. He was prone to hiding out in his room whenever possible, ostensibly reading volumes of Father's past sermons, but he was a creature of habit and took three punctual walks a day, morning, noon, and night to try and stay in shape, as he put it. And to snoop around in her opinion. He also had the grocery store detail now, tending the cash registers, counting money, transferring it in and out of different canvas money pouches. Faithful Rosebud Stella, the hefty cash register attendant, had asked after him this evening when her shift ended. Brother Devoute was aging, getting softer, turning grayer and more translucent in spite of his exercise regimen—he needed his mission family to check on him, make sure nothing was wrong.

Miss Sincere Sincerity arrived at the thick carved oak door and discretely knocked three times, the door so thick it must have absorbed the sound—did she knock loud enough? "Brother David, it's me, Miss Sincere. Are you in there?" No reply, only silence, no shifting of positions, no footsteps shuffling toward the door. She reluctantly turned the doorknob to see if she could peek in—maybe he was sick, or asleep, or not there. The door pushed open slowly, heavily, the hinges well-oiled and silent. She held onto the doorknob in order to quickly shut it in the event she caught him dressing, on the toilet, or some other private moment. The room revealed itself as the door swung open, whitewashed walls, too quiet, lonely, sparsely furnished with dark wood pieces smelling of furniture wax and fresh linens, and—something else, unpleasant, intestinal.

She moved tentatively, guilty at her intrusion, into a large utilitarian male cave devoid of any personal or family memorabilia except for a color photograph of Father and Mother Divine in full regalia in a silver desk frame atop the dresser. Mission style exposed rafters criss-crossed the ceiling, giving the space the feel of an ancient place of worship or even sacrifice. The small bed was made up with a simple white chenille spread and one white pillow, tidy as a hotel. Where was the smell coming from? Could there be a plumbing problem? To her left a stained glass window allowed in some cheerful dappled prisms of color reflected onto the white wall as the sun moved toward its Western descent into the bay. In the dimness to the side of the window, she could make out a punching bag hanging from the rafters—no doubt part of Brother Devoute's work-out routine, his secrete indulgence in things of the flesh. She moved to the window, creaking floorboards announcing her progress. As she neared the window the punching bag swayed lazily, and in one horrible flash as the smell enveloped her she realized it was not a piece of gym equipment but Brother Devoute himself, suspended from the rafters with a thick rope cinched tightly around his neck, his face contorted in a grimace resembling a smile, set forever in rigor mortis. His pants were soiled with his own feces and urine, beginning to dry and cake—he had been hanging for some time.

She stood there for a moment rather than screaming and running away, because she felt he deserved better—she stood there and looked full into his eyes to give him some measure of final respect. In a shaky voice that was barely audible, coming from somewhere deep within, she whispered "Brother David, we're sure going to miss you. How come you left us so soon? We need you. And we love you." Could her message somehow be transmitted to wherever his spirit was? She told herself it could, and that somehow it gave his death some meaning—she was part of his family after all. With a terribly heavy heart, she forced herself to move away from Brother David for the final time. She would never see him again because death was not acknowledged by the International Peace Mission. It signified that you were not a true follower of Father Divine's, that you had not achieved everlasting life because there was a flaw in you somewhere, or there must be a secretc violation of ethics. But Sincere Sincerity knew this not to be true of Brother David—a more devout faithful follower she had never seen. She was afraid because she had seen something in Brother David's lifeless eyes. She had heard, in her youth, that the eyes retain the very last thing they see in the moment before death. Looking into his eyes, she had seen fear and horror, not the peaceful release of life she had seen in the bodies of the very elderly followers that quietly passed on into the next life while at the mission. Brother David's eyes were fighting for life at the moment of his death.

He was finally alone with his personal mail, tonight about ten envelopes, most addressed to his formal title Reverend Major Jealous Divine—these were probably from his core followers, fawning, weeping personal stories about how he had changed their lives. He found them useful because they provided a personal look inside the inner workings of minds who required help or guidance—dependent minds. Analyzing the letters allowed him to better understand the inner workings of the weak-minded, why they followed, what they needed, what they lacked.

A discrete knock on his door jolted him out of concentration—now what? Another Rosebud delivering a message? He was in an irritable mood because of the encounter with the annoying has-been Giuseppi and the weird Druid, or Archdruid something—whatever that meant—who had caused him to become flustered. That should never have happened and it did. The man had appeared to be looking through him, as if he knew what he was—or wasn't.

"Peace, please come in." He pulled his head away from the comforting circle of soft light cast by his banker's desk lamp, pushed his correspondence aside, and arranged his face into his customary impassive, benevolent, all-knowing expression. Mother Divine entered, tall and imposing. He did not allow his shock to register on his face—she had never come to his private quarters before, and especially without an escort. "Why Sweet Angel! What a surprise this is. I would have thought you were retired for the evening."

Mother Divine moved a little forward into her husband's private domain, a bit uncomfortable but too self-assured to allow any weakness to show. She conveyed a dominance of her environment at all times, including now, her countenance one of regal composure—any and all situations were under her control. He registered once again how impressing Sweet Angle was in her role as Mother to his followers.

"Now that Brother David Devoute has finished his role with us I would like your recommendation for another Brother to groom as his replacement. Perhaps someone a little less interested, less inquiring." Her eyes glittered like cold diamonds, as cold as the diamonds that encircled her neck and fingers. She was only in her early twenties but somehow her soul had aged, hardened.

"Perhaps it's better not to give any follower an opportunity to get that close again, Mother dear. People are better off, happier, not knowing things, like children."

"I couldn't agree more Father Dear. Knowing that to be true, Miss Sincere Sincerity must indeed be an unhappy woman." Mother's eyes held his in a too-long significant gaze, cold as the Nordic snow from whence her ancestors had come.

"Peace Father Dear." She backed away and moved out the door, the latch softly clicking behind her. He wondered if his recurring dream would return tonight, the one where his bank turned into the Devil who then turned into his mother.

Putting this uncomfortable thought aside, compartmentalizing as he had read somewhere, he returned to personally answering a letter from one of his sympathizers who had sent him a recommendation for a family member who wanted to become a Rosebud. Unusual, he thought, and from the same woman, a Mrs. Nona Twining, who had worked at the grocery store briefly. Apparently one of her daughters wanted to be of service to the International Peace Mission Movement. The daughter's name was Ann Rosetta Born, nickname Dolly. Sounds vaguely familiar, he thought. But there were so many young girls out there who wanted to change the world—at least there was hope for a better world, young people that were willing and able to work for change. Each worker in the International Peace Mission represented many thousands of dollars per year in earning power, all given over to his Heavenly Treasury. The profit margin was very satisfying, considering the low cost of communal housing and buying food for them in bulk—he was always happy to sign another Rosebud up, indeed. He finished his composition and proof read it. Tomorrow he would give it to one of his secretaries to be typed and mailed:

June 6, 1947 A.D.F.D.
Mrs. Nona Twining
3100 Benvenue Avenue
Berkeley 5, California

My dear Mrs. Twining:
Your letter of the 26th ultimo is received and I AM highly pleased to know of your whole hearted stand for God. Surely you have brought yourself under MY Divine care and protection, giving MY Spirit free access to bless, to heal and to save you and yours.
I AM glad also to know that your daughter desires to be a Rosebud, for if she expresses the Heart of a real, true Rosebud and lives the Life I exemplify, she will be abundantly blessed from every angle expressible.
Continue to follow your heart's sincere conviction, in all things that concern you, so that you may dwell in peace and contentment and in the abundance of all good things materially, for have I not declared,
"The Spirit of the consciousness of the Presence of God is the source of all supply, and it will satisfy every good desire." (FATHER DIVINE)
Thus, trust in MY Name and I will bring you out, so that you and yours may have the privilege to become to be as this leaves ME, as I AM Well, Healthy, Joyful, Peaceful, Lively, Loving, Successful, Prosperous and Happy in Spirit, Body and Mind and in every organ, muscle, sinew, joint, limb, vein and bone and even in every ATOM, fibre and cell of MY Bodily Form.
Respectfully and Sincere, I AM
REV. MJDIVINE
(Better know as FATHER DIVINE)

2

CHAPTER 11

Palisades Park runs along the palm tree lined bluffs overlooking the endless expanse of Pacific Ocean in Santa Monica, California. It was fall, 1947—sunshine, puffy white clouds drifting by, 72 degrees—who would want to be anywhere else? Countless people come here to the edge of the city and pause, if only for a moment, to reflect on their lives, or just take a breath and relax—it's that kind of place, a sanctuary of peace and meditation. The perspective here is so enormous, the sky blending into the sea for eternity, it makes a person's earthly problems seem insignificant. Emil Born, father, husband, successful landscape architect, was seated here today on one of the benches perched just inside the fence line that keeps people a safe distance from the sheer unstable cliffs. He leaned back, crossed his legs, stretched one muscled arm out along the back of the bench and considered—how does one cope with the loss of a child? The child is you, and you are the child, one and the same. Dolly was his little girl even though she was grown up. What possibly could have motivated his beautiful little girl, a stunning woman now, to join a crazy cult for colored people? Tonight he would take out the letters from his daughters once again, which he would never, ever throw away, arrange them in date order, and search for clues as to what possibly could have happened up there in Berkeley. He knew there were a lot of strange people in that city, and that the college tended to attract misfits, in his opinion, so there were plenty of bad influences—she was a pushover for just about anyone, one of the things he loved about her—the trusting side. Maybe Dolly was just going through a phase and would be back for Thanksgiving Dinner just like she'd always been. He would make sure Lillian set a place for both his girls at the table.

For the hundredth time he went over his last telephone conversation with her. That was in May, when the flowers were first starting to bloom, carpeting the earth in every color nature could dream up, unfolding the promise of long perfect summer days. He noticed things like that, counted the years by the change of the seasons—after all, he was a gardener.

He tried to reason with Dolly when she explained Father Divine was God, if you defined God as someone who brought hope and solutions where before there was only despair. He reminded her of all the people who had done good in the world, helped humanity, but had remained close to their families. They didn't shun their parents and enter missions. Father Divine was encouraging people to isolate from their families so he could take advantage of them, use them as cheap labor for his businesses. When he delivered that point, Dolly had become angry, a new note of dislike creeping into her usually mild manner. He kept driving home point after point, in his logical fashion which was the only way he knew how to reason. You can't stop the world from being bad Dolly. That doesn't mean we should't try Daddy. It was like a tennis match except the score remained at zero for both players at the end of each set. After that last telephone call, Dolly managed to be too busy to talk on the phone. Genieve or Nona usually answered, or even Herschel, but Dolly never seemed to be around when he called. She only wrote a few letters after that, then nothing since June—over four months. It was Nona who dropped the bomb on him, a touch of triumphant spitefulness in her voice—Genieve had moved into a little studio that was attached to their friend's house near her school. She and Herschel were up in Whispering Pines in their Country home almost full time now, and Dolly had moved into the International Peace Mission in Berkeley. He felt like someone had punched him in the stomach and dropped the bottom of the elevator out from under him. He was terrified.

Later that evening he settled into the small nook of the house they designated as the library. Lillian was in the living room with eyes glued to their new RCA television set which was at the moment airing Pantomime Quiz. He flipped up a leaf of the drop-leaf table to make enough room to arrange Dolly and Genieve's letters open in date order for the years 1946 and 1947, the time period leading up to the Father Divine business. He tugged the chain of the reading lamp until it clicked on and started searching for any clue he may have missed before:

January 2, 1946

Dear Daddy and Lillian,

Thanks a million for the darling charm bracelet that you sent. You should have seen my expression when I opened it. Boy, I really treasure that. Herschel was sort of peeved because I made such a fuss over it. He wanted me to rave over the bathrobe he gave me. But I really did. Oh I guess he's just sensitive.

Dolly will write you but she's very busy with her work. And you both know how she is about writing. I would have written you before this, but I'm back to the working world now.

I work at a drugstore which is near our house. It certainly is handy for me. I work 5:30 p.m. and get through at 9:00 p.m. every day. So I once again work after school. It's quite hard because I have to add federal tax and state tax on every toiletry item the customer buys. It makes me nervous. I'll get over it I hope. Sure is different from Monkey Wards (Montgomery Wards ha ha).

Well I have to clean up for work so bye now.

Love, Genieve

May 12, 1946

Dearest Daddy,

Sure glad to hear from you—it's been a long time, hasn't it? I just finished giving myself one of those home waves—sure hope it turns out all right.

I took care of children last night to make a little extra money on the side. And when Genieve came home last night from work she couldn't stand the thought of staying home all alone on a Saturday night, so she went over to a girlfriend's house and stayed all night and said she would be here early this morning—but no Genieve as yet and it's 2:30 p.m.—and now I'm lonely. You know some people enjoy staying home by themselves, but I guess I can't. You see Daddy, Mother is often up at our Country home in Whispering Pines because she can't stand this weather here in Berkeley because of her arthritis. You see up there in the mountains it's dry and that's what she needs for her condition. It sure is hard and lonesome down here all alone without her. Guess I'm just a mama's baby. But for awhile there when we were all together, I would come home and sit down at my piano and practice an hour or two, then sit down to dinner. Genieve and I would do the dishes. It was all too nice, then she had to leave. She is just fine up there in the mountains, in fact, she is taking care of Joannie (Kathleen's little girl). Joannie baby is six years old and going to Country school up there. Guess you know all about it though, through Eloise.

Herschel is here two or three days out of the week because he's a traveling agent with First Federal Bank. But we aren't on speaking terms now. It's a long story, but to make a long story short—everything was just rosy after Mother left, and I would buy the groceries and fix dinner every night like I still continue to do. Then one morning he whispered to Genieve in a low voice so I couldn't hear in the kitchen, that for Genieve to give the $10.00 food money to him instead of me which was against Mother's orders before she left, because she said Genieve would give it to me and I would buy the groceries. Anyway Genieve, being loyal, came running into me and told me what he had said, which made me see fire to think he would be such a sneak instead of talking to me like a man. And if there is anything I dislike more is a sneak. So, I went into his bedroom and told him off, then wrote Mother about it—and when Herschel went up that following weekend, Mother scolded him, but good. Ever since then, we haven't spoken, and it's going on a month now. He just comes and goes now. And he has no kick coming as far as us being antagonist to him in any way since this happened, such as disturbing his rest with us playing the radio in the front room—we take it in our bedrooms if we want to listen to it late (after 10:00 o'clock). As that is what my new belief teaches me not to do. Do not be antagonist. But do unto others as you would like them to do unto you. And, love your enemies. By this parable is meant, hate the bad and sin in them, and love only the good in them. I don't hate Herschel, but a lot of girls would because of all the things he's done to me. But if he was to want to be friends with me, I would gladly be friends with him. But he's just a bull head and still hasn't grown up or otherwise he wouldn't be like this—he would talk things out like a man. One night when we were friends and everything was congenial, we took a walk one night to the drug store to get a cigar. And he started telling me how many bills he had and how sick he was just like a martyr or morbid person. But I just didn't side in with him, and I kept still. I used to feel sorry for him when he would tell me things until I found out why he was in debt and knew him better. Two years ago he pulled the same sob story on me and I loaned him $50.00 toward his income tax. And I never got it back. I had to take it by going up in the Country with Mother when she was so terribly sick and stay up there for three or four months. But I didn't mind that at all because I was very happy and there I met Bob who has a Country home across the road from us. Bob is a doctor (surgeon). He wants us to get married as soon as he comes back from Japan, but I'll tell you more about Bob in my next letter to you. After Bob left for the Army, Kathleen came up for her vacation and since I was not working and had quit work because of Mother's health (and to get my money back) I had to think about a job again. So I went down South with Kathleen and we had a room together with her little girl. And I worked at Yellow Cab Company in the office. It was just like Hell down there those five months, because the women I was living with made it very difficult for Kathleen and I. In fact I don't even like to talk about it. Anyway here I am back up North where I belong. I hate the South because it is nothing but a bunch of bad memories—here I am as happy even in spite of Herschel. I work at Cal, University of California, in the Registrar office. And I am happier here than in all the other four places I've worked in the past. A bunch of us girls go swimming during our lunch hour, and I am as brown as an Indian. One afternoon we dared to hike up to the Big C (which stands for Cal and is on a hill.) We did and was back to work in time.

I'm buying a tennis racket, a Wright Ditson, one of the best, and I'm having it strung and it will be ready for me this Monday. Gee!!! I'm so thrilled, it's like a dream come true after twelve years. Bob loves tennis too, and it's one of his best hobbies. Will he be surprised!!!

Well Daddy—if I don't end this autobiography pretty soon I'll have to send it by freight, ha ha.

How are you and Lillian, Aunt Edith and Charlie? I hope you are all well and happy and peaceful.

Love and Peace to you Daddy,

Ann (Dolly)

May 21, 1946

Dear Daddy,

Received your lovely letter, was really nice to hear from you again.

There's really so much to tell you, I don't know where to start, I guess I'll start talking to you about school.

One thing I know I'd never do was quit school, but I was forced to, had to earn my living, which I enjoy very much.

Herschel wouldn't see me through my last year of school so… But thanks ever so much Dad for the thought.
Would really like to see you again, it's been so long. We've all aged so too. Dolly is 21, I'm 18. Doesn't seem possible.
Oh by the way I'm working in a department store as a clerk. But I don't intend to make it my profession. Would love to get into the musical world.
Dolly and I have been living alone for quite some time, as Mother and Joanie (Kathleen's little girl) are up in the Country a lot, because the climate is better for Mother. Pretty lonesome at times, but we go out very much of the time.
I've really been on a strict diet, I lost 20 pds. I weigh 122 now, hope to get down to 115 pds.
Well Dad, I'd better close now as it's late.
Your loving daughter, Genieve
P.S. I don't get my vacation until Sept. 23rd. I get a week with pay. Wish it was sooner.

June 7, 1946

Hi Daddy,

Just thought I'd drop you a post card to let you know I'm on my week's vacation, and having a swell time and rest with Mother up in Whispering Pines. Wish you could be here to enjoy this also. You should see how beautiful Herschel keeps the grounds here. He has fruit trees, flower beds all around, and myrtle all down the side of the bank. I have fun keeping it watered at nights.
How are you Daddy and Lillian—take good care of your health and maybe we'll be seeing each other before long.—

Lots of love, Dolly

June 20, 1946

Dearest Dad,

Received your letter a few weeks ago and was very glad to hear from you. Well, I know you probably won't forgive me for not answering you way before this, but something went wrong. I just couldn't seem to write a letter. We've had Eloise and Darryle here for a week, and the other time I've been very busy.

I think that's wonderful of you offering to help me in my last year in school. Now as I've been out of school, I'm really anxious to finish my last year, but wouldn't that be hard on you Dad? What do you think I should do?

Am sorry to hear that Aunt Edith isn't too well. Rest is a great cure for most illness, I think.

I'm really glad your back is much better, I imagine that was painful.

I've been going to the dentist quite often with my teeth. I've had three fillings and have to have three more, guess I lack calcium.

Dolly and I went to the flower show some time ago and saw the most beautiful flowers from all parts of the world, we were wishing you could have been there, as we know how interested you are in flowers.

Well, time is short, and of course I can never think of anything of interest to write, so…I'll close for now.

Love, Genieve

July 27, 1946

Dearest Dad,

We received your letter a few days ago, and it certainly seemed good to hear from you.

Just finished my days work at Capwell's Dept. Store. Oh boy, Saturday is our busiest day of the week. I'm always glad to see Sunday come, it's my only day of rest, while Dolly gets Saturdays off, pretty good I should say.

Right now at the present time, Dad, I'm listening to George Gershwin's "Rhapsody in Blue"on my Philco radio phonograph. It plays 10 records at a time, it's an automatic record changer. It also plays 10 inch or 12 inch records. I saved my money and paid cash right off hand, no budget accounts or charge accounts for me, I don't believe in them. Didn't cost too much, a hundred & eleven dollars. The employees are entitled to discounts (thank heavens.). You know, now as I think about it, I've boughtened quite a few things, an electric automatic iron, bathroom scale, General Electric alarm clock, Bulova white gold watch, and a Bulova watch for Mother's Day, not to mention all the clothes I bought also, well Dad, what do you think about giving up my job to finish school? Jobs are getting quite hard to get now. I've thought it over and I decided by the time I finish the year, I won't be able to get a job. I'm really in question. I want a job to come back to and I don't want it said that I didn't receive my diploma. Oh well Dad, I think I'd better keep on working.

About telling you how much money to send, I really wouldn't know what to say, as I'm not used to that wonderful sort of thing. Send what you think I should have, or nothing if you wish. Being as I'm not going to attend school and don't have to have a certain amount, I wouldn't know what to say, what do you think?

One day at work we were quite rushed, and I got in a hurry and slammed the cash register down on my finger and my nail turned black and I believe it's coming off, oh boy.

For entertainment, I've been going swimming and to shows. By the way, I can dive and swim, bout time uh? Ha ha! Thought I'd never learn, but I did.

Kathleen came up last Saturday to take little Joannie down South with her and put her in a boarding school while she works. Mother and all of us became so attached to her, she came last March and went to a Country school up in the mountains until June, then Mother and Joannie came down here to live. Mother was living up there most of the time, because her arthritis became so bad, the dry climate seemed to help her, but now she's quite sick again, I wonder if she'll ever get over it. She can't even walk at times. I'll just keep praying.

By the way, the correct spelling of the street we live on is Benvenue. You were right.

The kind of music I meant was of course modern and maybe light opera, but that's just talk, I don't suppose I'll ever get anyplace, I don't have a speck of confidence in myself (darn it.)

I'm glad you're coming along nicely with your landscaping. That really is a healthy sort of job. I love flowers a great deal also, but I must admit I don't enjoy working in the garden, only like to pick them (lazy huh?)

Please excuse this pencil-written letter, as I couldn't find a pen, poor excuse I know. Ha!

I was just thinking back happenings of long ago, I remembered how I enjoyed and looked forward to those picnics we all used to go on. I'd love to go on one again. I'd like to do that sort of thing again.

That is certainly wonderful about you and Lil coming up next year, will be looking forward to both of you. By the way say "hello" to Lil for me.

Maybe you're wondering if I'm planning on marriage now as I'm approaching nineteen, but I'm not. This fellow I was going with wanted to marry me, but that's when I stopped going with him. I have a complex against marriages. Have seen too many unhappy ones, I guess.

Hope this long letter doesn't bore you, I'm getting writer's cramp and I imagine by this time you have reader's cramp, so—until I hear from you again Dad, goodby for now.

Lots of love, Genieve

Aug. 5, 1946

Dearest Dad,

I don't know how to tell you how much I appreciated that beautiful compact. It is just what I wanted and needed. Thanks again for that cute card.

I really had a wonderful weekend up at the resort. Les and I went swimming and dancing. He has a beautiful convertible car. It's powder blue. He likes all the sports I love, tennis, dancing, swimming, ping-pong, ice skating, and sailing.

It hardly seems possible I'm nineteen and soon (a year) will be twenty, gosh! Oh, well, I look very young for my age.

Well Dad, I have plenty to do, so…bye now,

Loads of love, Genieve

Sept. 11, 1946

Dearest Dad,

Received your letter of August 19th and am ashamed I have not answered before this long length of time, but I assure you, you were on my mind.

Lil certainly does have good taste. I received more nice compliments on my compact, thanks again Lil.

I'm glad you and Lil enjoy yourselves so nicely, as it is so important to enjoy the same activities together.

I'd love to have a picture of you Dad, but I'm afraid I'll have to have some taken of me at Capwell's, as I don't have a camera.

Well Dad, start looking for me, as my vacation starts Sept. 23rd and I think I'll take the Daylight train on Sunday morning, the 22nd of Sept. Can hardly wait to see those dear to me.

Am taking two weeks, but I'll probably spend the second week of my vacation up in Lake County. Maybe not, it depends what kind of a time I'll have down there.

Right now I'm listening to George Gershwin's "Rhapsody in Blue". It is a light opera. I appreciate all kinds of music.

My social life has certainly been busy. I've gone out every night for about 3 weeks straight, that is why I didn't have time to write anybody. But really, he takes me to all of the exclusive night clubs. We're also going to see the opera "Carmen". When he doesn't take me out, he comes over to the house and brings beautiful roses. Les bought me gardenias, gorgeous things. He goes to Vista Community College in Berkeley here, has a cream color convertible car and three sail boats. Pardon me for bragging Dad—ha-ha!

No, it isn't his money I like, it's him. He has a wonderful personality, sense of humor, and is a good moral boy. Enough of that for now, you're probably tired of hearing about him by now, but I enjoy telling you about my love life.

Mother has been down at Eloise's house and Jones's house for a month recovering from arthritis. Sure miss her. She will be back this Saturday. Funny how she recovers better away from us.

Say "hello" to Aunt Edith and all my cousins if they still remember me, and also Lil.

Well, I'd better end this letter for now, so will see you in a couple weeks.

Lots of love, Genieve

October 30, 1946

Wednesday 7:45 P.M.

Dear Daddy,

Here is the letter that came back twice. Is sure made me mad when they returned it the second time after I corrected it.

How are you and Lillian. Genieve told me Lillian has been ill. I'm terribly sorry to hear such news. I hope and pray she is well by now.

Daddy and Lillian I want to thank you again for that lovely compact. I don't believe in fact I know I haven't enjoyed a compact as much as I'm enjoying this one. It's so compact and practical, because lipstick and powder are the only things I use. And I have a certain lipstick I use so I am glad it didn't carry lipstick.

Bob is back from overseas (the doctor I told you about.). Golly we've been having perfect times in Lake County. We've gone to Lake County twice now. The first time his car broke down and it cost him 200 dollars to have it fixed. Poor kid and he doesn't have much money, because he's trying to get in at some hospital. I have no fear about Bob not landing a good job because he has his M.D. Which means he's both physician and surgeon. But his life work will be just surgery. Already Bob has done two brain operations and he's only 26 years old. Gosh but he's darling. He is real husky like Orson Wells and he has eyes that look like the blue blue sky. And you know it's uncanny how he looks exactly like you in his eyes from the profile. I tell him he's crazy going with a person like me that isn't educated, but he insists that I'm brilliant and wonderful so—I give up. Ha ha. You should hear Bob play the piano—he's terrific. He had a band one summer at a resort at Lake County while he was still at college. And he has cameras and does his own developing which look professional. He can't come over as often as Genieve's boy friend does because he's busy taking home calls for three doctors, and besides he lives across the bay in San Francisco. Next week he's going to Los Angeles to see if he can find something there. It's terribly hard for doctors to get in now unless they have a pull. After he gets started and money ahead he'll have his own business. I just wish he shared my faith but I guess you can't have it all. Mother, Herschel, and Genieve are all fine, except Mother's arthritis bothers her sometimes.

I just love working at "Cal". I have privilege to the library, and the pool, which I swim in during my lunch hour when it's warm. Also met some interesting people here, with different viewpoints about the world, and they all seem to know each other.

Take care of yourself Daddy and Lillian, and I'll be writing you soon again.
Lots of love, Peace, Dolly

Nov. 17, 1946

Dearest Dad & Lil,

Please excuse me for taking such a long period of time to answer but there's something about letter writing I dislike. How's everybody there feeling nowadays? I heard it snowed down there. What a thrill. It probably melted as soon as it reached the ground, am I right? I'd love to be there now. Dad, be prepared for a shock. I'm compelled to quit Capwell's. Here's the reason. I kept breaking out with these busted veins on my legs from standing all day at work, feeling worn out, etc. so Mother was worried and told me to go to a doctor and get a check-up, which I did. Sometimes I wish I hadn't. Well, so far I have kidney and liver trouble and found out why my eye sight is so poor. I didn't realize my eyesight was bad until I went to get my driver's license, I couldn't read the second line down of the big typing vision test, they wouldn't give me a license until I did something about my eyes so… Mother and Herschel are letting me stay up in the country for two weeks, then I'm going back to school and get my credits. I hate to think of the doctor's bills I'm going to have to pay. Maybe Dad, I'll have to ask you for that favor sooner than I thought. I dislike very much asking you to send something once a month, but I'm really in a spot now. Well, enough of that.

How are you and Lil? Are you still going to those exciting bridge parties? I bet they're plenty of fun.

I guess I'd better close this as I have to write the girls now, so bye for now.

Love, Genieve

P.S. Please excuse the wrinkled first page as I mistook it for Mother's paper, and am to write more.

Dec. 7, 1946

Dearest Dad and Lil,

I imagine you'r wondering why I haven't answered before this, but I'm waiting until I take my entrance test to see if I'm attending that school and more about it then I will write all the details.

But in the meantime, I received a doctor bill, and I don't know if I told you or not, but I quit work, so I'm sending you this bill. You can't imagine how I feel about this. I feel very much relieved, and that was a wonderful deed or deeds you are doing or going to do, but I feel like two cents waiting for change sending this. And then there is my glasses I have to pick up next week, which are $17.50. I really don't know what to do. I realize this is more than you can afford Dad. Just send what you can afford.

I'm not starting school until the first quarter, which I believe is in January some time or February, that much I know.

By the way, I forgot to sign your birthday card, I'm awfully sorry. I've never been that forgetful.

About my illness, I'm still taking my pills faithfully, and I do mean pills. The doctor gave me three different types of pills to take. One before breakfast, one after breakfast, one before and after lunch, and one before dinner. I suggest I should go on pill hill, what say? Ha. My kidney trouble isn't too bad now. I really feel conceited talking about myself so much, but you wanted to know, so...

Well, so much for all this.

The weather has been very gloomy here lately. I wish it would storm and have it over.

Speaking of compliments, I've had a number of people compliment on your picture that I carry around in my locket. They say you look like a blond Cary Grant.

I certainly hope you and Lil can make it up here sooner or later. It seems ages since I've seen you both already. I'll never forget that lovely evening I spent at your home. Oh well, maybe some time soon, it will happen again. I think I'm optimistic, don't you?

I'd better close for this time, so goodby for now,

All my love, Genieve

Dec. 10, 1946

Dear Daddy and Lillian,

We received your packages a couple of days ago and do they look interesting. We can hardly wait to open them. Those little packages "get me." Oh well, I'll try to have patience till Christmas. Thanks a million for them, I mean, whatever they are. The reason I haven't written you before is because I have such a terrific cold I can hardly see to write this letter, as my eyes are so watery.

We're out of school for two weeks until just after Xmas. Dolly is so busy with her work she doesn't have much time to write anybody. She has a whole new group of friends but I don't know them. She gets home after 7:00 p.m. and then we catch up in our apartment upstairs and she gets ready for work for the next morning.

I sure would like to see you. How is everything down there? Just the same I suppose. Well Daddy, I must close before I'm in tears with this "darn" cold.

Lots of love, Genieve

December 16, 1946

Dearest Dad and Lil

Well, here are some more words of gratitude. I really can't express in words how I appreciate what all you're doing for me. It really doesn't seem possible. It certainly seems possible when I pay those doctor bills though.

I found out that the school which I'm going to attend will start Jan. 29th.

I received the money order and also the presents. Really Dad, you're both too good.

I have my glasses now. It seems so strange to wear them, although they are only for reading and driving.

The weather has also warmed up considerably. It was so sunny today.

I certainly dislike seeing Christmas come this year. I was working last Christmas and could buy what I wanted. All I hope is that I don't receive any gifts. I'm going to work on Saturdays after Xmas.

I'd better end this pen scratch, as I have to go to the store, so…signing off with all my love to you both,
Genieve

December 17, 1946

Dear Daddy,

Here is just a little thought for the Xmas spirit.
I wanted so much to get you and Lillian something for Xmas together for the house, but believe it or not I am very poor this month—and for several reasons too. I did have a hundred dollars in my savings but a very dear friend needed it more than I did and was ill. Then too, I had to buy blankets for my bed out of this month's check, since Herschel wanted his blankets for his Country home, etc. So I am left with just enough to send my Xmas cheer on Xmas cards to the family. In fact the whole family is short of cash this Xmas so we all agreed to not give anything except to the children.
How are you and Lillian? I wonder about you two often, even though I'm not so sharp about writing.
I received your last letter and was very happy to hear you are planning to make a trip up here. But I hope you make the trip before next summer because I'm planning to make a trip back East, Penn. where I plan to live eventually, at Woodmont which is the center of the International Peace Mission Movement.
I received your gift and am very anxious to open and see what it is. Thank you, Daddy and Lillian. If only I had the money, I would like very much to have bought you both something real nice for your home. In a way I don't feel too badly about

not being able to buy gifts this Xmas because they say we'll bring these horrible inflation prices down if only we don't buy things we think cost more than they're worth.

Since I gave myself a cold-wave I'll have my picture taken and send you some, because you said, if I remember, you would like some snap shots. I do however have some pictures that I had taken last year which I was very disappointed in, because the photographer talked me into taking side poses. I'll send them to you though if you would care to have them and see for yourself if you don't agree. I'm really not as sad a person as I look in those pictures. I'm really a very happy person. Sure wish you would send me some good pictures of yourself Daddy—and you too Lillian.

Do you have any little pets around the house? If I can ever have a pet I would want a Cocker Spaniel—I think they're darling, don't you?

I suppose we'll go to the Country for Xmas. Hope it snows like it did last Xmas. I wish it were possible to see you for Xmas. Bob now has a job and is Dr. Alders' assistant. He is working like a dog. His schedule is as follows—7:00 he leaves for the hospital and is on duty for surgery from 7:30 A.M. to 11:30 A.M. Then he and Dr. Alders go to to his office to work (Dr. Alders office) and Bob is there until 5:00 P.M. Then at night he is on duty to take calls for Dr. Alder. So he's not free weekends like he used to be. But he is going to get off sometime this week to see me. I'm trying to talk him into going to a party at the Peace Mission with me.

Kathleen and Joannie are up here for Xmas. Wish she would stay but don't think she will.

I'm still working for the University of California. I will have been there almost 2 years this year. It doesn't seem possible. I guess time flies faster when you get paid just once a month.

I couldn't get used to waiting so long for my check but finally I got wise and started a savings and also a checking account. Well—I am out of words to write so I'll say goodbye and a Merry Xmas to both of you.
My love to you, Daddy and Lillian, Dolly
Daddy, please don't call me Ann, because it makes me think you feel distant to me—But, however, I do insist on my friends and Bob calling me Ann.

December 26, 1946
Whispering Pines

Dear Daddy and Lillian,

I want to thank you both for that beautiful and lovely wallet. Genieve and I traded, however, because I want the black one for a black purse I'm getting after Xmas. Anyway she said she likes the plain brown better, and I too liked the switch we made because I've always wanted a wallet with red on it. I hope with all my heart that you had a lovely Xmas and will have a very happy New Year.
It seems so funny having to write so small. I feel like I'm on a crowded bus. Herschel, Genieve, and I left for Lake County Tuesday after noon at 2:00 P.M. They let us off at 2 o'clock at work so Genieve and Herschel picked me up right from work so we arrived just in time for supper. You see, Mother, Kathleen, Joannie, Mr. & Mrs. Jones (from Santa Monica) came up a week before.
We were very much blessed by our Good Lord and had a very happy Xmas and plenty to eat. We had all agreed not to give

any gifts, but you know how persevering ol' Santa Claus can be, and he brought them down the chimney in spite of all.

I will be here until Sunday morning. Will take the bus Sunday morning and get home (Berkeley) about 1:00 o'clock.

They all left this morning except Genieve and I. Genieve and I will have a good rest and a lot of fun here alone. Genieve and I are more like girl friends than sisters. I hope I can get the little dickens up after I finish this letter to you. She loves to sleep even more than I do and it's already 1:30 P.M. She needs the sleep though because she's almost ruined her body dieting. She weighs 17 lbs. less than I do but I'm not going to loose it the way she did. I take much pride in being so very healthy and am very grateful to God and you and mother who started me out so well in life and took so good care of me.

She just got up and it's now 2:10 P.M. She's having a piece of pumpkin pie and a cup of coffee now. Guess we'll take a long hike out to the point after awhile.

Kathleen has finally decided to take a chance and live in Berkeley with us. We have it all planned how everybody is going to sleep and I think it will work out O.K. I hate to see her go back to Jones's. They're too dirty with their house for Kathleen and Kathleen really can't do the things she wants to do around there. At home we can play the radio when we want and what we want on the radio.

Herschel has really been swell to us girls. He gave each one of us, Genieve, Kathleen, and I a $6.00 cashier's check from H.C. Capwell's. So guess I'll get the pair of shoes I've been wanting. I didn't give anything this Xmas except to donate some things to the Peace Mission.

Guess I had better close Daddy dear and Lillian.

My love to you both,

Dolly

Jan. 3, 1947

Dearest Dad and Lil,

Thanks you so much for that lovely gift. It's so strange, seems like your gifts are so much needed. I was just thinking of purchasing a new one. That is such a clever idea, the wallet has so many openings.

Hope you received my very small remembrance. It was a little late, I realize, sorry.

Well, I start school the 29th of this month. It is such a wonderful future, to me.

The weather here is warming up so much. It was close to freezing.

I'd better end this note, so I'll close hoping this letter finds both of you in good health.

So bye for now,

Love, Genieve

January 22, 1947
Berkeley, Calif.

Dear Dad and Lil,

Received your letter the other day and also received the pictures which I thank you very much. That was quite a good picture of yourself. Didn't know I could do it.

I had a bit of social life the other night. Les and I went to a formal dance at the Masonic Club Saturday night. It was the Skier's Ball. Had a wonderful time. Although, I was a bit nervous. I haven't been to a formal in a long time. I had black elbow length gloves, black formal, and a huge white corsage (hope that's the correct spelling.) Enough of this.

How are you and Lil? Have you had anymore of those no-good back aches? Also, how is Lil's anemia?

Oh say, school starts Feb. 3 for sure. Maybe the first of the month you could send the check. And how much to send Dad, that is up to how much you think you and Lil can afford. I really dislike to set any amount. Anything you can afford.

Dolly and I are going swimming tonight. Sounds crazy, I know. We're going to the Y.W.C.A. They have all the convenience of drying the hair, etc. So…

Yesterday evening, we played tennis. You would think we are quite the sport things, doesn't it? I love all the sports.

I'll be closing for now. Until next time, goodby for now.

Love, Genieve

P.S. Please excuse my shaky handwriting, I seem to have nervous hands.

P.S.S. Also hope you recovered over your cold.

Feb. 2, 1947
Sunday

Dearest Dad and Lil,

Received your recent letter and the enclosed money order. Dad, I really think that is too much. I know you must be skimping on everything.

How can I ever thank you for all your goodness you've done. I'm not much for words, but I'm certainly a thinker. Thanks so much again.

The weather here is simply wonderful. It has begun to warm up. Can hardly wait for summer, although, I'll be going to school all summer, and maybe the fist of the Fall semester. Gee, I start tomorrow. I'm a little nervous, as I've been out of the habit of schoolwork for over a year and a half. I suppose I'll be somewhat rusty, but I'm going to try the best I possibly know how, and just have confidence and pray.

Well Dad, tomorrow is the zero hour, and I have to get to bed early now, as my hours are from 8:00 A.M. to 3:00 P.M. so for now.

All my love, Genieve

P.S. I think your advice is very wise, by that I mean about the social life.

P.S.S. How are you feeling these days Lil?

Feb. 22, 1947
Berkeley, Calif.

Dearest Dad and Lil,

Received your very interesting letter. Please forgive my delay in answering, as my time is somewhat limited. Going to school, homework, etc. But really, it seems wonderful going to school again. My subjects are Geometry, Math, English, and typing. I needed English and History for credits toward my high school diploma. I'm attending Merritt Business School, and they don't teach History, only to returning veterans, so I'll quit Merritt at June and attend Oakland High School for the summer session, (June to Sept.) where they teach History in the day time and back to Merritt for the Fall term (Sept.

to Jan.) and in January I should receive my diploma (God willing) if I pass all. Enough for this.

You recent letter Dad was beautifully composed. I only wish I had that gift of putting words so nicely together, and that have so much meaning to them.

How's all the family, friends, and Lil? I would like to see Lil again, as I enjoyed her company very much.

The most dreadful things have been happening lately. That shocking explosion at O'Connor Electroplating Co. I don't suppose you felt it, or did you? I was simply dazed while reading it.

Well Dad, I have to finish up my homework, so I'll be saying goodnight.

All my love, Genieve

P.S. Excuse my poorly written letter. My hands seem to be pretty shaky.

March 2, 1947
Berkeley, CA

Dearest Dad and Lil,

Received the money order for which I am very grateful. You certainly are prompt. Both of you are so thoughtful.

Yes, I'm attending Merritt from 8:00 A.M. to 3:00 P.M. every day, except Saturday and Sunday of course. I work at Capwell's on Saturdays for 6 2/3 hrs.

Last Saturday night, (yesterday) I went double-dating, and had a wonderful time of it. The boys and girl are too, from Merritt.

Next Saturday, we're going to see the life of Shakespeare at the Oakland Aud.

I limited my dates to once a week. I really like all my subjects. I enjoy school so much. It's so different when I was in high school. I seem to like this business school much better.

Hope this letter finds all of you in good health and remain likewise.

Really can't think of anymore to say, so I'll wind it up for now.

Lovingly yours, Genieve

June 23, 1947
Berkeley

Dearest Dad and Lil,

Received your sweet letter and feel horrible to think I have not answered before this. My excuse is in the next paragraph. We are being evicted the end of this month, and I have been going around in a daze. There just isn't a place to live anywhere, so Dad, be prepared for a shock! Dolly and Mother believe in Father Divine (as God) and we are going to stay at the Mission. It's a religion, and we will live with colored people etc. Really Dad, I'm desperate. Naturally I'll go with them. Where else would I go?? Enough, enough!!

You write such interesting letters to us, I only wish I had that gift. I appreciate the interest you take in advising us, it really helps.

Oh! Did you know, I'm working in the office at Merritt School for an hour every day. I do some typing, filing, etc. It is very nice. I love it, and didn't think I would like office work, but it just proves that I can't state my opinion unless I'm positive.

What type of music do you like? As for myself, I enjoy all types about.
Well Dad, I think I've covered everything, so I'll close for this time.
All my love, Genieve
P.S. I'll let you know our new address as soon as I know it.

June 29, 1947
Berkeley, Calif.

Dearest Dad and Lil,

I'm writing you this letter to tell you the miracle happened. Mother found me a studio at some friend's house in Oakland. The address is 1483-85, 8th and Chester. We were so thankful. Mother and Herschel are going to live in Whispering Pines, but Dolly wants to live at the Mission. Dad, you can't imagine how grateful I am toward your interest and willingness. You've done so much to help out concerning this problem of moving etc. I also appreciate the girls and Norman doing all they could too. Once again, thanks so much. So, I'll continue school, which is best that I stick to one school until I may obtain the diploma.
I'm terribly sorry to hear of Lil's operation. Kathleen was telling us about it. I'll pray hard.
Would love to come down for a visit and see you both, but don't think I'd better miss school.
Well, I'll close for now,
Loads of love, Genieve

P.S. I'm moving this Wednesday the 2nd of July, so send my letter to the address in the letter. Say "hello" to the family. Once again, I hope Lil recovers soon.

June 29, 1947
Berkeley, Calif.

Just wanted you to know that I received the tickets for Genieve and myself to come South. I will send you a $15.00 money order for the cost of the tickets when I can. I am staying here where I belong.

I sincerely hope you are all Well and Happy.
Love, Dolly (Ann)
P.S. Give Lillian my love.

CHAPTER 12

"Swing Low Sweet Chariot"—the Negro voices rose up together, billowing over and beyond the constraints of the music room, contraltos and mezzo-sopranos, harmonizing in an impossible way, mellow, reverberating, bouncing off the rafters and back down to resonate deep inside. Dolly was no coloratura soprano like her older sister Eloise but she was close, soprano maybe but weak. She was on the left side of today's Singalong Sunday semicircle near the rest of the light complected squawking high-voiced Rosebuds. How fantastic her life was now—she rarely thought about her so-called real family. Here she was, in a mansion, chanting and singing with her true family, hands clapping, surrounded by shining faces devoid of any emotion other than bottomless joy. She had entered Heaven on Earth, a sanctuary, just as Father and Mother Divine promised. It was like her life had just begun—there was a spirit of being and belonging somewhere, accomplishing things. They were all bound to a common cause.

Now it was time to put Father's International Modest Code to a tune, which was a great way to memorize, just like a nursery rhyme. The little ditty went like this, an endearing simplistic melody similar to the alphabet song:

"We're calling everyone, no smoking, no drinking, no undue mixing of sexes. So if you want a World of peace and joy, of purity and honesty, everybody's got to fall in line with the International Modest Code established by God Father Divine."

On the wall of the music room that doubled as a social room, a yellowed plaque proclaimed:

THE INTERNATIONAL MODEST CODE
ESTABLISHED BY FATHER DIVINE:
NO SMOKING.
NO DRINKING
NO OBSCENITY
NO VULGARITY
NO PROFANITY
NO UNDUE MIXING OF SEXES
NO RECEIVING OF GIFTS, PRESENTS, TIPS, OR BRIBES

After Singalong Sunday they filed obediently into the library for Individual Studies. Row after row of dusty magazines, pamphlets, loosely bound books and reels of tape held copies of Father Divine's sermons and proclamations going back to the beginning of the Movement in the 1920's. A young light complected brunette with freckles, one of Father's many secretaries, held out a glass fishbowl so the Rosebuds could pull out an index card which told them what date and title to check out. After study time there would be a ten question quiz just to make sure you were paying attention to the message. She, Dolly, who the ladies called Sister Ann now, thought the quizzes were too easy, but she was happy enough to get all the answers right, although competitiveness was discouraged. One of her favorite recorded messages of Father's was a statement given to the press in the 1930s when they had unjustly accused him of keeping follower's money for his own use. It went something like this:

"I did not and do not and will not receive compensation, remunerations, love offerings, donations, or anything of that sort for my spiritual work and activities from any individual. I'm a free gift to the World, gratis, to Mankind." She loved that because it proved how wrong her former family were about Father.

After the library the next event on the Sunday Rosebud agenda was the Garden Walk. She made sure to have a dark complected Sister as her buddy on the walk because segregation of any kind was prohibited, even if it was as innocent as having friends predominantly of a certain complexion—and there was always someone watching. Usually it was young Rosebud Lilly of the long black hair and fair complexion. She could feel Lilly's green eyes boring into her back right now, but she wasn't sure why the girl kept such a sharp eye on her—had someone told her she needed watching? Right now her walking buddy was Sister Stella, her queen-sized hefty cashier friend from the Mission Grocery Store.

"I saw Mother today—she looked so beautiful in her blue taffeta dress and pearls. She said good morning to me and smiled! We are so lucky to have such a wonderful beautiful person as our Mother." Stella was star-struck by the Divines, the estate, the dinners, the wardrobes, and wholly believed in their Godship, no question about it. Her large dark moon-face took on a look of rapture when she spoke of them. They walked and talked some more, and the topics were always the same, the Mission and its work, what assignment you were working on, what you did for the Movement and how you could contribute even more, do better.

The Garden Walk wound through topiary, roses, vines, succulents, fruit trees, and finally through the vegetable patches outside the back door of the enormous kitchen of the estate. This was the central hub of the Mission, the heartbeat, a place of gleaming, clanking stainless steel and copper, black iron pots, tin dishes, all manner of baking containers, and every imaginable kitchen utensil one could ever dream of, or need—and they all needed maintenance, especially the heavy silver cutlery that was kept polished to a mirrored finish. Linens galore were washed, ironed and neatly folded with precision creases, ready for the next feast. There wasn't a speck of dust or dirt anywhere, nothing out of place. An elderly dark complected woman, a Miss Blessed Quietness, ruled over this domain, and she was capable and intimidating to the extreme—strong as an ox with thick muscled forearms, short black wire hair flecked with gray, and thick eyebrows that overshadowed dark watchful eyes. The full length white apron tightly cinched around her middle was starched and flawless, flashing red enamel handles of kitchen tools peaking from the pockets. Even the Divines gave her a wide berth when she scowled at them during the rare times they ventured through the kitchen door as a shortcut to the main house. Dolly suspected she chose her name in an attempt to overcome her unquiet nature, but that was an unkind thought, so she put it aside.

Right now in the kitchen there was a pounding on the countertops as workers punched the homemade bread dough into shape, slap, bang, slap, the cooks keeping a conga rhythm to make a little game of it. Flour scattered up in white poufs with each slab of bread dough pounded down. Buttered bread pans waited near the ovens in a long line to receive the raw dough. The aroma wafting from the ovens was, well, Heavenly to Sister Ann. She walked obediently to the chalkboard and found her assignment for today—to remove the old grease from the deep fryer and replace it with new grease. The chalkboard was controlled exclusively by Miss Blessed Quietness. She, Dolly, *no Sister Ann* she quickly redirected, tried not to let the disappointment register on her face. The grease pot was just so heavy and, well, dirty and smelly. This was one of the lowest jobs on the totem pole and she wondered why she kept getting this assignment. But someone had to do it. Might as well get it over with cheerfully. They said work was supposed to teach you humility.

Today was Sunday, considered to be a day off, when they all feasted together, Mother and Father presiding at the head of the long banquet tables filled with mission workers, followers, and sympathizers from Berkeley and the surrounding communities—everyone was invited as long as you didn't have banquet service assignment which they rotated between the workers. The other six days of the week Father had decreed to be working days, but Sundays were special.

During the work week, Mondays through Saturdays, the mission residents here in Berkeley worked at the Mission Grocery Store, Mission Barber shop, Mission coffee shop, Mission Dry Cleaners and Laundry, or for the Heavenly Employment Agency providing domestic labor. She ended up at the employment agency cleaning houses because that was where they had most of the open positions. There was the promise though that with enough hard work and diligence she could get promoted to a secretarial position because she had some education.

Sister Ann went over to the heavy grease pot, gripped the sides with oven mitts, and hefted it toward the disposal area. She was getting strong from all the manual labor—cleaning kitchens, scrubbing floors, ironing, washing windows. Gee, she hardly had time to think anymore.

It was June 27, 1948. She had been in service and living at the International Peace Mission for a year —and she didn't have a dime to show for it, not that she needed her own money but that was the hardest thing to get used to. She didn't own anything. She had closed her bank account and handed over all her money and worldly possessions to the Movement, because that's what you did when you believed in something. It was the same as the Catholic Church, after all. Nuns and Priests didn't complain or question, did they? No, this was normal, the way things were supposed to be—you gave up your life to be a disciple of God, and he was here now, in the flesh. No waiting to get into Heaven—she had arrived.

After kitchen duty she and the other Rosebuds bustled upstairs to freshen themselves for Sunday Communion Banquet. It was 2:00 P.M. and the weekly banquets were served at 5:00 P.M. every Sunday like clockwork. There was a lot to do before the guests arrived. According to the weekly schedule assigned by Father's secretaries, she would be a circulator tonight, a foyer hostess that would graciously escort the guests from the community to their appropriate place at the banquet table. There were no place cards because they never knew who was coming—the only seating rules were light complected people must be seated next to dark complected people, and men and women were to be seated apart whenever possible—no undue mixing of the sexes in accordance with the International Modest Code.

Time for the feast now, and a few other Rosebuds circulated around the banquet hall, much like wait staff in an exclusive dining establishment, attempting to blend into the walls unobtrusively while simultaneously being attentive to any need a banqueter might have. She was wearing her best evening maid's uniform—black below-the-knee buttoned up dress, white starched collar, white apron and matching white cap, black low-heeled patent leather tap shoes with the metal taps removed. Gee, she never thought of herself as a maid, but everyone else was doing it, so she guessed it must be okay. And think of all the people she was helping—it made it all worthwhile.

The routine for Sunday Communion Banquet was always the same—the kitchen staff, led by Miss Blessed Quietness, would bring out each course and place the serving bowels next to Father and Mother at the head of the table. All eyes would be on the Holy couple as they nodded their thanks to the servers and perused the food offering appreciatively. Father usually kept the followers guessing, off balance—sometimes he gave a short sermon before commencing the feast, and sometimes he and Mother just dug in. Whatever he decided, the rest obediently followed. Tonight he was taciturn and the followers took this to mean he had important things on his mind, such as how to keep them all safe in Heaven, cocooned in luxury and immune from the evils of the outside world. Their fate was in Father and Mother's hands, and they all respected that, and trusted he would keep them safe—their lives were Father's problem, not theirs anymore.

Sister Ann stood at attention in the foyer and greeted the last few latecomers as they filed in, dressed a little self-consciously in their Sunday best—stiff suits, starched shirts, uncomfortable dress shoes, ladies in last year's fashion. Sister Ann's gracious smile did not falter. She looked just like Ingrid Bergman playing the role of a maid in an elaborate movie set, cast in a part that was just not believable. She stood out, even though she tried not to. Rosebud Lilly had the same assignment tonight, and they alternated escorting the last few banqueters to the table before the mission door was closed. Lilly's long black hair was cinched up into a tight bun in an attempt to contain the wild black mane for modesty's sake, but it only served to emphasize her watchful cat-like green eyes. Sister Ann felt Lilly's eyes on her, but she refused to let the girl make her uncomfortable. Now, with the guests seated, both Rosebuds moved to stand against the wall, hands properly folded behind them, Lilly toward the head of the table, Ann toward the end of the very long table, twelve chairs down from Father and Mother.

She became aware of a muffled shuffling sound coming from one of the guests, a broad shouldered outdoorsy gentleman with thick sandy blond hair. He lifted the white linen tablecloth and rooted around under the table to find the napkin that had slipped from his lap. The shoes scraping over the parquet wooden floor in an attempt to retrieve the fallen object were very audible in the anticipatory hush before the feast.

Sister Ann was there in a flash to assist, bending down to his level so as to be discrete. In a whisper she said "Sir, please allow me to bring you another napkin. You can just leave that one there and we will find it after the dinner."

"Thanks Dolly. I figured you'd have an answer to my problem." The man met her eyes and locked in, wouldn't let go, the eyes of the parent who has found the lost child that has taken the game hide and seek a little too far. A little gasp escaped as she drew back, various waves of emotions playing across the porcelain face—surprise, fear, shame, anger—finally freezing into a tight smile.

In a low voice she spat "How did you get in? You can't be here—get out!"

"Of course I can. Anyone is invited—Mr. God himself has invited everyone who is hungry, and who wants to receive the truth. And oh boy I would sure like to receive the truth—it's about time. Take off that ridiculous maid's costume—we're getting out of here now. I've had enough and so have you." His voice had risen, the Nordic Viking loose, slow to anger but uncorked now, while the entire banquet room watched in morbid fasciation as the juicy family drama played out before their eyes—they were getting more than free food, they were getting a dinner drama along with the meal, something to talk about during the feast and at least a week afterward, something to cluck about and shake their heads knowingly. Emil stood up authoritatively and moved to put his arm protectively around his daughter. With a deft faint to the right his Dolly dodged the embrace and made a break for the kitchen, pounding the double swinging doors back so hard they hit walls, swinging backwards into the banquet room, swinging still as the people kept their eyes glued on the doors, hoping for an encore performance of an even higher degree of drama. The doors finally came to a standstill, and people suddenly remembered Father and Mother. All eyes turned expectantly to the holy couple to gauge their reaction and take cues as to how to register all this—but only a lack of emotion was broadcast from the couple. The observant among them would have noticed Father's almost imperceptible nod to four muscular dark complected men in suits that had materialized from the shadows—they promptly and roughly escorted the agitator out through the front door and into the purple twilight settling over the Bay.

At least now he knew Sister Ann wasn't a spy—the scene created by her biological father proved that. He would tell his new favorite girl, Rosebud Lilly, that she didn't have to watch her anymore, she was in the clear, a legitimate follower even though she seemed different from the others and had come to them under the unusual circumstance of a letter of recommendation from her biological mother. He was convinced, and there was even past evidence, that the IRS, FBI and most certainly the local police were not above planting spies in his organization to get information on his cash flow. And they were not above trying to set up a morals code sting either, citing the Mann Act or something of that nature. Anything to get a piece of his pie, chip away at his financial empire through taxation, or just the satisfaction of ruining a successful colored man—not that he was colored, but the narrow-minded saw him that way, he knew that. That's all he needed, more bad publicity—it would precipitate a run on his bank if followers demanded their money back from his Heavenly Treasury should there be a prosecutable scandal.

He would use the family drama from last night's communion dinner as the backdrop for a future sermon on how to let go of the past, rid oneself of controlling people, family members, old relationships, and accentuate the positive present. He, Father Divine, better known as God, was well aware of one of the basic laws of human behavior, hard wired right into the brain—the psychological chains that bind are stronger than physical ones. He was a master at untangling these old chains and subtly installing new chains, better, more secure chains made of gold, the ones you didn't want to break away from.

Enough philosophizing—right now it was time to take care of business. Lately there always seemed to be something irritating and petty to attend to. He was scheduled to quietly meet with the guards that had ended last night's dinner drama to find out if they had taken care of the agitator and made certain he would not return. There was something in the set of the agitators's jawline that looked unusually determined, purposeful, a Scandinavian glacier that would be extremely resistant to going away unless convinced by force. With this in mind he walked through the garden and down the thick grassy slope to the colonnade that ran along the front of the white marble pool house. Here it was far removed from the bustle of the estate, a peaceful sanctuary for a swim—which he avoided at all costs because he never learned how to swim—or just to reflect on the beauty of the surroundings. The enormous pool was tiled in a pale aquamarine, the color deepened by the reflection of the dome of the sky above and the infinite sweep of the blue ocean as a backdrop. The furniture cushions for the wrought iron pieces were done in black and white cabana stripes set off by yellow umbrellas—Sweet Angel Divine's decorator knew what she was doing, he had to give her credit—of course, with unlimited funds it was hard to go wrong. Even the landscaping was well thought out—if you were here in the early morning or evening, when the sun was at a certain angle, the flowering jasmine vines released their scent gently around the pool area. Oh yes, this was Heaven on Earth, bought and paid for in cash.

Off in the left corner toward the shallow end of the pool—the only safe place to be as far as he was concerned—the four men in suits were seated around an ornate wrought iron table shaded by a large yellow umbrella, their heads bent over various sections of the local newspaper, pages rustling in the breeze the only sound to be heard—no laughter, no talking. Fedoras were pulled down over their faces, so anonymous and so alike that it would be impossible to identify them individually except by the clothes, which could be changed if necessary. He didn't know much about these four men and didn't want to—all he needed to know was that they worked security for him. They were not followers, and how could they be? They saw the dark side of his operation, made the problems disappear, and were well-paid enough to make their silence worthwhile.

"Gentlemen, good morning. I trust everything is well today, and the little annoyance from last night will not trouble us again? I did begin to ponder how such an event happened at all given the surveillance of a highly trained professional security team such as yourselves."

They shifted in their seats uncomfortably like little boys being reprimanded by a teacher. One large fellow raised his head enough to look Father in the face and said deferentially, "With all due respect sir it's near impossible to prevent these kinds of disturbances, which by the way have not happened before this, if you are going to have an open invitation to the general public to come every Sunday for a free banquet, no matter who they are. If someone has a mind to make trouble, these dinners are an open invitation, an easy target. It's a miracle it's been as peaceful as it has been.

He stood up taller and tugged at his vest, fiddled with his buttons, stuck out his chin importantly. "Yes gentlemen, miracles do tend to surround me. But this should serve as a good reminder for you all to be more alert to those who don't quite fit in, if you see what I mean. The agitator had a certain determined and tense carriage which, according to the psychology of body language, portended his intent to do something other than just partake of the feast. What I'm saying is, let's not let agitators from the community in so casually, understand? There must be some way you can think of to screen them without anyone knowing what you're doing, isn't that true?" All four anonymous suits quickly nodded in assent.

"So, although I don't need to know the exact details, is last night's agitator still near us?"

Another muscle-bound fellow, who had been looking down, holding back, saving the best for last, sat up taller and said proudly, in a deep baritone voice, "After we roughed him up a little I found out whereabouts he was from and told him to git on the nearest set of wheels and git the Hell out of town but quick. I told him he wasn't wanted around here, not by his ex-daughter or anyone else. He told us, after a few twists of the arm, that he was here to take his daughter back home to Santa Monica. I told him not his ex-daughter or anyone else around here likes crazies from L.A. and he'd best be gittin' back home to the rest of the crazies." He emphasized the ultimatum by slapping his sizable hand on the sports section of the open newspaper. "He won't be comin' back sir, you can bank on it."

He, Reverend Major Jealous Divine, nodded to the men signaling the meeting was over. He started the trudge back up the grassy slope toward the estate, wondering why they put the stone steps so far out of the way—they should be in a direct line from the pool to the house. Lately the walk down to the pool and back had become a bit of an effort. Was it possible to get old and tired even though you had endless riches here on Earth? He had created Heaven around himself, a golden impenetrable cocoon, he had access to anything he could possibly desire—but he was tired now, tired and unsettled after watching the passionate and brave struggle of one man to rescue his daughter, take her back to safety. His followers were his children, yes, but only in name—he didn't have anyone of his own flesh, someone to fight for like that, someone to risk death for. He was alone with himself, after all was said and done, and he was not part of anyone.

The room was definitely humble compared to the public rooms of the International Peace Mission West. This is where the Rosebuds lived, in the maid's quarters that had been expanded to include a wing of the second floor. Each room contained two hard twin beds with matching nightstands. Each bed was assigned a separate small dresser for the few personal items the Rosebuds kept—toiletries, extra uniform articles, stockings, undergarments, sewing boxes, and the like. On the dressers and nightstands were photographs of Father and Mother Divine in formal wear, making full unwavering eye contact with the camera, watching over each girl's room.

Right now she, Dolly—*I'm not Dolly anymore, I'm Sister Ann* she had to remind herself again—had been given the day off from her current Monday through Saturday assignment, a cleaning job with the Heavenly Employment Agency, to recover from last night's trauma caused by her estranged father Emil Born. She was laying face down on the hard bed crying because she sent her own father off in such a mean way. But it was just like Mother Divine had told her when she took her under her wing—to follow God you had to forsake the comforts of this world if you wanted to remain in Heaven and do a greater good. Your family would always pull you back, interfere, cause you to live a smaller meaningless life if you allowed them lure you back in. Only the chosen few were great enough to live life according to Father's principles. She herself, Mother Divine, had separated from her family in her teens to follow Father Divine and the International Peace Mission Movement, and she had come to find a deeper meaning in life, a fulfillment that would not have been possible living an average life. She had assured Sister Ann that in time, she too would find the greater truth, a divine fulfillment. She just had to give it time.

A quiet knock at the door, and then it cracked open just enough to show a familiar grizzled head. "Are you okay Sister? It's me, Miss Sincere. Can I come in?" It was Sincere Sincerity, Mother Divine's personal assistant. She had arrived silently, as usual, materialized from nowhere, unaccountably present near the scene of an event, like she had a sixth sense.

Sister Ann sniffled and looked at the door through swollen eyes. She glanced in the dresser mirror as she sat up and didn't recognize herself at first—rumpled frumpy clothes, dirty blond hair that had darkened from lack of outdoors recreation, swollen red blotchy face. Where was her former self, the swimmer, the tennis player? She didn't know anymore, she was lost even to herself. She felt like a she was really two people—Dolly Born from Santa Monica, daughter, sister, aunt, and Rosebud Sister Ann, a vital part of the International Peace Mission Movement.

"I just want to say, Sister Ann, we are all so proud of you, how far you've come. You truly have a higher calling, and the light shines out of your eyes when you don't even know it, like right now. You're a true Rosebud in the spirit, an inspiration to us all, and Father Divine is with you even in your most difficult times. He watched what happened to you last night and said it was a test to show you how strong you are, even if you don't feel strong at the moment. If you weren't strong, you wouldn't be here today. You're a very important part of our family, and we are here for you even when it feels like you are alone. Father and Mother know your heart Sister, and it's pure."

With a sob, so drained her body felt like it had turned to rubber, she sat up and leaned into Miss Sincere Sincerity's bony side, against the senior Sister's starched and spotless black cotton work dress with the lacy white collar—there was a reassuring whiff of Ivory Soap mixed with lemon polishing oil, the smells of good honest labor.

Then Miss Sincere got to work, as she had hundreds of times before with new wavering, unsure Rosebuds—she told the sad story, with a few embellishments, of her life before the Peace Mission Movement, how she had cried a thousand times just like Sister Ann was doing now, how dark and depressing her thoughts had been until she had been rescued by Father Divine, pulled literally out of the mud of the streets to move into the light. Father Divine had turned her life around, enabled her to be a part of ending the suffering of others through denial of self, to be a part of the bigger picture. She sympathized with Sister Ann, but she knew there was a reason for her being here, she must be hearing a higher calling, a voice telling her there was work to do, no time for self-absorption and self-pity. The people in her former life would in time forget about her and she would forget about them. Humanity as a whole needed her more--the task at hand was too important to abandon.

Indoctrination had reached the next level, and Sister Ann stopped crying and started listening, absorbing, hypnotized by the idea of being a part of Heaven on Earth. Groupthink had insinuated its way into her consciousness as well as her subconscious, and she had begun the transformation, the metamorphosis into a member of the hive.

CHAPTER 13

Emil was slumped against the cold window of the Southbound train looking out but seeing nothing, not the magnificent sweep of the Pacific coastline, the mountains sloping down to the sea, the formation of pelicans scanning low over the water. Summer was in full swing and carefree surfers clutching their longboards to their sides happily trotted over the sand to the waves, girls spread out blankets with picnic baskets to weigh down the corners, brightly striped beach umbrellas were positioned against the sun. The train sounded the whistle, a happy sound, a sound bearing the good news of shiny modern transportation taking people to wonderful destinations.

He saw none of this because his thoughts had completely blocked out all external stimuli since the moment he boarded the train in Berkeley, the repetitive motion of the wheels clicking along the tracks lulling him into a meditative state. He'd spent a sleepless night in the hotel near the train station after the four colored thugs had roughed him up, thrown him into the street and told him never to come back. They had looked like they were enjoying it too, which didn't surprise him. The really shocking thing was that he didn't recognize his own daughter, the little girl whose every expression he had known from the moment of birth, the mirror image of himself, the beautiful woman she had grown into. The person he saw at the International Peace Mission dinner was Dolly, yes, but there was an essential part of her that had gone missing, he saw that when he looked in her eyes. The hatred in her expression was something that struck fear in him, as if Dolly had been taken over by another force, snatched away from him and he didn't know where to find her again. It was actually worse than death, really, because death was predictable, understandable, but this was like something straight out of science fiction, a person of your own flesh being taken over by an unseen force, an enemy you couldn't see.

He came back to the present now, shaking the gloom off just long enough to realize he needed to use the the restroom. Steadying himself on the handrails leading down the isle to the rear of the train, apologizing because he was weaving, brushing against passengers more than the motion of the train warranted, he found the low narrow door and moved inside the tiny enclosure to answer the call of nature. He splashed water over his face and looked in the mirror. He looked like a hobo, a bum, with a black eye, swollen lips, and he could still taste road grit and blood in his mouth—the thugs had worked him over pretty good, four against one, the cowards. He, Emil Born, was not a quitter, not afraid to take a risk, but suddenly he was angry, yes, very angry. Over the last year he had never for a moment given up on Dolly, calling, writing, and finally appearing in person in front of a crowd of people to rescue her, only to be scorned, ridiculed, used as a punching bag and dumped on the roadside. And not even a phone call afterward from her to apologize, find out if he was okay, explain herself. He had called home this morning to tell Lillian what happened, and Lillian said the phone had not rung at all, no call from Dolly to find out if her father was okay—the pink Bakelite phone just sat quietly on the telephone table, silent, disinterested.

Nona and Herschel were getting along very well up in the mountains, snug and secure in their large cabin on an even larger 1 acre parcel of land. It was just far enough away from the tourists, but close enough for a ten minute walk to the Whispering Pines Resort, where they held a membership. There was swimming, dining, dancing, and mixing with all kinds of interesting and beautiful people from places like Los Angeles, San Francisco, Sacramento—wherever the successful called home. All of them had one thing in common—the mountains, lakes, and open space recharged them from the stress of the dollar driven city life—being successful required regular bouts of managed relaxation. The days passed serenely, marked by frothy health shakes, massages, eucalyptus steam baths, swims, nature hikes, healthy gourmet meals, and more massages. Then arise and repeat in a loop until your body was recharged and renewed, polished to a sheen and ready to take on the next fiscal challenge, maintain your spot at the top. As an added bonus Whispering Pines Resort personnel were exceedingly discrete so you could unwind, within reason, without repercussions.

Right now she and Herschel were lounging by the resort's Olympic sized pool, wearing matching straw hats that covered most of their faces, lightly perspiring because it was in the eighties, hot but not too hot. In the evening it would drop down to the forties, perfect for hot tubbing—the fun never ended. Nona tugged at the skirt of her one piece suit, as if the extra inch would cover any flaws. If she got tan enough, it would disguise the fine little spider veins on her thighs—but they were going away anyway, with all the health food and massages. The sun angling down through the pine forest threw shade patterns on the water and turned the pool area into an inhalation therapy session, the pine scent penetrating deep into the lungs, opening seldom used tiny air sacs, renewing the simple act of breathing. It was fabulous, really. She should have met Herschel long ago, because this was the way she was meant to live.

Their eyes were focused lazily on the silly couple in the swimming pool, the lithe young woman floating on an air mattress, posed like a swimsuit model, wearing a rubber bathing cap covered with plastic flower petals, giggling in a high-pitched voice every time her very senior balding male friend surfaced from diving under and around the mattress, pulling it along like a tug boat. He looked old enough to be her father, and he was winded from all the activity—the girl was too much for him. Nona wondered if the old fart actually believed she was attracted to him.

A slightly French male voice from behind her lounge chair interrupted her musings. "Excuse me Mrs. Twining, sorry to disturb you, but there is an urgent call for you. You can take it in the lobby behind my concierge desk, so you can have privacy. It's a Mr. Emil Born calling." The concierge, whose enamel name tag announced Maurice, was swarthy, intense, and deeply out of place in a health resort setting—his eyes indicated he had alternative ideas to being healthy. And he was young. Nona wondered briefly what sort of services he offered. How did they convince these people to work in such remote places? He bowed slightly, trailing a whiff of scented hair oil, and led the way to his desk where the call was waiting.

"Hello Emil, who died? I just can't think of any other reason you would page me at the resort, unless you just miss my voice. Wish you were here." She hoped the sarcasm in her voice was evident. After that she was silent, listening as Emil related the bizarre event at the International Peace Mission West. It really didn't sound like anything Dolly would be capable of, and she couldn't picture the little girl who loved shopping for clothes in Westwood Village wearing a maid's costume, unless it was for Halloween. But then she quickly refocused to the present, the person Dolly had become, the hatefulness toward her family, the estrangement, the New Thought, as Dolly called it—and Father Divine's personal letter to her acknowledging Dolly's desire to be a Rosebud. Perhaps this should be allowed to run its course, and interfering would only serve to make Dolly more determined to resist. And she was still mad at Dolly for her behavior toward her family—and she still loathed Emil for breaking up the family. They deserve each other, Dolly and Emil, she thinks.

"I am so sorry this happened to you Emil. Herschel and I have decided to leave Dolly alone for now, let her explore on her own. We are sure it won't last long—how could it, with her background? She won't be able to live like that for much longer. I'm sure she will be calling soon, just give her time to think. If I know my daughter she's probably thinking of us right now, wishing she was vacationing—she loves it up here."

"I blame this on you Nona. You should have nipped it in the bud before it went this far. But you were too wrapped up in yourself I suppose, to see what anyone else might be going through. I'll never understand why you encouraged the girls to move to Berkeley when they were doing just fine here. They have roots in Santa Monica, like I thought you did. You're the only person I know who moved away from Santa Monica voluntarily—usually this is a place people never leave unless they have to. Now look at the result—Dolly got mixed up with the wrong crowd and we may have lost her, all because you were bored and just had to try something new. You're still unstable, even at your age, still trying to find yourself, self indulgent, you're such a….."

Click! Nona slammed the receiver down, gripping the handset tightly as if her hands were around Emil's neck. She hated him, and it's no wonder he fathered a problem every bit as bad as himself. Genieve was more like her, but Dolly was her father's child, absolutely. She could use a break from both of them—no use letting two people ruin your life.

She returned to take her place at poolside. Herschel had not moved, the lower half of his face below the straw hat displaying complete relaxation—she envied him his lack of family drama, his ability to distance himself from problem situations. She resolved not to tell him the latest details because what good would it do? His idea had been to distance both of them from Dolly and now her father was calling, disturbing their peace at the resort. She really didn't want her past to ruin her future and she was convinced Dolly would eventually turn around, come back to her senses.

"What did Emil want?" Herschel feigned interest in a bored voice.

"He called to find out if he should plan on Genieve and Dolly for the holidays." It was the only thing she could think of for the moment—she wasn't good at impromptu white lies.

"But we're still in summer. Isn't that planning a little far ahead?"

"Emil and Lillian were wondering whether to make reservations in Carmel-by-the-Sea. They book up far in advance for Thanksgiving and Christmas."

"Oh, well that explains it. I wish he could have picked a better time to call. But that's good news—maybe just you and I can plan a trip, perhaps a romantic cruise to the tropics. Imagine you and I drinking Mai Tais on the beach at night in front of a full moon, warm breezes blowing..." He smiled slightly from under his hat and drifted off. He was going to be very affectionate later tonight, she could tell.

Surrounded by luxury, with the piney mountain air expanding her lungs, it was easy to distance herself from problems. Later in the evening, with each long deep stroke of the masseuse's hands, the issues of the day melted away into insignificant set-backs that could be dealt with some other time, if ever. She wanted to learn to be more like Herschel, relaxed, indifferent, attentive only to the important things, the things you could control. Nona realized she could not control the unfortunate events surrounding one of her children, so she started to slowly let go of Dolly in her mind. Eventually it would work itself out, that she knew.

Six months later, Emil is driving up Wilshire Boulevard toward Westwood Village where his overpriced attorney somehow afforded an office with a view of the entire Village. Irritated at all the traffic going into the Village—where were all these people coming from, and did everyone suddenly need to own a car? He heard on the news recently that Santa Monica now had 65,000 residents, and it looked liked most of them drove. Up ahead the light was turning yellow, and the person in front of him was taking their sweet time, trying to make him miss the light—probably a woman driver. Disgruntled, he tapped the brakes on his new two-tone green Buick Roadmaster, green because that's how he paid for her, with green cash earned from his green landscape firm. He was doing well, oh yes, and could finally see his way to purchasing a piece of the rock, a large parcel in Thousand Oaks with one house and plenty room to add two more. But not before he got some legal advice.

He glanced in the rearview mirror to check on the status of his fading scar running along his cheekbone from the scuffle with the Peace Mission thugs this last summer in Berkeley—the physical scar was fading but the emotional ones would stay with him. His ex-daughter Dolly never did call to see if he was okay after his working over—for all she cared he might as well be dead. Thanksgiving had passed, no call, no card. His forty-ninth birthday, three days after Thanksgiving, had passed—same silence, no call, no card. Genieve came down to celebrate Thanksgiving with he and Lillian, and said she had called the mission several times and they either told her Sister Ann was not there, or that she didn't want to talk to any relatives at all. So it was obvious where her loyalty was, and it wasn't with her family, who she appeared to have forgotten.

Emil had been doing more research on cults, and learned that legally Dolly was entitled to inherit a portion of his property should he pass away—and he inevitably would pass away—and at that point Dolly could do whatever she wanted with her portion of the inheritance. His research had led him to a few stories where cult leaders required followers to turn their inheritance over to the group—meaning the cult leader, or be rejected by the cult, apparently a fate worse than death to the mindless followers. That would happen over his dead body, period. Nope, not allowed. He had worked hard all his life to build something of value, and he would rather burn the money in a bonfire than let that crook Father Divine get a penny. He could always revise his Will and Trust at a later date, after Dolly had apologized and explained herself, but for now, she was out of luck after pulling a stunt like this.

So today he was meeting for the fifth time with his attorney to sign the Final Will and Testament. After he passed away, and after Lillian passed away, everything was going to Genieve and her children, if she ever had any, and he knew she would. His Genieve was a good daughter, normal, healthy, motivated to be the best she could be. It made him feel good that he was able to give someone a secure future that really deserved it. And keep it away from those who didn't.

"Hey, watch where you're going!" Some angry guy with black slicked back hair and New York plates was leaning on the horn in the right lane next to him. What the heck was his problem anyway? He was in his own lane, doing just fine.

"Go back to New York if you don't like it!" Emil usually didn't yell out of his car but this guy really deserved it—he looked so surly, so New Yorkish. And his car was ugly. Which meant the jerk was jealous. The guy stepped on the gas to speed away, blowing a thick cloud of black smoke out the rear tailpipe which promptly entered the cab of the Buick and momentarily overpowerd the new car smell.

The open window let the coastal air blow in and cleared the smoke out in one block, and now Emil made a left off Wilshire onto Westwood Boulevard, the familiar dome of the Bank of American building rising up ahead. The dome really gave the Village a sense of place. It had been on the corners of Westwood, Broxton and Kinross since 1929, the first building erected by the Janss Investment Company when they developed the Village. He kept going, feeling at home, easing down the tree-lined streets, then made a right on Weyburn and a right on Glendon. He knew he would easily find parking here because Glendon was a side street off the beaten path. He wished Lillian were here with him—they had met so many times here in the Village when they had to sneak to see each other. But he couldn't bring Lillian to a will signing with him—by its very nature it was a private matter. Lillian would approve anyway—they were almost always in agreement, and once again he realized just how lucky he was to have her, his true soulmate.

Sure enough, there was a parking spot right in front of the building, a three story Mediterranean office complex built around a courtyard, complete with a large central fountain and Pygmy date palms underplanted with ferns and pale lavender impatiens. Good landscaping really was the most important aspect of any building, he noted with satisfaction. He strode through the courtyard, past the trickling fountain, and to the back staircase so he could get a workout rather than take the elevator. On the third floor landing he made a left, until he came to the door plaque announcing: FELIX MATRISCIANO, ATTORNEY AT LAW, WILLS AND TRUSTS. He pushed the door open resolutely with the confidence that comes from knowing he had the power to secure both his own future and the future of those dear to him. It was a great feeling, it validated him and made all his hard work completely worthwhile. It was time now to sign into law who would be protected years into the future.

CHAPTER 14

Father Divine frowned, re-reading the letter from his attorneys Sperling and Fletcher. Someone, one of the snooty denizens of Holy Hill whose family had been established there for generations, had taken up a petition and had a Cease and Desist order issued against his weekly banquets—the nerve! As if he was the only person who did any entertaining in the area. That's what these huge properties were for, wasn't it? The half mile long driveways, the marble columns, the intricate tile work, the fountains, pools, tennis courts, servants, the...but what really bothered them was that he was a Negro—as the narrow-minded labeled those of a dark complexion—and they thought he attracted the wrong crowd. That's what this was all about, same story as always, period. The familiar anger rose up in him, the righteous indignation and powerlessness when he was reminded that even though he had made a fortune, owned multiple estates and businesses, and was God to most of his followers, he was a perennial outsider to these people, and they were going to keep it that way. They were the inner circle, the families who really ran things, the power structure—and they would never let him in. He had sent invitations to his neighbors engraved with gold on quality linen stationary, proper, tasteful invitations, and they had all, each and every one of them, gone unanswered, even though there was a finely scripted RSVP at the bottom of each. The universal lack of response from the neighbors was louder than a punch in the nose. And now this, the reminder once again that there is a difference between money and power—he had the money, but they had the power to control policy, which controlled the money.

He kept reading, counting all the petty complaints, each one like a bee sting because he knew they were dredging up laws that no one had enforced in years, if ever, until he came along to upset their status quo:

Raucous parties until past midnight.
Loud voices outside the home.
Flood lights outside the home keeping the neighbors awake and blocking out the stars, scaring nocturnal wildlife away.
Interfering with neighbors' quiet enjoyment of their homes.
Cars clogging the narrow winding streets posed a danger.
Landscaping on a nearby property flattened by tire tracks.
Singing and clapping echoing off the hillsides and across the canyon.
Petty property crimes such as littering, stealing garden items, urinating in public, etc.

He considered just not responding—that would show them how unimportant they were to him. But he knew if he showed defiance, they would come gunning for him even more. Perhaps if he purchased another building in a commercial area, he could continue his operations and maybe even expand the dinners. But then certain prospective followers would be uninspired by the surroundings, and he had set up this particular location specifically to attract more well-heeled followers and sympathizers—and yes, donors. It was a fact that money attracted more money, and if he downgraded his banquets, which were his main fundraising venues, he would end up attracting only the poor, and he had worked very hard to shake the stigma of being known as a religion for poor colored folks. That was fine when he first started out in Harlem, but he had higher aspirations now, and was even entertaining thoughts of running for political office. That took friends in high places, the kind that wanted to be wined and dined at the Holy Hill estate--he was in a quandary. He pushed the chair back and stood up from his reading desk and glanced in the mirror—did those wiry gray hairs on his temple grow in just recently? He never noticed that many before, and moved in to take a closer look. Once again he had an overwhelming desire to just run away, retire, go fishing like normal people did at his age. But if he walked away with all those people's money he would never see the light of day again. You can't retire from being God, he reminded himself. He was obligated to carry on and maintain the charade. He wished sometimes he could turn back time to when he was a preacher doing pretty well for himself, before the time he had reinvented himself as God. That was a hard cross to bear, especially as he entered his senior years.

He moved away from the mirror and in a dreamlike state entered his bed, slipped down between the satin sheets and pulled the covers over his head, grateful he didn't have to give any of the Rosebuds spiritual guidance in his private quarters tonight. He was taking a break from Rosebud Lilly who had become demanding—he briefly wondered if she was a sex addict, an unfortunate affliction that so many of the young girls came into the Mission with. On this last thought he slid into a heavy dreamless sleep, and he slept the sleep of the dead.

The cover of the local Berkeley newspaper, Monday, December 13th 1948 issue, featured a profile photograph of Father Divine, head held high in defiant joy, being hustled away in handcuffs by two Berkeley policemen on each side of him, with the caption:

> INTERNATIONAL PEACE MISSION'S LEADER CAN'T KEEP THE PEACE
>
> At 10 P.M. last night Father Divine's peaceful banquet once again turned rowdy and neighbors are fed up. Police were called to the scene of a loud party that the neighbors say goes on every Sunday, and they've had enough. The officers asked the party goers, who had spilled out of the banquet hall and down to the pool and cabana, to disperse but most refused, saying they were on private property and had a right to stand by the pool and talk all night if they wanted, it was a free country. While the police were questioning the party goers, a crowd of neighbors surrounded the estate, a few wearing loungewear and smoking jackets, clearly disrupted from an otherwise peaceful evening at home by the ongoing noise and light pollution. Fearing an escalation of civil unrest, police informed Father Divine and his guests that they had fifteen minutes to disperse. Father Divine had them wait in silence for ten minutes, and then they filed into police custody. Processed by the county jail at 3 AM, clerks were frustrated, because the guests often refused to reveal their given names, instead using names they had adopted in the religious movement. Sixty-six people were arrested, including twenty whites. Most pleaded guilty to disturbing the peace and incurred $5 fines, which Father Divine paid with large denomination bills. When clerks came up short of money to break the large bills, he reportedly told them to "keep the change."

There were a couple follow-up articles about goings on at the International Peace Mission West, mostly hearsay evidence from people in the community that were outraged a cult was allowed to operate in their safe well-established neighborhood. No one mentioned the other religious organizations around Holy Hill—these groups were for the most part under the radar as far as the citizens of Berkeley were concerned. Of course, their leaders didn't claim to be God, didn't hold weekly banquets for anyone who wanted to show up, didn't have a Rolls Royce, didn't require their followers to forsake their families and give over all they owned to the organization. And they didn't open businesses that directly undercut the local businesses. Father Divine was high profile and people were either outraged or enjoying the snow—he was a talking point.

Today Divine had another meeting, one considerably less stressful than his recent attorney consultation regarding the parties. This was his weekly meeting with his secretaries, a room full of women competing to be the one who delivered the most relevant information of the day. Sometimes it was rewriting or rephrasing his code of conduct, sometimes it was a personnel issue, and at times there were reports of various goings-on the secretaries thought he should know about. Mostly it was the gossip of women—petty, small minded, but mildly entertaining and calming because there was no challenge in it for him. All he had to do was sit there and look sympathetic or concerned—whatever the occasion called for. To the women his very presence solved any issues they may have, like a soothing salve. The head secretary, a titular position that tended to shift according to Father's whims and tastes of the moment, was currently held by Rosebud Lilly. Now, in the soft morning sunlight scattered in prisms through cut glass windows, he adopted a serene smile and pushed open the heavy dark door into the jewel toned Queen Ann themed sitting room filled with light, brocades, velvet and Persian rugs, walking softly to his favorite peacock blue mohair wing backed chair. He leaned back, the chair releasing a whoosh of air scented with the familiar lemon oil and a touch of incense the ladies usually burned in the evenings. He caressed the soft mohair arms and raised his eyebrows as a signal to the ladies he was ready to hear their stories.

In the semicircle before him, toward the right corner, sat his own Sweet Angel, Mother Divine, a real surprise because she usually didn't attend the secretarial meetings. And right next to her, the ubiquitous Sincere Sincerity, looking a little too alert now, bright piercing eyes accentuated by the dark complexion. Sweet Angel wore a watercolor green silk dress cinched at the waist with a wide black patent leather belt and matching open-toe pumps—she was in stark contrast to the rest of the ladies' attire, standard issue Rosebud uniforms. She looked like a blond goddess, he noted with approval. People admired and wanted to emulate the attractive, a fact of which he was constantly aware, and why he always appeared in public meticulously groomed and dressed to the nines—anything less than a three-piece suit was unacceptable.

He slowly perused the small gathering, trying to gauge the mood. They all looked a bit uncomfortable, as if they had been arguing just before he made his entrance. Rosebud Lilly was giving him a pouting look, narrowing her green eyes to catlike slits, no doubt to send as loud a non-verbal message as she dared to register her disapproval about not being summoned over the last week to his private quarters. He realized he needed a replacement. Some of his ladies knew how to move on, but some became bitter, a potential problem that could eventually find its way to the newspapers in the form of a kiss and tell—enough of those and people might start to take the stories seriously.

Lilly shifted self-consciously in her chair and leaned forward. "Father dear, we had two people come to the door yesterday looking for what sounded like the Rosebud True Light. It was an attractive couple, a tall man and a red-headed woman, in their forties, well-dressed, well-spoken, and they said they were the parents of a girl named Patricia Hirshfeld. It was Sister Sincere Sincerity who answered the door and spoke with them, and she can tell you more Father Dear, if you wish to know the details of what was said." She looked toward Sincere, who was peached on the edge of her hard wooden chair, leaning forward eagerly in anticipation of dropping a bombshell on Divine, hoping to make him sweat just a little if she could. She really thought very little of Divine, and her dislike had only grown after the deaths of True Light and Brother David Devoute, whom had been a good man and a faithful follower. She was pretty certain Divine had something to do with the deaths, although she knew there would never be any proof. She calculated that the fact Divine might have an inkling she suspected him would be good for some leverage if she ever needed it—it never occurred to her she had no back-up, no one to come looking for her if she too disappeared.

Sincere drew in a long breath, pausing for dramatic effect. "Yes Father Dear, that's how it happened, yes indeed. The front doorbell rang and I answered. The couple were very polite but insistent. They said their daughter had emotional problems, and she disappeared from their home about a year ago. They hired a private detective who told them he had evidence their daughter had joined the International Peace Mission Movement. The couple say they own a publishing company so they were able to post photos of their daughter in various publications with a reward to anyone with information on her whereabouts. Apparently someone contacted them saying the girl was seen lingering around the Berkeley campus, and at that point they hired a local detective, which led them to our door."

"You told the unfortunate couple that it is not in our Code of Ethics to delve into the past of our followers, I assume? That we don't know anyone's name other than the one they give us, their own chosen names, and they don't bring identification from their former lives into the Mission?" Father fiddled with the buttons on his vest, needing something to do with his hands.

"Yes Father, I did tell them that, and I told them we had no knowledge of any Patricia Hirshfeld or anyone fitting her description. The woman showed me a black and white photograph of the girl they were looking for. I told them it looked like a lot of young girls but no one in particular. However, privately, I thought there was a resemblance to True Light. I expressed my sympathies and told them there was nothing we could do for them, their daughter was not, and had never been, seen here."

Father carefully arranged his face to reflect deep concern but not nervousness, and leaned toward Rosebud Lilly. "Miss Lilly, please explain to us why you thought this was about Rosebud True Light, who is unfortunately no longer with us."

Lilly whispered, not comfortable in the spotlight, "Because the woman who said she was the mother looked exactly like True Light, so much so that they could have been twins, even down to the red hair—and her voice was identical to True Light's. The man who said he was the father looked like her too."

"Thank you for this information ladies. There are so many unfortunate occurrences happening in the World of Man. You are all immune to the evils surrounding us, because you chose to join my Flock, and as my Flock you are and will forever be protected in this Heaven on Earth, because you put your trust in me. There is nothing for you to ever fear, I will take care of you as my children—I have shown you this better than I can tell you, and I have called you to walk in my shadow."

This reassurance elicited many Amens from the ladies present, Sweet Angle Divine leading the chant, many heads bobbing yes, yes, indeed it was so. Patricia Hirschfeld was quickly forgotten—she really was not their problem, and her parents' problems were worlds away from Mission life, the center of their universe and their refuge. These people had no business bringing their troubles to the door of Father Divine's Heaven on Earth. The followers recited a few more repetitions of Thank you Father and moved the meeting agenda forward to the next topic.

Later that afternoon, sitting alone in the library, he made a mental note to have his real estate attorney check to see how much the International Peace Mission property and the grocery store building downtown had appreciated in value since he purchased them. Not that he would ever sell, of course. That would give the neighbors too much satisfaction, and that was the last thing he was ever going to do. But Berkeley was oddly unwelcoming, quite surprising for such a liberal minded town. It was subtle, but it was there, nevertheless. First it was the lack of people of note at his banquet, the ignored invitations, the neighbors' complaints, then the dropping off of the Mission grocery store sales—odd because the prices were lower with far superior merchandise and selection—and now in today's local newspaper the editor had allowed a small blurb about the parents of the missing girl tracing her to International Peace Mission West. That was unnecessary, and people tended to believe the worst if it was printed in a newspaper. George Baker, he who had successfully reinvented himself as Father Divine, felt rejected by the townspeople of Berkeley. Maybe conventional wisdom was true, that the East Coast really was more evolved, both socially and financially. At this thought he allowed himself to reminisce, waxing nostalgic about the Autumn colors on the trees back East, the snowfall during Christmastime, the wonderful established ethnic neighborhoods of New York City with their rich history, the Italian restaurants, the French bakeries, the rolling verdant hills of Pennsylvania dotted with truly historic estates with acreage.

Here he sat, in mid December with perfectly sunny beach weather, warm enough for a swim, but alone in a place called Holy Hill, where he had no history, no friends other than followers, in a town filled with heady, cold intellectuals puffed up with a lot of theory but little action—yes let's face it, phonies. These were not his people. Maybe it was time to consolidate his efforts, go back to the corporate headquarters and the home of his heart, the Woodmont estate. The address was burned into his memory, the center of his movement and the home he considered his crowning glory—1622 Spring Mill Road, Gladwyne, Pennsylvania.

"Peace Father Dear". Mother Divine had quietly glided into the library from somewhere down the hall, probably on her way upstairs after her new post lunch regimen of a brisk walk several times around the property. "I didn't mean to startle you." He had turned around a little too quickly.

"Tell me, Sweet Angle, what is the weather like today? I haven't had a chance to go outside yet."

"It's perfect, just like always—a little foggy in the morning, then it burns off and it's clear and sunny, and the Bay is bright blue."

"Isn't it almost Christmas? I thought it was supposed to be snowing and we would be wearing our winter clothes—scarves, gloves, full length coats. Something is missing."

Mother Divine sighed, sat down and rested her chin in her hand, indicating she felt the nostalgia too. "I miss the Seasons back East—it reminds me of my girlhood in Canada. It feels like we just got here because every day is almost the same. We've been here three years and I feel no attachment whatsoever, although it' beautiful. It just feels like one long endless summer, like time is standing still. I want to go home but it seems our work is here, isn't that right Father Dear?"

"Sweet Angel, no one is minding the store, so to speak, at Woodmont and our people need us there—you can tell by the letters if you read between the lines. Maybe it's time for us to go home for Christmas and see how we feel."

Mother Divine allowed herself to show some enthusiasm, a departure from the usual Nordic chill of control that was her customary aura.

"My suitcases have been collecting dust Father Dear. I'm going to go right now and have Miss Sincere start putting some things together for me. This will be a perfectly wonderful Christmas." She swept out of the room with just enough enthusiasm that he got a peek at the young girl she must have been before she was saddled with a title and a diamond tiara—there was still a part of Sweet Angel that just wanted to play in the snow at Christmastime.

CHAPTER 15

The year is 1950, the start of a new era. The Great Depression is a receding memory, incomes are rising, families are moving to newly built suburbs, and the kids are glued to black and white television sets watching Howdy Doody. Dad goes off to work and Mom stays home with the kids and cooks, flipping through the red and white checked Betty Crocker Cookbook for interesting and nutritious meals. The milkman arrives at the door and leaves full glass bottles, takes the empty ones away. The Helms Bakery Truck driver toots a double whistle and they all race out trying to catch him before he pulls away. People don't think much about crime except to watch in fascination as the FBI searches for the Brink's Robbery suspects—a million in cash and a million and a half in checks vanish, the work of slick professionals, the crime of the Century.

Some notable events:

The movie Sunset Boulevard staring Gloria Swanson and William Holden is released.

The actor James Dean lands his first television role in a Pepsi commercial.

Chuck Cooper becomes the first Negro to be drafted into the National Basketball Association by the Boston Celtics.

There is a failed assassination attempt on President Truman by Puerto Rican nationalists.

Congress passes laws that restrict communists and communist parties in the U.S., affirming a popular sentiment that the Reds definitely aren't welcome here in America—we like our freedom too much.

For the most part, 1950 marks the beginning of a period when most everyone feels hopeful, confident that America is the absolute best place on Earth, that we are on top of the world. Everyone has an opportunity to do better, the possibilities are limitless, if you only put in a little elbow grease, a little effort, into whatever work you do. It's pretty much guaranteed you're going to get ahead.

Nona and Herschel were walking through downtown Berkeley this early spring evening of 1950. The salty breeze was whipping a few loose strands of hair across Nona's face, there was a hint of a fireplace somewhere with roasting marshmallows, and for a moment she was young again, filled with possibilities. She loved this city, its energy, and had come to feel she had history here because she had been a resident almost four years. She and Herschel had friends both in Berkeley and Whispering Pines. Her Santa Monica life seemed a little distant now, not a bad thing. Her daughters and son enjoyed coming North to visit too—all in all she felt she was in the right place at last.

Up ahead a familiar black awning jutted over a window that cast warm light onto the sidewalk. "There's the Bodhi Tree bookstore I told you about Herschel." She briefly wondered if the cocky pseudo-intellectual book store clerk was still there. Gee, that was three years ago she mused. They stopped for a minute to browse the books displayed in the window, and inside, sure enough, she recognized the same clerk's indolent movements as he restocked the shelves, giving each volume deep consideration, moving slowly in the cozy glow of the reading area. How interested—and worried—she had been at the time over the Father Divine pamphlet the clerk had handed her. Since then a lot had happened, and for the most part she had learned to let go. People entered your life and left it, including your children, and there was little you could do to control that. Best to just let go, accept and enjoy the ebb and flow of life.

"I can't believe they have the latest Agatha Christie book, A Murder is Announced, right in the front widow. This looks like the kind of store where they would carry only formal works of literature."

"Well Herschel, this is a college town and they have to appeal to the literary crowd—you know, hardback, quality paper, highbrow authors."

"Yes, but they still need to a make a living. At least they're smart enough to put the popular stuff on display to draw in the common man, right?" Herschel chuckled and put his arm around her, drew her in closer to him.

They moved on into the evening, down the street, window shopping the arcades and alcoves of downtown Berkeley. Quite a few of the stores were geared toward the student population. Nat King Cole's velvet voice purred his latest hit "Mona Lisa" from somewhere nearby. Nona knew she would remember this moment, suspended in time, for the rest of her life—she was at peace, secure with her place in the world, accepting, and the evening felt magical.

"Let's walk by the Mission Grocery Store just for old times' sake, okay Herschel?"

"Seems like something best forgotten, but if you want to, let's go." Herschel was feeling indulgent.

Down the block, around the corner, and there it was, the little grocery store—but wait, something is different—the sign now read GIUSEPPI'S MISSION GROCERS.

Nona, momentarily taken aback, exclaimed, "What? How can this be? I thought Father Divine put Giuseppi out of business."

Herschel snorted knowingly. "The swindler probably dumped the business when it slowed down and sold Giuseppi his former customers back, cheap, in exchange for keeping the word Mission in the business name. Slick."

He shook his head knowingly—he's seen it all in the banking business. The crook probably even made a deal to get a portion of the profits in exchange for using the Mission's name. He made a mental note to ask his business loan manager at First Federal if he knew any details of the deal. People had been disappointed when Giuseppi's closed—the feisty little Italian man had been a favorite in the community, but he just couldn't compete with the low prices of the Mission Grocery Store. Father Divine was not a favorite at the banks either—he never needed loans because he always paid cash, delivered in large suitcases. He made interest, he never paid it.

"I say good riddance Nona. The grocery store was nothing more than a gimmick to hook people into the cult. When it didn't work out quite as well as the crook planned, he packed it in and left town, but I am sure he still made his almighty profit off the community before he pulled off in his Rolls Royce."

They walked on into the evening, headed back to their pied-à-terre, each deep in thought about the many wrongs of the International Peace Mission Movement, both on a business level and a personal level, Nona's daughter Dolly being a topic that was tacitly agreed to be off-limits. They both shook their heads, amazed that Father Divine got away with what he did.

Later that evening, Herschel checked the real estate section of a couple newspapers and sure enough, an out of town agent had placed an advertisement for the mission:

> FOR SALE: A spiritual retreat in the heart of the city. Once in a lifetime opportunity to purchase the former estate of the International Peace Mission West. Unobstructed views of San Francisco Bay, Olympic sized swimming pool and cabana, two tennis courts, professional kitchen, maid's quarters, four thousand square feet of living space. Too many upgrades to list. Price available upon request. Serious inquiries only please.

He shook his head again, wondering at how these cult people operated. If things didn't work out in one city, they hightailed it to another city, taking the gullible along for the ride. He felt bad about Dolly, but she wasn't his daughter, and she did become difficult toward the end, after all. Dolly was not his responsibility, and there was no emotional connection—she was the offspring of Nona and another man. He sat and mused for awhile about how well Nona had seemed to move on from Dolly's enlisting in the International Peace Mission Movement. Maybe she still thought it was just a phase, and Dolly would come to her senses. Herschel knew better. People took him at face value, a strait-laced banker and businessman, but he had a deep side too. He noticed right from the start that Dolly had lacked a certain basic connection to her surroundings, that she seemed to be just a reflection, really, of what was going on around her, a reaction to other people's ideas. Maybe she was cut out from birth to join something like this—if not Father Divine then maybe it would have been a convent. Some people were just born like that. He felt bad for Nona but gee, her other kids—adults actually—were so great—Genieve, Eloise,

Kathleen, Nona, and Norman. They gave her strength, grounded her. He had a brief wave of regret for not having children of his own, but then reminded himself that he had been spared potential heartache and unpredictable outcomes. Giving your life up to have a family was risky business, indeed.

CHAPTER 16

Sister Ann was diligently cleaning seemingly endless floor to ceiling rows of windows in a large French Country style estate in Gladwyne, Pennsylvania. The home belonged to a new, very wealthy client of The Courtesy Employment Service—same as the branch in Berkeley, and unfortunately she did such a good job at cleaning she was still employed there, never promoted to secretary as they had promised.

Gee, she thought, it was spring and there were still patches of frost on the ground. The Christmas snow had been pretty, and a novelty because most all her holidays had been spent back home in Santa Monica, but the cold became tiresome very quickly, and the icy muddy slush puddles on the ground and the dead trees were depressing. She didn't have the right clothes for back East so they gave her some hand-me-downs—fuzzy sweaters with pills on the arms, coats that were well worn and musty, frayed wool scarves and hats. She felt like a hobo, but she tried not to feel like that and concentrated on all the good she was doing for those in need. She never actually saw anyone in need, but it was generally accepted among the followers that they were in service to help and give of themselves—to someone, anyone, who needed it, wherever they were, even internationally if Father and Mother deemed it necessary.

She thought of the recent miracle she had witnessed in the meeting hall right here at Woodmont. Father was giving a particularly moving sermon from his raised pulpit, and right in the middle of a sentence he looked up and paused, as if listening to a voice from above. He shut his eyes and said he was listening to a little boy praying to him for help all the way from India. Father left the room for a time and the lights lowered as he shut the door softly behind him. Time stood still, impossible to say just how long, with only the sounds of collective muffled breaths in the room. After a time Father entered the room from another door, larger than life, a calming magnificent presence that caused the lights in the room to shine brighter, and all of a sudden he was encased by glowing little pinpoints of light, like stars, a cone of light seemingly coming from the Heavens. He said he had just gone to the boy in India and saved him from dying of a terrible sickness that had infected many people in India. But because the little boy had believed in him and prayed for his help, he personally visited the boy's bedside, touched him on the forehead, and the little boy sat up, feeling better, the fever all of a sudden gone from his small body. The family couldn't see Father, only the little boy could. When the boy was safe Father returned to his flock, his Heaven, at 1622 Spring Mill Road, Gladwyne, Pennsylvania—right where Sister Ann now lived, with Father and Mother, in Heaven on Earth. And this all happened within the one hour during the sermon—such was the power of God.

Even with all the wonderful things happening around her, Sister Ann often missed Sincere Sincerity, who had been her rock when she first joined the Peace Mission Movement. Miss Sincerity never made the move from Berkeley to Pennsylvania that winter because she was found dead in her room right before Christmas. It was so shocking, and she wanted desperately to find out just what happened, but no one seemed to know anything other than to intone, she is no longer with us here on Earth. If anyone was going to live forever, it was to be Miss

Sincere Sincerity, a tough old survivor who was as healthy as a horse, and a loyal follower of Father and Mother Divine—and she was even the personal assistant of their own Mother, Sweet Angel Divine. Sister Ann knew Mother must miss her terribly, her constant companion, servant, and advisor. It was so strange though, that when she covertly observed Mother Divine for any signs of sadness, there was no sign of anything—it was as if absolutely nothing had happened. The same serene smile Mother normally adopted was there, frozen in place.

Another missing person was dear Sister Stella, her queen-sized hefty friend with the very kind soft moon-face—Stella would give someone the shirt right off her back if they needed it. Sister Ann could see her now, smiling, so proud of the most important job in her entire life, that of cashier at the Mission Grocery Store. Many shoppers waited longer in Stella's line just to have a few words with her as she checked them out. She brightened everyone's day, made them feel important. It was quite a shock to Sister Ann when Stella confided in her that she didn't want to leave Berkeley and all the nice customers she had met—she finally felt like she belonged somewhere, was a valued member of a community outside the mission. She made Sister Ann promise not to tell, but a Mr. Giuseppi, who used to own an Italian grocery store nearby, approached her and said he was the new owner of the Mission Grocery Store as of next month, January 1950, and asked her to stay on as head cashier. She signed the paperwork in secret and went to live at a friend's house until she could save enough money for an apartment of her own. She said she loved Father and Mother Divine with all her heart, but she had gained enough confidence to go out on her own. She had her whole life before her, and she wanted a family and a house with a white picket fence some day—with a large kitchen and a fireplace. It sounded nice, but also very materialistic and unlike Stella—but that just proved you can never really know the heart of Man. You can only count on God.

Sister Ann kept her mind in the present by using the power of positive thought, like Sincere Sincerity had taught her to. It wasn't easy at first, and her mind sometimes drifted to pleasant memories of her past, her family, her former possessions. Sincere had said this was a normal part of letting go, a grief period until you accepted your new life as one of service to God rather than oneself. This life of service was the authentic identity, not the past life before joining the Peace Mission Movement—there is clarity in service if one can learn to let go of the controlling ego, which in the end can provide no meaningful sense of fulfillment. Only a life of service to others can bring meaning to one's life. She had pondered this often, and remembered her former life as Dolly, watching her mother Nona go through an endless series of re-inventions and five husbands—the constant turmoil, the extreme highs and lows of her life. What did it all mean? It seemed like a bunch of craziness. But as soon as her mind drifted to her Daddy Emil and her sister Genieve, she had to physically get up and start working, or talking, or anything to distract her deep sense of sadness and loss, a sinking feeling right in the pit of her stomach. After a lot of practice and moral support from her mission family members, and photographs of Mother and Father Divine on every wall and tabletop, thought control was finally working a little and the memories were fading. Some people didn't like memories to fade, even the sad ones, but the Peace Mission Movement required your all, and memories would only get in the way. The key was to stay busy, keep your nose to the grindstone.

"Miss, are you almost finished? We have guests tonight and I want to start setting up this room." The lady of the house, no doubt. Sister Ann could tell by the refinement of manner. A woman about her same age, mid-twenties, beautiful, a blond blue-eyed Doris Day lookalike—judging by her surroundings the woman had married very well, had a large dowery, or both.

Climbing down the ladder, eyes downcast, Sister Ann said in a barely audible whisper, “Yes ma’am. I have only one row left.” She had never used the word ma’am before but her Sisters in the Movement said this was the proper way to respond to those in authority, especially if you were working for them.

“Very good. I am sure we will be pleased with your work.” The woman turned away then, called to another area of the house no doubt, perhaps required to fawn over an older overbearing husband who required constant and servile attention. Sister Ann shook the rag out and snapped it with this last satisfying thought.

“You drift through the years and unless your life has meaning, unless you are making a difference, one day you wake up and all the years are behind you, with little ahead but decrepit old age. Most of the time when you get old your children desert you, leave you to rot because they have their own families and you are forgotten after having given up your entire life for them. Here you are safe, and we will never desert you—your hands are kept busy with good works and your hearts are filled with the Spirit of God. You will never be alone and you will always be a valued member of the family.”

These were Mother Divine’s latest reassuring words to her, spoken in a soft voice as they walked the cold soggy winter grounds together in a tight little group of Rosebuds. Mother’s forte was getting to know each individual Rosebud or Sister and making them feel like they were of paramount importance to the Peace Mission Movement. She excelled at both public speaking and interpersonal relationships—poised, confident, always tastefully dressed. Who wouldn’t want to emulate her? Mother also had an arsenal of pithy statements at the ready for members of the press—she and Father were a topic of fascination, humor, respect, controversy, or derision depending on which reporter and newspaper carried the story. One of the latest stories, geared toward the growing Civil Rights Movement, lead with a quote from Mother, or Sweet Angle Divine as the reporter called her, advising that "A Negro God was atonement for the injustices perpetrated against those of a darker complexion by those of a lighter complexion. You need to overcome your prejudices."

Since coming back East, Sister Ann noticed a few things were very different from California. Having spent most of her life in Santa Monica, she had a laissez-faire attitude toward racial topics—to her, it wasn't really a topic at all, and most people she had grown up with had very little, if anything, to say about it. Her hometown had plenty of colored people, and the kids went to the same schools so it was never really much of an issue. She remembered when she was in Camp Fire Girls, her colored friend Mey had taught her to dance. They wore the same Camp Fire Girl uniforms, listened to the same music, tried to win the same merit beads for civic service. Here, back East, the people seemed, well, meaner, more on edge, ready to fight with each other. She heard that some colored people were even forced to sit in certain sections on public transportation or restaurants. And they talked about lynchings—it was so horrible Sister Ann could not even imagine it. She just kept her nose to the grindstone and hoped she was helping—someone, anyone.

One evening, sitting in the library bent over a weighty tome of past sermons of the Reverend Major Jealous Divine, studiously taking notes of the highlights, she noticed Father Divine himself considering her, looking at her quizzically from a dark corner of the room as if he was trying to recall something. He always looked somewhat odd to her because he seemed so tiny. Only behind the podium did he seem larger than life. She bent her head over more so the sheaf of blond hair concealed where she was really looking. Maybe he was remembering the fiasco caused by her former Daddy Emil Born when he made a scene at the banquet a couple years ago. She was quite in awe of Father

Divine, but she gave him a wide berth, remembering the Greek fable of Icarus, the boy who flew so close to the sun that it melted his newly crafted wax wings—in the fable he fell fatally into the sea. Sister Ann instinctively knew to keep a safe distance from from Father, although she couldn't quite say why she felt like this. He was God, after all, so the discomfort didn't quite make sense—or did it? After some time, Father seemed to lose interest in her and quietly made his exit. Sister Ann briefly wondered if he was reading her thoughts.

After a time, Sister Ann noticed a few green blades of grass popping through the snow, then some dots of green on the tree branches which would eventually become leaves. She guessed this was the East Coast version of spring. Instead of feeling revitalized though, as in springs past, she realized she felt an unnamed longing that she couldn't quite put her finger on. Spring used to fill her with hope, but she felt a bit down this year. It was probably the change of climate, she reassured herself. She would get used to it.

But her dream last night was still with her today, and it had been so clear that it seemed like it really happened. Even with the power of positive thought it was impossible to control one's dreams, and last night's dream made her want to cry. In it she was at Whispering Pines Resort, dancing under the stars on a warm night with the man she was going to marry, Dr. Bob Wallen. An ancient stately oak tree grew from the center of the elevated dancing platform, forming a leafy canopy that seemed to engulf them in a little bit of magic. The nearby foothills outlined a backdrop against the silvery full moon. It was one of those nights when the air was the same temperature as your skin, and you felt your clothes fade away, so it was only the warm breezes that clothed you, as if the night air itself were your gown. He held her close and his face was softly smiling, his dark eyes were filled with love—she felt safe, safer than she had ever felt in her life. The band was playing "I Love You For Sentimental Reasons", doing a beautiful job, and Bob was mouthing the words to her. Then the number came to an end and they walked back to their table which was perched just over a trickling stream that ran alongside the dance platform. This was where he was going to propose, she just knew it. But instead of proposing, he excused himself and said he would be right back—she thought he may have forgotten the ring. Hours passed, it got chilly, fellow dancers filed off the platform to go home, and the band packed up. He never came back for her, and the dream ended with her panicking, looking everywhere, running into the surrounding dark woods to find him, branches grabbing, ripping at her, and fear grabbed hold like a vise. Then the dream ended abruptly and she sat up in bed, throwing the covers off, her heart pounding.

Right now, in her bleak room at the end of the hall in the servant's wing of the estate, peering into her sparse closet filled with practical work clothes and sturdy shoes, photographs of Father and Mother Divine reminding her of the choices she made, she allowed herself just for a moment to wonder what her life would have been like if she had married Bob instead of pushing him away with her insistent Peace Mission rhetoric. Then, taking this moment of weakness that Sincere Sincerity had warned her about to practice thought control, she reimagined how miserable and meaningless her life would have been as a boring housewife who cooked and cleaned all day, and took care of ungrateful children who eventually would abandon her no matter how well she treated them. Armed with that thought, knowing she had transcended the commonplace and normal, she chose an outfit for today, quite similar to the outfits she wore every day—one suited to a solid eight hours of drudgery in someone else's fine home. At least here she was working for a purpose, the International Peace Mission Movement, and she was doing a lot of good for those in need. She only hoped she would have a dreamless sleep tonight.

CHAPTER 17

The line was out the door and down one side of the narrow hallway. Nearby a janitor was mopping, the strong scent of the ubiquitous Pine-Sol cleaner lingering in the air—maybe government building managers bought it by the case, Emil mused. The temperature was turned down to sixty-seven degrees and there was an echo, topping off the impersonal feel bouncing off the shiny linoleum floors. The sign over the double doors announced what the attraction was that warranted such a line: CITY OF THOUSAND OAKS PLANNING DEPARTMENT. The area was quickly growing post World War 2 because Thousand Oaks had plenty to offer and was reasonably close to civilization, namely Los Angeles County—where there was life, unlike here, where cows dotted the hillsides.

Emil hated standing in lines, especially government run operations like this one. Where was the incentive to work harder or faster? It was almost impossible to lose your job unless you just didn't show up. But here he was because there was no way out of it, and he even had to be deferential while they committed highway robbery on him with the outrageous price of building permits. He was a little shocked how small the whole operation was—after all, he was used to Los Angeles County offices, huge cavernous Art Deco spaces that actually looked important.

He was here to pull permits for his new property, his pride and joy, purchased cash after watching his pennies and saving for years. There was no way he and Lillian could afford Santa Monica, so one day they took a drive up the coast and cut though Malibu Canyon Road to Thousand Oaks, only thirty miles away and under an hour to drive. And what a drive it was--sweeping ocean views all the way up, and through the canyon breathtaking cliffs and rolling hills dropping off into emerald green wooded riparian valleys. They made a routine out of it—every Sunday come rain or shine they went to Thousand Oaks to familiarize themselves with their prospective future home town. What you could get for the price just over the hill—Santa Monica slang for inland from Malibu—was astounding. Huge parcels with ancient oak trees, mountain views, clean air, uncrowded streets, solidly built homes. It was too hard to resist, and of course if they missed Santa Monica they could always visit on Sundays. Naturally their friends would visit them, and they would make new ones too. Lillian could sell Avon here just as well as she could in Santa Monica, and he could pick up occasional landscaping projects in between building his rentals behind the main home. They had it all planned.

He waited patiently for his turn in front of the City Planner, trying hard not to show his irritation. At the counter there were two men at the desks, taking their sweet time, chewing the fat with the locals in line. The smug looking fellow with the see-through comb-over hairdo the color of brown shoe polish signaled him forward.

"Hello Mr. Born. This permit is an application for two houses on a parcel that already has an existing home built in 1947. That right?" The Planner looked down his nose, clearly sizing up the rich out-of-towner.

"Yes sir, that's right. I have the money order ready if you're okay with all my information. It's for eight thousand dollars, which covers permits for the two additional small houses on my parcel. I've gone over all the City requirements and think I have them covered, but if there is anything else I need to do please tell me." Emil hoped the Planner swallowed his subservient act—he'd practiced it in front of Lillian a few times to make sure the City didn't hold him up unnecessarily just because they had the power to.

"Nope, looks like you're good to go Mr. Born. Don't forget, you'll be getting regular visits from the Building Inspector. We need to monitor the progress of every new structure to make sure they're up to our Code."

Emil nodded politely. He knew the less said the better. It was too easy to bury oneself in unnecessary conversation with government officials. It might jog their memory and then they might pull out another hoop for you to jump through. He backed away unobtrusively from the counter, hurried down the hall, and out the door to the parking lot. The green two-tone Buick Roadmaster stood out from all the other jalopies here in Hicksville. He did miss the big city sophistication but he wanted to be a landlord, wanted to have a large parcel, something to show for all his hard work—and it was beautiful here, he had to admit. One day it would be a city as large as Santa Monica, and he had beat the crowd. He had a lot to be proud of.

He glanced at the gold Lord Elgin pocket watch Lillian had given him for Christmas a few years ago. He remembered how surprised he was when he opened the box. Engraved *Emil from Lillian 12-25-47.* The year Dolly had disappeared into the cult. Lillian had assured him she sold a lot of Avon products that year and could more than afford the expensive watch. Right now the watch told him it was almost time for dinner. Lillian would be fussing over the stove in her new kitchen, in domestic Paradise with all the little gadgets, towels, doilies and what-nots that women seemed to find so necessary. He resisted the temptation to feel lucky—it wasn't luck, that was for sure. He had earned it.

Cruising along Thousand Oaks Boulevard at a leisurely pace gave him time to check out the pedestrians. The town was so small he usually saw someone he knew. Doing work on his home and preparing for the addition of two more homes on the property had brought him into contact with just about everybody—hardware store workers, handymen, carpenters, plumbers. Up ahead was the little hole in the wall eating establishment closest to them, Lupe's Mexican Restaurant. He liked driving by there early mornings because he often got a whiff of homemade tortillas. Maybe if he could catch Lillian before she started her nightly food prep, he'd take her out. He was feeling good, getting to know the area, feeling connected to his adopted home town. After all, considering what he was building, he was going to be here for good.

As he passed Lupe's, movement caught his eye on the right up the driveway, a dark shape hunched over a white sack, lugging it along secretively, arms wrapped around the bundle protectively—the eccentric elderly woman who owned Lupe's had slipped out the back door and was headed toward the rear of the property toward her house, a simple wooden shack amid an avocado orchard, tomato vines obscuring the entry. The rumor was that she carried sacks of money right out of the register throughout the workday and squirreled it away somewhere on her property. Most of it never saw the bank. Supposedly she paid all her bills in cash, counting out each dollar as if it were her last. He could relate to that, paying cash. The banks were not your friend, that was for sure.

Now he turned right, then a quick left onto Los Robles Road and into his long graveled driveway. He never tired of noticing that his driveway was almost as long as some of his landscape clients in Bel-Air. He could think of no reason his property shouldn't have the same sense of arrival that the Bel-Air properties had—small grey crunchy gravel, bougainvilleas, and no less than three huge six hundred year old white oak trees. The house was small but who spent time inside with a property like this? Not him, no way. He was an outdoorsman. And now a landlord—as soon as the back two houses were built. Every time he looked at the back of the property the stacks of materials for the houses grew taller, wider—piles of lumber, bags of cement, pipes, wires, pavers, roof tiles. And four saw horses, yes sir. For the times he could round up a handyman to help him.

The front house had an addition that came from an unusual source—a chicken coup builder in nearby Simi Valley. In 1947 when the home was built it was almost impossible to get your hands on enough lumber to build. The post war building boom was in full swing and the price of lumber sky rocketed as the supply quickly dried up. The enterprising coop builder always used the best lumber and had a surplus. He somehow convinced folks around here to buy them and simply attach them to their houses for an added room. As luck would have it, the chicken coup builder specialized in larger coops that were about the same size as a small library or bedroom. The telltale slope of the add-on rooms was barely noticeable and everyone was thrilled at the ready-made added space for their homes.

Right now, as always, he looked at the mailbox and wondered if the letter was here, the one he had been waiting for going on three years now. In his imagination the letter would be addressed in Dolly's delicate flowing hand with the upward swooping pen strokes. He would open it carefully, unhurriedly, so he didn't rip the letter inside. It would begin with *Dear Daddy*, and end with *I'll be home soon*. When he moved from Santa Monica in February he had chosen the Post Office's one year forwarding option for the mail, and the one year call forwarding from General Telephone. It cost a little more but was well worth it not to miss Dolly's letter or call which would surely happen this year. He knew his daughter well enough to know she would eventually come to her senses. He longed to show her his hard earned property and assure her that one day it would go to his daughters—assuming Dolly's cult fad was over. He had taken care of both his girl's future. All Dolly had to do was come back home and be part of the family again, return to her normal self, then he would revise his Will and Trust to include her. But he would definitely add a legal stipulation against any proceeds going to the cult—he would have to speak with his attorney about that. You can't take it with you but you can control what happens to your life's savings.

He pulled the car just halfway up the driveway, leaving the back of the property clear so he could work on the houses tomorrow. Up in the kitchen window, sure enough, there was Lillian with her head bent over the sink, probably peeling potatoes judging by her posture. Boy, did he make a great choice with Lillian—it had been scary to leave that old bag Nona because of his daughters, but it had paid off so many times in his life he just could not count the ways. Lillian was his soulmate and had enhanced and complimented his life many times over, as he had done for hers. He wondered how many men felt so lucky to have found just the perfect person to go through the years with. And to cap it off, make it all so right, his daughter Genieve thought the world of Lillian.

Now he walked intentionally slow toward the three mailboxes at the front of the property, gravel crunching deliciously underfoot. Three mailboxes because the City had approved his parcel having three separate addresses. He guessed if a person paid enough—and stood in line long enough—the City would approve just about anything. He crooked a finger under the metal pull and opened the first mailbox, ducking his head low to see all the way back inside the long box. A letter could get stuck in the back of such a large box. He reached all the way in to feel the sides to make sure nothing got caught. He repeated this daily ritual two more times. The second two boxes were empty because the mailman, with whom he was on a first name basis, made sure to get it right. The first box for the main house had the usual stack of cards and letters, bills, and advertisements. He closed the box with a hollow metallic clang and lowered the red carrier signal flag which one of the local kids habitually flipped up as a joke.

More gravel crunching as he slowly walked to the front porch. He wanted to give Lillian time to hurry to the mirror and dab on perfume and lipstick as he knew she would when she saw the car in the driveway. She kept her Avon essentials right on the dresser for easy access, neatly lined up atop an antique perfume tray—this after ten years of marriage. She wasn't taking him for granted, ever. Hey, he was a great catch, and getting better every year—handsome, smart, in shape, articulate, and now the owner of a large property purchased cash. Stand in line ladies.

In the after dinner torpor they lounged on the tweedy couch, the cuckoo clock softly ticking in the background, the southwest facing picture window glowing red and orange from the sunset over the Santa Monica Mountains. Soon the sky would turn purple and the wild birds would settle in, each in their snug roosts in the oak trees. Lillian poured over the latest issue of Vogue Magazine with a concentration usually reserved for calculus equations. No wonder she was at the top of the Avon sales awards every year—she took cosmetics and fashion seriously and she knew her arsenal well. Actually he just realized that Lillian often dressed like the latest cover of Vogue, which most of her clients subscribed to—no coincidence there. They probably chatted for hours about how to be fashionable in Thousand Oaks. He wondered where these people went when they got dressed up. He made a mental note to explore that further—they needed to get integrated into the town because they were going to be here a very, very long time.

Now he reached over Lillian's silk stockinged knee, leaning into the perfume cloud, for today's pile of mail, sinking back into the couch, then dealing out each piece of mail one at a time like a stack of cards into Lillian's lap. His heart stopped just then—a letter in a feminine flowing hand, no return address. He held it closer, flipped it over—the return address was on the back side of the envelope, something he used to argue about with his daughters. He maintained it was supposed to be on the front, and they argued that it could be either way, but it looked better on the back. This letter was from Genieve. He tried not to be disappointed, but her writing was so similar to Dolly's, just for a moment he allowed himself to hope. But no, this wasn't what he had been waiting for. He slid his thumb expertly under the seal and extracted the letter. A short one from Genieve, all the way from Santa Monica. He smiled—Genieve loved to write rather than call, even though it was no longer considered a long distance call. She had come home permanently after her sister had left town at the end of last year with the Father Diviners, as he called them. There was nothing keeping Genieve in Berkeley anymore—the hope that Dolly would come back to them was extinguished when she walked by the vacant Peace Mission building one day. Dolly never even said goodbye when they left for back East, and in fact there had been no word from her since she moved into the Peace Mission West in 1947. The cult had swallowed her up, as Genieve put it—there was no more Dolly, she might as well be dead.

"Who's that from honey?" Lillian was curious and knew Emil secretly waited for Dolly's letter to come. Lillian could pretty much read his thoughts.

"Genieve. Says she wants to come see us this weekend. She bought a car because she got a raise at Prudential—it's old but it runs perfectly. She wants me to check it out for her—as long as the breaks are good, that's the main thing. I'm just so proud of my girl. They gave her the front desk with an engraved name plaque. I guess her business degree is paying off."

"She's like her father. Good looks and brains, along with persistence. They always pay off. I'm looking forward to seeing her. I have some Avon samples I know she'll love."

Genieve was an amazing daughter, that was for sure. Loyal and attentive to her Daddy, loved Lillian, loved her mother Nona and even her mother's fifth husband, Herschel the stick-in-the-mud. She was a real people person, popular, a positive life force. Emil was certain only good things would come to her. She stuck with her Merritt College business school even in the midst of what must have been chaos, got the diploma, and put it immediately to good use, taking a position at the new Prudential Insurance Company on Wilshire Boulevard and Fairfax Avenue in Los Angeles. He chuckled when she told him she could walk to the La Brea Tar Pits for lunch but hoped she didn't fall in.

"She doesn't talk about Dolly much anymore but I know my daughter and she thinks about her all the time. She blames herself for not stepping in sooner. She told me once that she was so wrapped up in her studies and trying to get ahead that she deserted her own sister."

"Oh honey how horrible. You never told me that. You can't stop someone from doing what they want if they've made up their mind. Dolly is doing what she thinks she needs to do, strange as it seems to the rest of us. If she were miserable she would come back. Maybe there is some joy in it for her. Look at the Catholic nuns for instance—their life seems strange to us but rarely does a nun leave the Church. They wouldn't have it any other way, and I don't think I've ever seen a nun that wasn't smiling. I'll have a talk with Genieve, woman to woman—she shouldn't blame herself because her sister has a religious calling."

Dolly would forever be himself in his most perfect form, innocent, filled with possibilities, but her face was fading a little after three years. He remembered her now mostly from photos and flashes from the past when she was young. Her voice now seemed far away and he could barely recall the sound of it. He didn't want the memories to fade, didn't want the hurt to become less, because it meant he was moving on, leaving his girl behind. He believed time heals all things, blots out the past, but when it was your own flesh and blood, maybe that was not a good thing. He vowed never to let go, ever. Later that evening he carefully placed Dolly's letters in his keepsake box far, far back in the bedroom closet, deeply buried among the shoes he thought he might wear one day, the suits that were still perfectly good even though they had long since gone out of style, the rain gear that was enough for a monsoon, and his mother's sewing kit he refused to throw away even though she had long since gone to meet her Maker. He wouldn't read the letters again, wouldn't take out the lock of blond hair that she had enclosed in a card for him, but they were the physical embodiment of her, a tangible part that couldn't get away, and they would stay with him, secure in his home, forever.

CHAPTER 18

Another Holy Communion Banquet was underway today this chilly spring evening of 1950 at the Mount of the House of the Lord, Woodmont, in Gladwyne Pennsylvania. Father and Mother Divine sat at the head of the table in carved high back chairs, swaying ever so slightly to the music, eyelids lowered, half smiles arranged on their faces, while the aging Rosebud Choir warbled songs in papery elder voices that they had composed for Father and Mother. One of the Sisters was pounding at the piano as if she could produce a true note from the choir by hitting the keys harder. The banqueter crowd had thinned a little from years past at Father's Missions, and the regular attendees had grown a little long in the tooth, a little grayer, a little more frail. The Peace Mission Movement seemed to have matured and Father Divine noticed fewer young people around Woodmont. He recognized the regular Sisters and Brothers, but somehow his flock had stagnated, aged, wilted, his human capital had dwindled—he couldn't quite put his finger on it, or stop it, but the whole thing seemed to be fading. The elderly followers looked at him piteously, needy eyes eagerly sucking up what little energy he managed to radiate. Actually, the most enthusiasm he could muster anymore was at the banquets. They all loved to eat—who doesn't? At the end of every meal though there was always a little sadness, and the after dinner revelry had gotten a little shorter, tamer, and the sermons a little more brief.

He and Sweet Angel Divine had been back home for good since this past Christmas season, California already a dimming memory. But he did long for the energy of a college town—it was different, there were things happening, it seemed to be moving, people in motion, going somewhere, while here there was only the staid Pennsylvania countryside. When he looked around his magnificent estate on his daily walks he took in the gigantic mature trees, the endless expanses of rolling lawns, the Colonial estates with discrete servants tending the entries as limousines carrying important people either arrived or departed to mysterious and wonderful destinations. He, George Baker, realized this is what it meant to be at the top. But at the top of what? In his mid-seventies he was closer to eighty now than seventy. Seventy had been bad enough. He was still considered an inconvenient oddity that the neighbors had to put up with, and he could feel the subtle disapproval, the distaste that he lived in their neighborhood. The only family he could surround himself with was the followers, those poor lost souls that accepted him as God on Earth—because they had nothing else. Well, he had little else too, as he had lately begun to realize. Money and property, yes, but there was little to feed his soul, no one to carry forward his good works.

Of late he often reflected that maybe the celibacy he required of the followers had backfired—it was a conundrum because it was impossible to give yourself entirely to the International Peace Mission Movement and care for a family as well. One of the slogans he repeatedly brainwashed his followers with—*you can't be soldiers of God if you are slaves to the flesh*—may have come home to roost. He would have a talk later with Sweet Angel to see if she had any ideas of how to continue the legacy of The Movement. The 1950 prosperity and building boom was beginning, the Depression over, people were filled with hope. Fewer people were looking for an answer to their problems, a roof over their heads, a free meal, security against bad times. Everything was great now, America was booming, and the Press reported mostly good things. Who needed a Mission? America herself had become Heaven on Earth.

Now, on his nightly after dinner walk, he was thinking. Something had to be done, he couldn't just sit and wait to die because all he had built up would disappear—or worse, be divided up among the weak-minded followers who would fritter it away as they had frittered their own lives away following a fantasy. Just then a strong gust of freezing wintery air stung his face, threatening to snatch his black wool Fedora—thankfully this one had ear flaps so it clung stubbornly to his bald pate. It had been an especially long cold lingering winter and spring was making only a weak appearance. He leaned into the wind and walked on along the wooded street, deep in thought, not seeing much of the beauty of the frozen Earth. To his right he passed a circular driveway where a white limousine had just deposited a young man in front of a columned grand entry. A young lady was waiting to greet him and they wrapped around each other in a warm embrace as the chauffeur looked dutifully away. Reverend Major Jealous Divine trudged forward, boots crunching on the bare frozen ground, a few dead leaves rustling in the breeze, in step with none.

By the time he got back to Woodmont it was late evening. The cold new moon lit the path up his long driveway with a silver sheen, and a faint scent of charred white oak drifted toward him—diligent housekeepers always kept a fire burning in the winter. Built on seventy-two acres in the Châteauesque architectural style, it didn't look like any other building around, that was for sure. It was ornate to the point of being whimsical, stacked to overflowing with pointed russet roofs, spires, frescos, stone facades, and archways. Completed in 1894 for

Alan Wood, Jr., a steel magnate, the style suited the wildest fantasies of the new money crowd. It passed through Mr. Woods' family, one of whom was a follower of the International Peace Mission. The property was eventually given to Father Divine as a gift from the family member, although some said he paid for it from a suitcase filled with $75,000 in large denomination bills of undetermined origin.

Father Divine now moved purposefully across the marble entry, past the dark carved oak winding staircase, through the formal dining room centered by the magnificent shimmering Murano glass chandelier and toward the kitchen. Just before pushing open the swinging doors he stopped—there seemed to be a drama unfolding in the kitchen. A woman was wailing, accusations were flying, voices in the background indicated a high level of stress with strained high pitched voices. Through it all the reassuring smells of leftovers from dinner muted the discord.

"We gonna put you both out with mo' than you all deserve—you lucky to get that five dollar. Way you been carrying on with that woman, it's a wonder you gitten anything! You gonna rot in Hell, that's fo sure!"

"You can't tell me who to love. We love each other, and that's the truth. We ain't doin' nothin wrong by lovin' each other!"

On these last words he heard the back door to the kitchen slam with finality. He quickly moved to the window that looked out on the driveway, making sure to stay behind the heavy velvet curtains for cover. After all, he, God, was supposed to know everything so he took care never to be caught spying. The window was a little fogged up from warm bodies inside protected against the frozen earth outside by his thick castle walls. At the bottom of the driveway a Yellow Cab Company car waited for the woman as she made her way unsteadily down the icy driveway wearing only a thin wool coat, a stringy scarf and clutching a small overnight bag that she held like a shield to her breast. The headlights of the cab illuminated the mist hanging in the air, defining a cone of wet light that the woman moved toward. The driver got out as she approached and opened the back door, then summarily shut it and jogged around to the drive's seat. The car pulled cautiously away and disappeared into the cold damp night.

Sadly, a fallen angel—he was sorry to see her go. The goal was to add followers, not lose them. Why did some find it so hard to follow simple rules that were for their own good? He suspected this was the Sister they had told him about at one of the more confidential meetings, the one that was caught under the covers with another Sister. Two middle aged ladies in bed together, doing things he would rather not know about, giving in to the call of the flesh. Well, at least they did in fact partially adhere to the International Modest Code in that they did not unnecessarily mix with the opposite sex, but Evil Temptation eventually came to them all and not everyone could overcome it. Some never got caught but these two did and must be made an example of. The Movement called it being Put Out. The fallen follower was given a five dollar bill and asked to leave, taking all his or her belongings. Since they were not allowed to have personal items, this meant only a change of clothes and transportation money, usually to the nearest Salvation Army. The longer they had been in the Peace Mission Movement, the harder it was to leave because contact with family and friends had been eliminated, cut off, usually for many years. All money earned while working for the Movement was immediately handed over, so if they were Put Out there was literally nowhere for them to go, no one to turn to. Most followers made sure they towed the line.

He turned away from the window and headed back to the entry, toward the magnificent winding staircase with carved black walnut handrails inlaid with mother-of-pearl. The staircase led up to his inner sanctum, which contained the exact furnishing as his former suite in Berkeley—the housekeepers made sure his rooms were identical in every way so he always felt at home wherever he was. He was taken care of and catered to so meticulously that even his special toiletries were in the exact same spot at any given location.

Tomorrow he would speak with Sweet Angel about what to do regarding carrying on the legacy. She always had ideas about how to maintain control, and he admired her for that. She did inspire a little fear in the followers, he could tell, but someone had to be the one to dish out retribution. It wouldn't look right coming from him, because he was benevolent, all-seeing, all-knowing, a healer, a savior to mankind—let Mother Divine take care of the particulars while he distanced himself to follow his higher calling.

He pushed open the heavy door to his suite, moved inside and noted with satisfaction that firewood had been neatly stacked atop the grate in his fireplace, kindling below, with long wooden matches placed invitingly on the hearth— all he had to do was strike a match and he would have some nice contemplative time to himself before retiring. Before sitting down to enjoy the fire he walked to his dresser and resolutely grasped the wax candle formed in the shape of a crucifix with Jesus clinging to the cross. It had sat atop the dresser for a couple years, unused for the purpose it had been created for. He never understood how anyone could want to burn a candle that had been so painstakingly formed. But it was clearly meant to be burned or the artist would not have put a wick in it. With conviction he struck the match and held it first to the kindling, then to the candle on the hearth. The white wick sputtered in protest a little but gave in to the unavoidable fate for which it was made.

Hours later, somnolent and mesmerized by the dying fire, he arose and moved toward his bed. The candle fascinated him, how it burned so cleanly and purposefully down the cross, rivulets of hot wax running over the body of the Jesus figure, melting the head first, then the torso, until the figure on the cross and then the whole cross itself was a flattened puddle of warm amber scented wax with only a thin line of black smoke dissipating in the heated air. He wondered if the candle artist had an intended message—discomforting, succumbing to the inevitable, ashes to ashes, dust to dust.

The next morning, the fate of the crucifix candle still fresh in his mind, he knew today would be different from other days, there would be a new path to follow, a new fork in his road. Some inconvenient realities had to be faced, brought to light, discussed with the steely willed Sweet Angel Divine. She was so young, she had her whole life in front of her, and she appeared to be willing to do whatever it took to remain on top. If she were a man, Father mused, she would be a politician, and probably a dirty one too, if that was required to win. Just then he heard her footsteps, which he knew by heart, a steady cadence, approaching his downstairs office. A brief businesslike knock to announce her arrival and then, without waiting for an answer, she pushed the door open, wearing the official public smile, dressed sedately, stiffly, in the female version of a suit—a shapely jacket cinched tight at the waist, wide lapels, fitted pencil skirt brushing her knees, proper pearls with matching pearl and diamond button earrings, blond loosely waved hair falling just below the delicate earlobes. She smelled of Ivory Soap, never perfume, and managed to look like the cover of a fashion magazine. A wealthy modern business lady—suddenly he felt dowdy, used up, an old man in the presence of his successor whom he is forced to train to take over the job.

"You look lovely Sweet Angel, and very stylish I must say. But I know there is a lot more to you than your good looks—you're a smart woman and I want to ask your opinion of something I've been thinking over a long time."

Mother Divine's antenna was up now—she was on high alert because this was a departure from the norm. Father Divine didn't ask for her opinion on much of anything unless it involved overseeing the house or matters involving the Rosebuds. She raised her pale face expectantly toward Father, a husband in name only but her business partner in the strangest endeavor she could ever have imagined, her co-star in a bizarre real life drama far stranger than any fiction writer could have dreamed up.

"Tell me, what would happen if one day I were to become incapable, for whatever reason, of performing my duties? Who would take over the role of Spiritual Leader, Father, God, Reverend, or any of the multitude of names I have been blessed with?"

Mother Divine, Sweet Angel, Edna Rose Ritchings—which one of these personas should answer, she wondered. Was this his way of telling her he was sick? "Father Dear, that is such an unlikely event, are you sure you want an answer? It would be based on conjecture only."

"That's fine, then let's speculate. Who would take over?"

"Well, preferably a young person, a male, a person of a dark complexion. He would have to be clever, attractive, and have charisma. He would need to be educated in business too. In other words, someone just like yourself but younger."

"I knew you would be able to put it into words Sweet Angel. Especially the charisma factor. You absolutely need to have charisma for people to follow you—it matters little what you say, if you don't have charisma, they won't listen. I want you to find me such a boy, a little brown boy who I can train, shape his mind before it gets polluted by the ways of this world. Tell me, where will you start looking?"

She squeezed her hands together, knitted her brow, shifted uncomfortably in her chair. How could she tell him that she had always intended on taking his place the minute he became too infirm to function? She calculated she would not have too much longer to wait, and time was on her side, she only in her twenties. She had patiently waited, learned the functionings of the Movement, quietly studied the financials until she knew the entire labyrinth by heart. "The orphanages are a good place to start. There's plenty of unwanted children in the world. But we would want to avoid adoption at all costs because that means legally he would be our son which could be quite awkward with all the Peace Mission's assets. Perhaps a foster home situation would work better, or something of that nature."

He's thinking how amazingly organized and easy it was for his wife to come up with a perfect solution—almost like she had been anticipating it, and judging by her body language, dreading it. He knew the child would create extra work, but he couldn't leave the Peace Mission Movement to a woman, especially a light complected woman. She just wouldn't be able to conjure up the anger, the repression, the righteous indignation that he or someone like himself could. She was too frosty, too privileged looking, and her voice was too soft, too well modulated. No, not the the type at all. He needed an angry, smart, dark little boy from the ghetto. Mother Divine would be the one to teach him the snooty manners, because he would need those to succeed, to have credibility with the business community who were necessary for the financial success of the movement.

He reached toward her, laid his hand on her shoulder, very subtlety guiding her toward the door. "You have been so helpful my dear, and I thank you for that. This will have to be done very quietly, very privately, and I know you will handle it well, as you always do. Find me this boy so we can get to work solidifying the future of our Misson. And keep me informed of your progress. I don't want any time wasted." He shut the heavy door softly behind her, sealing himself back inside the control room.

Three months later, in the gloriously verdant summer of Gladwyne, Master Timothy Montoya was presented to Reverend Major Jealous Divine. Dressed in an identical suit to Father's, he was marched from the main house by an authoritative Mother Divine, who gripped his hand tightly so he couldn't pull away and fidget. They were going to the poolside cabana for lunch with his future mentor—Father thought the casual poolside meeting would put the boy at ease. He knew that Timothy was used to impoverished surroundings and he didn't want to overwhelm him all at once. It was 80 degrees and the eight-year-old tugged at his collar as if to let air in—being California born and bred he was unused to anything but T-shirts, shorts, and jeans. He walked awkwardly, feet rebelling against the constriction of the shiny dress shoes—and he's never seen people dressed this way around a swimming pool—didn't they know how to swim? He was dazed and confused. Even the air was different here—it was like a heavy hot wet blanket on top of him, constricting his air intake. He didn't like it and he wanted to go home to the beach where he could feel normal again.

The boy's mother had recently been recruited into the International Peace Mission Movement by a West Coast recruiter—one Miss Simple Hope, a dark complected frizzy haired young social worker type, who was employed strategically at the Self Realization Center in Pacific Palisades, one of the wealthiest enclaves of Los Angeles County, at the foot of Sunset Boulevard just before it hits the ocean. The magnificent facility, dedicated by a Hindu monk and meditation guru, was always open to the public, welcoming them to meander along the path circling the lake, or explore the moss covered mysterious Far Eastern shrine with the stone etchings on the walls. Even in summer it smelled damp, cool, green. Nestled among the ferns were statues of Buddha figures meditating over burning incense cones, and depending on the time of year, flocks of chortling avian residents—swans, ducks, herons and the like. Jade benches were sprinkled throughout to encourage quiet reflection—it was said that jade contact with the body imparted a higher energy to one's meditation. It was the perfect place to strike up a conversation with various lost souls seeking refuge, looking for something deeper. The gift shop was placed strategically at the end of the lake path so one felt obligated to at least go in and say hello—after all, they were gracious enough to let you in for free. Perhaps you could purchase a bookmark or an art magnet as a token of appreciation, to vindicate your intrusion into this private sanctuary.

Miss Simple Hope was savvy when it came to sizing people up—she could spot a possible Peace Mission sympathizer at the front gate, even before they ended up in the gift shop. It was something in their carriage, something dejected in the set of their shoulders, some underlying sadness, a giving up. The day Timothy Montoya and his mother came through Miss Hope knew she would find a willing ear, someone who could use a life saver thrown at her before she gave up and sank. After befriending Mrs. Montoya, who was poor as a church mouse after her husband abandoned them, she easily sold her on the idea of living in a mansion in Pennsylvania, doing a little housework to earn her keep, and letting Father Divine take over the child rearing and the expensive education. She desperately wanted to do her best for Timothy, and if she had to leave California to do it, so be it. She clung to the teachings of Father Divine as a drowning person clings to any floating object they find. Miss Simple Hope sent a photograph of Timothy to Father Divine with the message that the boy just might be what Father was searching for. He was an attractive child with an appealing wit, milk chocolate brown skin and a shock of shiny light brown hair and eyes to match. He was perfect. The photograph made its way to Father and soon Mrs. Montoya and her son were sent a one-way first class ticket on the train to Pennsylvania.

Today at the pool Timothy—recently re-titled Master Timmy by his new family—met his benefactor for the first time. Mother Divine let go of his hand and rigidly backed away up the hill toward the house.

"Master Timmy, you look so handsome in that suit—and it looks just like mine! We must have the same tailor." Father thought a little humor would put the boy at ease. Standing up, he pulled the chair out, and he's thinking the boy looked hot, scared, and stiff. This was going to be a challenge, to turn this raw material into someone who could eventually take over his Kingdom, his Heaven on Earth. "Sit right here Master Timmy. We can have lunch and get to know each other a little, okay? I hear you like spaghetti and chocolate cake, and that's exactly what we're having today. I hope you're hungry because the ladies made way too much for us." Father grandly lifted the silver domes off the serving bowels on the lunch cart. Good, he thought—Timmy's eyes got bigger. Food was the universal ice breaker.

"Do I have to eat the salad first?"

"Timmy, there is no salad. Nothing green, don't worry. Today we can get away with just the good stuff. You can even eat the cake first if you want. I do it all the time if the ladies aren't watching me, trying to control what I eat. Desert is the best part of the meal, right?"

Father and Master Timmy shared a conspiratorial glance, looked around for the food police, snickered a little, then dug into the cake. He knew very well that instilling the idea of persecution, even though right now it was only dining rules, creates solidarity and loyalty—us against them. The meeting was off to a good start.

Later after the lunch and some small talk appropriate to eight-year-old boys, Father Divine gestured to the attendants waiting discretely in the background.

"Please take Master Timmy back to Mother Divine—I believe she has a surprise planned for him." Father smiled benevolently and handed Timmy over to a female attendant, one of the small army of women attending to the daily details of running an estate. Just before Timmy was walked back, he turned, and with a funny expression almost mimicking that of a grown-up's he said "Thank you Father for the best meal I've ever had." Timmy smiled devilishly, conspiratorially, delighted with the secrete he shared with Father—they'd beaten the system, got away with it, and had fun. Partners in crime.

Father acknowledged it with a nod. The boy was perfect—easy to mold, engaging, and a little naughty. The project was off to a good start.

After the lunch, on his way up the grassy slope to the estate, surrounded by acres of newly mown green fragrance, he heard a scraping, digging sound coming from below and came upon a woman bent over one of the flower beds lining the walk path. She was pulling weeds from the beds and turning the soil, slowly, methodically, on her hands and knees, blond hair falling forward over the side of her cheek. "Peace to you Sister. That flower bed looks beautiful. Thank you for taking such good care of my garden—I mean *our* garden." Father shuffled back a little, a minor conversational gaffe which would probably not be noticed. She looked up from her gardening, blinking like a mole hit by the sun, unused to the light. Sometimes when a follower made eye contact, even if they were new to him, he could see a soul, a glorious but fading presence that once resided behind the eyes. But in this case, he saw only tired blue eyes, a little sad, but nothing there to speak of. He thought she looked a little familiar but he couldn't place her. It didn't matter, anyway. The poor woman was busy with only the task at hand, and probably after her hard day's work would fall asleep in the deep solid dreamless sleep of the uncomplicated and untroubled. They nodded at each other and he moved on up the hill.

Sister Ann was a little relieved Father Divine didn't stay and talk. There was nothing to say, really. She was just trying to focus on today's assignment, complete it, and continue to be the best person she could for the International Peace Mission Movement. One day at a time, one year at a time, but time had no meaning anymore for Sister Ann—there were no clocks in Heaven, after all.

EPILOGUE

He did die of course—a little hard to explain even for Mother Divine, who concocted the plausible, she hoped, explanation that he needed to spend some time in the other Heaven, but had a plan for a return at a later date, in another bodily form. He had, by her account of their last conversation, instructed her to preside over the Mission and take care of everything until he returned. Sweet Angel Mother Divine was now in charge—and she made sure everyone knew it.

Father Divine's exodus from the Earth happened in 1965, on a cold September morning at Woodmont, when he failed to arise at his usual early hour. His housekeeper and personal assistant, a Miss Jenny Love, repeatedly knocked on the door and after getting no response, pushed the door open to find a small lump under the covers of the huge bed. The lump didn't move when called, just remained horizontal, ominously quiet. She crept timidly up to the bed and still didn't see her dear Father Divine because the covers were pulled up all the way over his head. She tapped him—no response. There was something she didn't like about the feel of the body, a stiffness. She braced herself and pulled the covers down. All the way. Her mind registered the scene in seconds—naked man on his back dead, deflated as an old party balloon from the night before. She promptly fainted, and she would never confide in anyone what she saw, ever. When she regained consciousness, the room was abuzz with activity from the house staff, and they did indeed question her thoroughly as to what the last thing was that she remembered before passing out. She demurred, citing amnesia due to the fall.

The death was a media frenzy and the newspapers were in their element with catchy headlines like *God Finally Dies But Says He'll Return After His Heavenly Vacation*. During the funeral procession reporters tried in vain to get a statement from the tight lipped attendees. The followers were furious that their God had died, just upped and left them, and that they were made to look like idiots by the press, who were circling like jackals. It was tawdry, yes it was. And so entertaining.

Master Timmy, then twenty-three, got on the first train from Westwood Village, California when he learned of the passing. All these years he had been groomed by Father Divine to take his place, and now it was upon him—and he was ready. He even knew where the hidden safe was, and the combination too. Years before, Mother Divine had very kindly arranged for him to be sent away to college at UCLA at age seventeen, thinking that since Timmy was originally from that area, he would be more likely to stay away. In fact, she practically packed his bags for him and pushed him out the door, but now Timmy wanted back in to claim the throne. He was done dabbling with the PhD in Philosophy—that could wait. He knew if he didn't grab the kingdom, Mother Divine would surely take over. Which she did, and sent Master Timmy packing again in no uncertain terms. She made it clear he was no biological relation, had no legal rights since he was never adopted, and was just one of many charity cases that Father Divine had helped out of the goodness of his heart. Timmy still to this day claims the assets of the International Peace Mission belong to him, but the courts won't hear it due to lack of evidence. He gets a few hits on his website every once in awhile, but that's about it.

Mother Divine, aka Sweet Angel, aka Edna Rose Ritchings, presided over the Movement from the time of Father Divine's death in 1965 until 2017, when, at age ninety-one, she, too, surrendered her body to the inevitable. She ruled for fifty-two years without Father Divine, even managing to fight off Jim Jones, the head of the People's Temple, when he attempted to take over the Peace Mission Movement by claiming he was the reincarnation of Father Divine. Sweet Angel ruled with a velvet glove, smiling benignly, presiding at the head of the banquet table accompanied always by Father Divine's photograph in an ornate silver frame placed strategically within view of the banqueters. Sweet Angel never failed to ask the photographic image for its blessings upon the meal, and she often paused and looked up as if listening to her husband's voice projecting to her from the Heavens. Father Divine's calm black eyes followed her impassively throughout every banquet, seeming to bestow approval on the orderly progression of the ritual feast. The only thing missing was Father himself, and his rhythmic stentorian proclamations about how to make the world a better place. All that is left now of the International Peace Mission Movement are a few elderly followers, some magnificent real estate holdings with unclear beneficiaries, rooms full of dusty memorabilia, volumes of writings on brittle yellowing pages—and footsteps clicking in the empty banquet hall of eternity.

Her Grandpa Emil's property was only two miles from her home in Westlake Village. She drove slowly along Los Robles Road, searching for remnants of the good 'ole days when she used to come from Santa Monica with her mother Genieve to visit her Grandpa Emil and his wife Lillian. Things had changed a lot, but the way the oak trees framed the mountains remained the same. And the sun setting in the west still lit up the big sky with flaming pinks and oranges before fading to purple, silhouetting the magnificent oaks. Up ahead were the three lonely mailboxes that waited in vain for mail addressed to occupants long gone. They were crooked and bent now atop posts that badly needed repair. She turned up the long driveway for the three cottages, gravel crunching familiarly under the tires, and parked next to the front house, next to the siding with the peeling paint, next to the enormous six-hundred-year-old White Oak tree. The neighbors on either side of her property were pretending not to notice, but she could feel them check her out as she pulled up in the black Mercedes, so out of place in what was now called Old Town Thousand Oaks, a shabby remnant of the quaint small town Thousand Oaks once was.

She, Colleen, granddaughter of Emil, is the determined type that gets things done by putting one foot in front of the other and completing the job—no whining that it's too difficult or unpleasant. It it's worth it, it gets done. Period. She picked up the bag with the protective goggles, the dust mask, and the gloves. She was going to clean out the entire three houses, one room at a time, sift through the remains for something close to the heart. Her mother had lived here almost forty years, the property put into an Irrevocable Trust by her father, the chain going from Emil, to his daughter Genieve, then to his granddaughter Colleen. Genieve passed away last year in 2013 at age eighty-six. She almost never threw anything away, so Colleen knew the project would be slow going—but worth it because it was all hers now. She's thinking *thanks for taking such good care of all of us Grandpa. Where would we have been without you?*

There were photos spanning over sixty years showing how the three houses used to look when her Grandpa was alive—he and Lillian kept them looking like doll houses, and of course the landscaping, highlighted by the three ancient white oaks, was to die for. The houses had been filled with friends, parties, and happy tenants who usually became friends as well. It was sad to see how neglected everything had become. Her mother never appreciated the property, in the way that some people who get things for free don't. It just wasn't close enough to her beloved Santa Monica--but hey, it was free.

Colleen ran her hand over the oak tree's rough bark as generations before her had for six hundred years, a way of acknowledging its steadfast presence over human dramas played out under its canopy. Now she pulled open the tattered screen, pushed open the original wooden door, giving it a kick on the bottom to help it along, and went straight to the kitchen, the heart of the home, and set her bags and purse down on the dining table. There were no food smells anymore, no aroma of her mother's famous banana nut bread in the oven. Instead, the musty smell of ancient shag carpet pervaded, and the dry smell of dust. She ran her hand over the linoleum counter top and it was gritty—was it better just to tear the houses down? But no, not a chance, no way. Last week she had posted an old photo of the houses on her Facebook page with the caption:

> "Old walls and doors know something we can't understand, the true nature of time. The drama of human lives is written in the buildings. We will be gone; only places remain." - Anonymous Russian author.

How can you tear such a thing down? Better to restore than to demolish. With that thought she put on the mask, gloves, and goggles and headed for the master bedroom to get to work, the floor creaking underfoot in the exact same place and with the exact same sound it had made when she was just a toddler visiting grandpa. Advice from friends had been consistent, warning that it would be almost impossible not to get distracted and hopelessly lost in the treasure hunt, because surely every item uncovered would hold special memories, some filled with laughter, some with tears. So to Colleen, organizer extraordinaire, that simply meant she would have to time herself to limit inefficient lingering.

With that goal in mind, the first stop was the master bedroom dresser. People universally keep their most treasured possessions on top and inside dresser drawers. And sure enough, there was the first treasure, side-by-side as they had been Colleen's entire life and probably long before that—a hand carved doll-sized teak chair and matching teak photo frame with a picture of her mother Genieve and Genieve's sister Dolly, a mythical figure in the family, disappeared into a mysterious cult in the 1940's. They were dressed beautifully, skirts and cashmere sweaters, glossy hair brushing their shoulders, looking out over the edge of the cliffs at Palisades Park in Santa Monica toward the limitless sweep of the Pacific Ocean. Genieve must have been around eighteen and Dolly twenty-one, both beautiful, one brunette and one blonde, but alike enough to be twins. The teak set had been a present to Genieve from Dolly, purchased from a gift shop at the Whispering Pines Resort. The resort was still going strong in 2014—maybe she would take a drive up north when the house project was finished, see if it was still as great as Grandma Nona had gone on about.

At the thought of her Grandma Nona, Colleen sighed. She was sitting in a museum, sifting through the past, everyone gone now to meet their Maker—Genieve, Emil, Nona, and all Nona's children. Dolly would be eighty-nine years old this year if she was still alive, which seemed doubtful. Most of Nona's family really, passed on into the Great Unknown. Why did the past have so much draw, a hold that won't let go, a perfect thing, a perfect moment, always better than the current moment, and here she was now, looking for something she was not even aware of but that needed to be uncovered. But there was something here to be found, she could feel it.

She shook off the momentary nostalgia by checking her watch—it was necessary to keep moving forward if the project was going to get done. It was impossible to hire anyone to do this task unless she wanted everything just thrown away. Nope, not a good idea. She moved to the clothes closet to see what items might be donated to charity. Pushing the hangers aside was almost impossible—the closet was stuffy and so packed with clothes the hanging rod was bowed with the weight. After discarding a tatty pink bathrobe, a puffy faded red car coat and various pill-laden garments, she was able to step inside to get better leverage to clear all the stuff out.

After a few minutes fighting with hangers her foot hit something in the back left corner of the closet floor. Great, more junk to go through. She bent down and rummaged blindly through the hanging clothes, getting a face full of old dusty wool, pulling the box of junk forward into the light of day which it probably hadn't seen since who knew when. The item was a shallow black cardboard box with a lid, very tidy looking considering the rest of the house. But dusty, and very old—hopefully hidden money. A million dollars would be nice. She lifted the lid. Old letters, but why all the way back in the closet? After shuffling through them but not reading she looked at the postmarks and for a moment it didn't register—the letters were in date order, beginning in January 1929, so her mother would have been only a year and a half old. These letters must have belonged to her grandpa Emil. Maybe when Genieve moved in after he died she never cleaned out the closet, or she knew about them and just left them there for old time's sake. Genieve was like that, saving baby teeth, pet tags, antique perfume bottles—anything attached to a memory. She put the box aside, glanced at her watch to be sure she remained on schedule, and assigned the box a separate project of its own, to be perused on another day.

Months later, after reading all the letters and touching the lock of blond hair that Dolly had sent to her Daddy Emil, Colleen finally understood the meaning of loss, especially the loss of a child, a sister, an aunt. To see it in writing was so very different from hearing the same story repeated over the years of her "weak-minded" aunt who joined a cult. Dolly didn't seem real then, but she did now. She had been a real person with thoughts and feelings, not just a family story to be recounted. If it was true the cult had at one time millions of followers, that meant millions of other people had lost someone to it, a former child, husband, sister, brother, loved one. Just vanished into thin air, never to be heard from again. It actually seemed worse than the loved one dying—with death at least you know the outcome, had some understanding, some closure. Not knowing or waiting in vain for someone's return was far worse. Genieve said she called many times over the years and was told there was no such person, or that Sister Ann didn't know her, or that she was dead, or she didn't want to talk. There was not even an attempt at a consistent story from the cult, almost like they were taunting the outsider. Colleen decided to try anyway, so she read a book on cult mentality and behavior for guidance on how to communicate with brainwashed cult members.

She picked up the phone and dialed the number to the International Peace Mission headquarters, the Woodmont estate, and although mysteriously no one had heard of Ann Born, even though she had been with the cult for sixty-seven years, was eventually advised to contact the Westminster Evangelical Home for the Aged, one of many businesses owned by the cult. The phone rang in the lobby and a worker answered, a Miss Scarlett Brown. They chatted a bit about the nature of the call, and Miss Brown informed her that Ann had died many years ago, but asked for Colleen's name and number. At least the person admitted to knowing Ann, so it was encouraging. Later that day the director of the Westminster Evangelical Home for the Aged called to inform her that Miss Ann Born was still alive. After stating her purpose in calling, that she just wanted to hear Ann's voice because her mother Genieve had recently passed, the director, Miss Eliza Kindness, agreed that Colleen could talk to Ann. At that time, Sister Ann was eighty-nine.

The line went silent for a few breathless minutes, then Ann was put on the phone, an elderly voice that carried the lilting undertones of the eternally youthful—it matched Genieve's voice almost exactly. It had to be aunt Dolly.

"Do I know you?" Dolly sounded wary.

"I'm Genieve's daughter, Colleen. Do you remember your sister Genieve?"

"I have a lot of sisters." Dolly sounded evasive. Her voice sounded like she was trying to convince herself that the cult members were her sisters.

"I mean your biological sister Genieve."

She must have handed the phone away because Miss Kindness got back on the line and said Ann was tired, and couldn't hear well.

"I would like to send some pictures of Ann when she was young—it that okay with you?"

Miss Kindness agreed and gave the address, a seedy area of Philadelphia according to the Google map street view.

One month later, Colleen called back to see if Miss Kindness had received the photos. She did, and said the photos had made everyone happy, and that they seemed to ring a little bell of memory in Ann. Miss Kindness commented that "She still has that beautiful voice." Miss Kindness sounded like she had some sympathy and understanding, for which Colleen was grateful.

Dolly had been found, made real, spoken with. Her photos had been received, shared with her—hopefully—and that was it, mission accomplished. At least Dolly was being taken care of, Colleen hoped. She left it at that—let sleeping dogs lie. For awhile.

Now it's 2021, and Dolly is ninety-six if she's still alive. The calendar on Colleen's phone informs her of the birthday every year, the passage of time marked by an impersonal electronic reminder message that she, for unfathomable reasons, doesn't want to delete. Perhaps she is like her grandpa Emil, who didn't want to forget because it meant forgetting part of oneself, and that just wasn't right. Maybe it was hard-wired into a person's genetic code, the need to connect with the rest of your genetic line—that would explain the success of the multitude of genealogy websites. Which made people like Dolly, who could just walk away from it all, such a mystery.

Colleen called the Westminster Evangelical Home to find out if Dolly was still alive, but the number was disconnected. After a bit of research, she determined the building and the business had been sold in 2019, but the corporate entity that owned the home was listed as active, meaning still in business—and the President was Eliza Kindness. Scarlett Brown was listed as another officer of the corporation. A search of two other corporations owned by the cult revealed they were foreign corporations, and after even more digging, Colleen found the funeral home normally used by the Westminster Evangelical Home for the Aged. She called to see if there had been a death certificate issued for Ann Born—but the funeral home was permanently closed, the founder meeting the same end as his clients, passing away in his nineties. She then turned to the Philadelphia vital records website, but it was required to have a date of death in order to get a death certificate. There was one place left to call—The Woodmont Estate, headquarters of the International Peace Mission Movement, where Father Divine is interred in his The Shrine to Life, a white marble and gold encrusted mausoleum tucked away in a remote corner of the the 72 acre property so as not to emphasize the inconvenient fact of his passing.

In early 2021, Colleen sent a brief email to Woodmont's contact address asking if Ann Born was still alive, or if not, the date of her passing. She also called the phone number on the Peace Mission website. A Mission worker answered, took down her name and phone number, and said she would call back with Ann's status or date of death so Colleen could at least obtain a death certificate. There was no call back, and no answer to the email either. In the current age of information of every kind—one might say even too much information, Colleen was never able to find the fate of her aunt Dolly. Apparently it was possible to make someone disappear without a trace. Dolly never warranted a mausoleum, never warranted even a headstone or death certificate. Her life was obviously meaningless to the International Peace Mission Movement even though she gave herself over to it entirely. Maybe she stopping living that day in 1947 when she entered the cold marble hallways of the mission.

Father Divine built his empire with the labor of trusting followers, do-gooders, the indigent, the naive, and the lost. He fanned the flames of alienation and mistrust, breaking up countless families to gain manpower for his Peace Mission Movement. It all seemed so callous, but it worked—and he got away with it.

Colleen hoped he was enjoying the fate which comes to us all—ashes to ashes, dust to dust.